# Apocalypse M

Thomas W. Everson

# Dedication

This dedication is to two women:

The first is my wife, whose spirit, strength, and willpower I tried to model in this novel.

The second is my mother, who despite losing her battle with cancer, showed incredible fortitude until the very end.

# Contents

# Acknowledgements

Thank you to F. Staines, Angela Williams, Lillie Baird, and B. McNerney for beta reading and providing incredibly useful feedback.

Thank you to Jake Murray, my illustrator, for an amazing cover as usual.

Thank you to Tim Marquitz for editing this novel at an amazing speed, and giving me some extra perspective which helped me make the story a little bit more visual.

# Chapter 1:

**Present day:**

Inside a dimly lit room with one door, and no windows, Morgan sits with her wrists and ankles shackled to a chair. She's not going anywhere. She's not sure how long it's been now. It could have been hours, or even days.

General Truman, a soldier, and a doctor are there. All eyes are on her.

"This may sound cliché, but we can do this the easy way, or the hard way," General Truman tells her.

"Piss off," Morgan snaps at him.

He punches her in the gut, and she heaves. She fights back vomiting, getting away with just heavy coughing.

"Where is the key?"

"Gone. I burned it. Didn't your puppets tell you I destroyed it in the car?"

"We're sifting through your stuff. We found a hard drive, and I've been told it's recoverable."

"Good luck with that."

"Tell me what your goal was. Your real one."

"I told the whole world," she spits out. "I gave everyone the zombie apocalypse it's been dying for, and I beat you to it. I know what you had in store."

"You're destroying the lives of millions of people. You're worse than Hitler." He sneers and points his finger in her face. If he were any closer, she'd bite it off.

"You realize that by likening me to Hitler, your entire argument falls apart right? Hitler killed millions. I've killed none. I've simply taken away their ability to control themselves, until my demands are met."

"Isn't that worse?"

"Even if I hadn't, they were mindless sheeple already. The world needed to be shown that your faux-Utopia would have ended them. I'm not sorry for what I've done."

The general turns his back to her. He tries to restrain the anger in his voice, "You're clearly a very intelligent woman. You've demonstrated that. We need passionate people like you to step into leadership roles for the future. Help us fix this, and I'll arrange a meeting with the president."

"Declassify the program, all of it, and then shut it down. Tell the public the *truth* about what you and TEAL were doing."

"I don't have that power."

"You just said you could get me a meeting with the president, so clearly you *know* people who do."

"They won't shut the program down. They shouldn't. Humanity has a bright future, if we can come together. If you've heard the news at all since the outbreak, you know this is being called a terrorist attack, and the government won't give in to demands."

"Then you tell the president she can kiss my ass. You won't get anything out of me. Go ahead and try to cure them without me."

The general grunts in anger and barks at the soldier guarding the door, "Take her to room five."

"Yes, sir!" he replies.

He removes the chains but keeps the cuffs. When he's standing her up, she lunges at Truman. The soldier subdues her, and the general glares. He nods to his subordinate. He carts her out of the room into the dark hallway. Farther from the double doors they came in from, they reach the fifth room. Inside, a room with overly bright lights awaits. She's shoved from behind, and her face hits the floor first. She tries to get back up, but Truman is there to keep her down.

"I'll give you a little alone time to rethink your answer," he says in a huff.

The door is shut, and there's no way out. The room has a single vent in the ceiling, but there's no air flowing. It's hot, and sweat is already starting to bead on her skin. After a minute, Truman's voice blares over a loudspeaker.

"Agree to help us and this will end. All you have to do is say you're ready to cooperate and you can come out."

She's left alone. She punches a wall with her cuffed fists. Bringing the program to the public's attention has been accomplished, but the government still needs to take accountability with their intent to "inoculate" every American citizen, turning them into programmable slaves. *I have to hold out.*

The light and heat give her a headache. Even sitting in the corner with her head down in her knees, there's no relief. The light seeps in anyway. The best she can do is focus on steady breathing, and trying to sleep. As she's drifting off, a loud horn is blared over the speaker, and she startles.

*This must be the real torture. And here I thought I'd have to go all the way to Guantanamo Bay for this.*

*

General Truman watches her through monitors as she tries to get comfortable against the wall.

"How long do you think she can endure?" he asks Doctor Tseng.

"I'm not sure. It depends on her current level of fatigue. She's going to need food and water to start. She'll be no good to you dead."

"No food. Only enough water to keep her hydrated," he says, and then redirects the soldier who escorted her in. He's taken a spot at a computer console, and is monitoring her. "Blare the horn once an hour."

The soldier nods and looks at a large digital clock which now says 00:02. Truman and Doctor Tseng exit the room to continue their conversation.

"This woman is a terrorist, and I intend on using enhanced interrogation techniques to get the information I need. Keep her alive and alert."

"I'm a doctor first. I will stand by the Hippocratic Oath."

"You'll do whatever the hell I need you to do." Truman pokes his finger in Tseng's sternum.

Tseng scoffs at him, but Truman stands his ground.

He returns through the secured hallway to the makeshift command center. He oversees the group, currently tasked with reverse engineering a cure for the infected or locating the key.

*

Morgan is tired. Micro-naps aren't working to restore her mind or body. Lying down, she puts her face into a corner and plugs her ears, anticipating the next horn blow. The fatal move of creating a second wave had sealed her fate, and removed any possibility of escape.

*If only I'd taken a boat.*

*

**Two and a half years ago:**

Morgan accessed her favorite reddit page /r/anonymous. She was a silent supporter. Nothing pleased her more than learning of the exploits of the anarchist world she wanted to join. A world where she saw freedom of the mind, and where the oppression by the government and corporations was torn down.

*They have too much control. Every one of them that says they're for the people is a liar.*

The thought of upheaving a complacent, sleeping society excited her. The only issue was that, even though she was capable, she wasn't sure where to dive in. Taking on the entire system was alone was impossible. Even if one of the corporations controlling the country was taken down, there were still hundreds more. It was a hydra.

Scrolling, she saw a thread which caught her attention. It was titled 'Unkillable Super Soldiers.' In the thread was a small paragraph, and then a link.

> 'The US government and TEAL Inc. have created soldiers who can't be killed. We need to know more! If the government can create immortal soldiers, then what can we possibly do to fight back?!'

She clicked the link, and it opened to a video on an external site. From a distant hiding spot, someone filmed United States soldiers making a raid into a desolate town filled with people who appeared to be of Middle Eastern descent.

The US soldiers in the video enter into a firefight. With pinpoint accuracy the US soldiers make headshot after headshot on their targets. Militants return fire, but despite bullets clearly piercing through some of the US soldiers, they keep going. In the end, the US forces are on top with zero casualties. A soldier says something, but she can't hear it at first. Rewinding, she turned up the volume and it became audible. 'Scrub the site! Burn it all!' The screen went dark.

Rewinding again, she moved the video forward one frame at a time. The US soldiers were definitely hit, but in the end, they moved as if they hadn't been. They didn't even flinch. *This isn't real, is it? Could this have been staged? Or maybe from a movie?* She read the description under the video several times.

> The super soldiers the United States military doesn't want you to know about! The military has a contract with TEAL Inc., and they've somehow created people who heal at an extreme rate! We can't let them murder people and dominate the world! Expose them!

Wanting to see it one more time, she hit the rewind button. The buffering icon came up, but the video didn't load. She refreshed the page, and received a 404 error. The entire page was now non-existent. Going back to reddit, the thread had disappeared also.

Pandora's Box was open. An urge inside her told her to stop lurking and investigate.

*

**Present day:**

She couldn't be sure how much time has passed, but she had a good idea. The horn blares for the eighteenth time. With the lack of sleep piling up, her head was swimming. Thoughts were running together about the nanites she altered. Morgan bursts into laughter, delirious.

"This is *your* fault, you know? That video was leaked and nothing could stop your secrets from coming out!" she yells at them through her laughter. "If it wasn't me, then it would have been someone else!"

"We're aware of the leaked video. It was under control. Tell me about the key," Truman responds through a speaker. "Help me stop this, and we'll make sure your permanent cell has a window."

She spits at the ground, still cognizant enough to act in defiance. The horn turns on and blares non-stop, forcing her to cover her ears.

*

"Push her farther. Keep the horn on for an hour. I'll be back then," Truman instructs the soldier.

The soldier nods, and Truman exits the room. He thinks about the next technique he'll use on her. *With lack of sleep, she may be defiant but could also let something slip,* he thought while passing more enhanced interrogation rooms.

*Many harder people before her cracked under far less pressure. Perhaps slapping or shaking.*

No matter who was really to blame, be it Morgan for creating the world's worst plague, Corporal Reyes for letting his guard down, or the soldiers who failed to fully scrub a site, it was his ass in the end because he oversaw TEAL's Project N program. He had to check in with the president soon, and she would be expecting updates or useful information.

Past secured double doors, and through the large basement-turned-command center, he calls the elevator to go up to the Pentagon's main level. The evacuated building is quiet. Passing one of the doors, he takes note of how calm it is outside. *It's only a matter of time before they find their way here.* The horde is coming, and he's hoping to be prepared with a nanite antivirus.

*

She can't take it anymore. The horn has been on for so long, she's sure there'll be permanent hearing damage. She beats her head against the wall in an attempt to knock herself out. Her head is pounding already, and she can barely think, so the harm will be less than continued consciousness. After several strikes against the wall, the horn turns off and *they* intervene to stop her.

*If I had nanites in me, I'd be able to fight them off.*

She doesn't, and blood runs down her forehead. Her ears are ringing. She's woozy, and when the soldier carries her from the room, she drops all of her weight and lets him do the work. Hauled to another room with striking similarities to the first room, she's chained back to a chair.

*

Truman enters Morgan's holding room. He lets her breathe for a moment before pushing her farther. Doctor Tseng enters and pulls the stethoscope from his neck. He checks her vitals and listens to her breathing. Returning the stethoscope to his neck, he pulls a flashlight and checks her pupils. Snapping his fingers in her ears results in a slight twitch in her eyes to the side he's currently snapping on.

"There's likely no permanent hearing damage, and the wound on her head is superficial," Tseng informs the general while patching her up from a small first aid kit.

"Do you have anything to tell me?" Truman addresses her.

"Water…" she barely gets out.

The doctor nods, and the soldier leaves, returning a few moments later with a small paper cup full. Tseng takes it and holds it to her lips. She can barely get it down.

"Where, or what, is the key?" Truman asks.

She struggles against her bindings and shakes her head. He slaps her face. Not too hard, but enough to jolt her back to reality.

He gets a little louder. "Tell us where the key is."

She shakes her head, and he strikes her on the other cheek.

"No…" she whispers.

He raises his voice to a yell. "If you don't help us fix this, the world will eventually be consumed by your infected, and no one will be left!"

She's silent, and he slaps harder.

"Tell us how to stop the nanites!" he gets in her face like a drill instructor.

Morgan stammers to respond, "The key…it's…not here…"

"Is it a device?"

"It's a…thing…that I…you have to…"

Her head droops and drool spills from her mouth. He slaps her again, and she perks up for just a moment.

"Arturo…" she mumbles.

"Where is the key?" he yells at the unconscious programmer. "Who is Arturo?"

Tseng checks her vitals again.

"Wake her up," Truman demands.

"Based on this interaction, it's my opinion that even if I do, she's going to give you gibberish. Give her an hour, then wake her," Tseng says.

Truman grumbles. He may have time if the president is still putting out fires with other nations. He shakes his head and leaves the room, slamming the door.

*

**One and a half years ago:**

Morgan had isolated herself from the world. In an abandoned warehouse at the New Jersey port, she sat and scrubbed through classified information on a burner laptop. There hadn't been a moment in recent history where she'd felt secure, since first breaking into the Pentagon's servers to search for files on TEAL. The warehouse was on no one's radar, and she wasn't dumb enough to hack them from there.

It took her six months to program an exfiltration worm to grab what would seem like a lot of random files, while its true mission was to find anything TEAL related. At its implanting, she was incredibly close to spending the rest of her life in a detention center. She had accessed the Pentagon's servers from a public Wi-Fi spot near Central Park. She had a virtual private network set up, and proxy servers across the globe she was bouncing off, but the US government was good.

In hindsight the whole plan was stupid. By the time she broke through their security using some programs written by fellow Anonymous members, and planted her worm, she received an alert from an accomplice that the Federal Bureau of Investigation was on their way to her location. To escape, she concealed herself amongst a large student body studying the effects of climate change on the park's trees.

Black vehicles rolled up and began searching people they thought were suspicious. But she'd made her way out in the opposite direction they came before they could get to her.

She had to wait for the worm to collect enough data, and then risk capture by breaking into the Pentagon again to pull it out. Until she didn't have to. Upon fishing for patsies on the deep web, several Anonymous members volunteered to retrieve the worm and send it, as long as she shared any damning information with them.

They had no idea what they were retrieving, or that it would likely land them in prison if caught. She was asked several times for *juicy bits* to dox politicians and shame them into oblivion. Their minds were on trivial things like sex scandals, corporate favoritism, or international controversies. *Such small minds.*

Taking a mental break, she communicated through encrypted messages with her cohort, who'd saved her that day from the FBI. They were currently the only other one who knew her true goal at the moment.

God-Complex: Find anything yet?

Apocalypse M: Still looking...there's just so much junk.

God-Complex: I bet. When you find their super serum info, let me know. I want to know how it works, maybe even use it on myself. How much do you think the formula would go for on the deep web?

Apocalypse M: I'm not interested in selling it. My goal is to expose and dismantle. A lot of this is redacted. Whole pages blacked out.

God-Complex: Eh, that's the government for you. Keep digging, and I'm sure you'll find the truly classified stuff. Just don't fall too far down the rabbit hole, Alice.

Apocalypse M: Mmm. Likening me to a fictional girl who was probably insane. Thanks for the encouragement.

God-Complex: She was, I'm sure of it, and you might follow her path if you continue on alone. It would go faster if I were there.

Apocalypse M: We can't ever meet.

God-Complex: Two heads are better than one.

Apocalypse M: You just want to take credit.

God-Complex: Nah, I need some real human interaction.

She clicked the X to shut the messenger. A little paranoid, she snuck quietly down to the warehouse's bay doors and peeked out to see if any unmarked, black, government-type vehicles were rolling up. After about ten minutes of nothing happening, she figured she was okay for now.

Returning to the laptop, she continued digging. Hours passed, and she had to peel back multiple layers of security to access certain files. Anything not pertaining to the TEAL program got dropped into her computer's Recycle Bin.

Progress was slow, only finding small amounts of information at a time. The choicest piece was a document where someone had missed redacting the word *nanites*.

*Nanites?* Nanotechnology was an idea people had theorized. Every couple years an article popped up on popular tech and science websites stating groups had been attempting it. To date, there hadn't been reports of anyone succeeding. She scribbled the word on a note of things to look into later.

She spent countless hours at the computer, and fatigue made her eyelids heavy. Lying down on the cold, hard floor, she stared up at the steel beams overhead.

*Could these nanites really heal a mortal wound? They'd have to be extremely complex, both in their mechanical workings and in the programming.*

*

It was weeks later when she finally got into the hardest to access files. The first was a letter to the government, addressed to their previous President. Alphaeus Lang waxed poetic about thwarting sickness, disease, and death in the letter, promising things like immortality. He was vague in his details about the nanotechnology, about how it worked. His intentions in the letter seemed pure.

A second letter by him detailed how TEAL Incorporated intended to provide the nanotechnology to the public, for free, so everyone could have access to a long healthy life, as well as be better members of society. He toted how the nanites would then work to eradicate drugs, both legal and illegal, because the nanites would be programmed to disallow the chemicals from even taking effect.

*Is he trying to be the next messiah? Humanity's savior? Smells like bullshit.*

He was responded to, and their work together began. A high ranking military officer, General Truman, was assigned as the liaison between Lang and the Pentagon. Lang appeared to be left out of some correspondences, where General Truman and the then Secretary of Defense discussed application of the nanites to the military, and dominating foreign enemies.

*Same shit they've been doing.*

Then it came. The damning piece. The one which would put the noose around the beast's head and hang it. The government's internal memo which perverted Lang's ideas. It may as well have said they planned to control the population with the nanites.

'Phase 1 is currently in progress and being actively evaluated to ensure there are no long term negative effects. There have been significant amounts of data collected on increased healing, increased strength, and increased mental capacities. Dozens of missions have been run, and more are scheduled to happen with increasing frequency.

Phase 2 is in preliminary status based on data being collected. Within the next year, the hope is to roll out Project N to all of the US military.

Phase 3 will require the establishment of three beginning classifications for those who will receive the nanites. Those classifications will be broken down as follows:

- Government

- Military

- Citizen

The three classifications will determine what programming will be allowed, as we do not want unauthorized individuals to be able to compromise the security of the new infrastructure. Once the new infrastructure is operating efficiently, we can make amendments to the number of classifications to expand the horizons of the United States of America. While there will be classifications, there will still be fundamental, and equal rights when it comes to the pursuit of life, liberty, and happiness.

This phase will be the most critical, as some industries will suffer, and some will fall. With the inability to become sick, there will be less need for doctors, nurses, and pharmaceutical companies. Health will instead be regulated by the upkeep of ones nanites, and therefore TEAL will require the funding to expand its branches to include clinics in case of any programming or technical complications.

Phase 4, the inclusion of the global community, will need to be soon after the beginning of Phase 3. US citizens could potentially be inoculated with the nanites under the premise of treating potential outbreaks of infectious diseases. There would be no reason to immediately reveal the nanotechnology. This would eliminate uncontrollable elements, such as international travel, where a US citizen would carry the nanites to foreign countries. Once the inoculations are nearly completed, the nanotechnology would be offered to allies first, and then the rest of the world as a means to bring everyone under one banner.'

Though they were two halves of the same coin, this side was worse. She read between the lines; government officials would be grandfathered in, and they'd take control of not only the US, but the world. *No doubt with these* classifications, *they'd be able to control exactly what a person could do with their lives. Under the guise of developing humanity and curing all sickness, all people had to do would be to submit completely to the United States government.*

"Servitude in exchange for immortality?" Morgan mumbled to herself as she added to her handwritten notes, including this file's location.

She leaned back in her chair and tapped the pen to her mouth. *If they get this off the ground, there would be little room for a resistance. The sheeple are already complacent in the shadow of the government and corporations.*

"The living-dead need a wakeup call."

There was a solution: take control of the nanites. But how? She was sure she wasn't going to find files on how to build nanites in the government's documents. If she were to hack TEAL's servers and somehow find blueprints, it would probably be impossible for her to duplicate one. She needed ones already created. She needed one of the soldiers in Project N.

*

**Present day:**

Morgan awakes to being shaken rapidly and Truman yelling in her face. If her hands were free, she would coldcock him. Her head is pounding, her ears are ringing, and the room is spinning.

"Damnit, tell me what I need to know! Where is the key?" His words are finally clear enough for her to understand. "Does Arturo have it?"

"Truman, did you ever stop to think of the consequences? Did you not think someone would figure out your plan? Phase four, global domination. I've saved the world. They may hate me now, but I'll be memorialized as a martyr and savior."

It would be wishful thinking for her to believe she could escape, or that maybe God-Complex would have tracked her, and that an Anonymous army would swoop in. But reality is different. She's sure death by Truman's hands is certain.

He slaps her, bringing her back into the moment. Her eyes water, and she has to blink several times to clear them.

"It's only a matter of time before we devise our own cure, one that won't trigger your kill command. We've enlisted your friend, Reese Gordon, or God-Complex as you know him. He's working with us, and TEAL techs. They're getting close. Once they have it figured out, you're out of luck. But if you help them, I'll help you."

"Don't piss on me and try to tell me it's raining. You're a liar. That's your job isn't it? Lying and killing? You're nothing but a mercenary for the government. A thug who wants more power than he has now."

He slaps her again, nearly knocking her and the chair over.

"I'm trying to build a better world! To *unify*! What's your excuse?"

"A better world where everyone's enslaved? Where diversity no longer exists in favor of *your* ideals?" she shoots back. The little rest she had was enough to put some fire back into her. "Let me go, declassify everything, and shut it down. Then I'll give you the key."

He unleashes an assault of slaps.

"Tell me where the key is first," he yells, "and then I'll talk with the president about going public."

"I'm not a moron…"

His face has been turning deeper shades of red the more she resists. Succumbing to the idea that this is where she dies, she hopes he's reaching that threshold, and she prays for it to be quick. The timeless trope TV and movies like to beat to death of dying before saying anything is what she wants.

"So, how many states are infected now? Has it reached the Midwest yet?"

Truman balls his fist. Morgan grins evilly at him, a little crazed. His knuckles connect to her cheek. Blood pours into her mouth, and she spits broken teeth at him.

She drools. Despite the pain, she still speaks defiantly, "Admit this happened because you tried to play *God* and created something you couldn't hope to control forever, and it got away from you. You're a failure!"

"What the world knows, and will only know, is that a terrorist hacked a new technology and attacked the USA. In the end, humanity will be cured, and everyone will know that the *terrorist* lost."

"Then we have nothing to talk about."

He assaults her more, and harder. She's endured the torture up until now, but an emotional dam bursts, and she begins to sob. Tears and bloody drool mix in her lap. Helplessness builds steadily, and she cries out.

"Just kill me!"

"Where is the key?"

"Kill me! Fucking do it! Kill me!"

The assault is interrupted by a soldier entering the musty room.

"Sir, phone call for you."

"I'm busy," Truman snaps.

"Sir, POTUS is on the line."

Truman mutters a string of obscenities and storms out of the room. While he's away, the doctor enters and checks Morgan's vitals. Lifting her chin, he shines his flashlight in her eyes, but she zones out.

*

**One year ago:**

The lists of the *super soldiers* in the program were extensive. They recruited enough Marines to have a unit in each US state, and then ten international units. She spent weeks combing and profiling the people in the lists, and settled on one who looked like an easier mark than the others. Once she found *him*, she prepared for an encounter.

In addition to hacking his e-mail and social media accounts to profile him, Morgan had stalked Corporal Antonio Reyes around New York for an entire week. He had just finished a tour in the Middle East and was on leave.

She sat in the corner of a pub, eating fried calamari and sipping an alcohol-free margarita, watching him and some others chat and drink.

Trying to dress fashionable, she searched 'girl geek chic' on the internet and tried to match the first image she came across in an attempt to play at what this Marine would find interesting. What she came up with were boots, black knee-high socks, a flowered skirt, and a blouse. She'd even purchased some fake, geeky glasses and put her hair in a bun for a sort of librarian look.

But it hadn't been her only preparation. Checking her purse, she was fearful she'd forgotten to bring the Taser X26-P she had to travel to Vermont to purchase. It was there.

*Did I plan well enough for this? If he is some sort of a super soldier, will a Taser be enough to take him down?*

Having combed through numerous files regarding Project N, she was ready to confirm it actually existed.

*I hope the amps don't fry the nanites.*

Corporal Reyes was having a lively debate about favorite football teams, and he was defending the Seattle Seahawks with passion. During a lull in the conversation, he looked about the room and made eye contact with her. She played shy and looked down at the table to play with her food. Bringing her eyes back up, she made sure he saw her looking. This piqued his interest enough to leave his group and head over.

"Hey," he said, nodding at her slightly.

"Hi." She fidgeted in her seat and pretended to be coy.

"Your boyfriend step out or something?"

She smiled bashfully and tucked some loose bangs back behind her ear. "I don't have one."

This put a smile on his face, and she felt awkward. Her life had no time for boyfriends, especially now, and were it not for needing him for research, she wouldn't give him the time of day.

"May I?" he asked.

"Sure," she was quiet.

"So, why are you all alone on a Friday night, miss...?" he asked while looking back at the bartender and waving him over.

"I'm Rachel," she said, holding her hand out for a handshake.

He shook her hand. "Antonio."

"I'm just taking a break from work, that's all."

"What do you do?"

"I'm a curator at the Metropolitan Museum of Art."

She had rehearsed the lie a hundred times in the mirror before going out that night. She wanted it to sound boring enough so he wouldn't think to ask too many questions about it.

The bartender brought two drinks over in short glasses. Morgan easily recognized the amber liquid as whiskey. Corporal Reyes pushed one over to her.

"Doesn't sound like my kind of thing." He laughed and downed his whiskey in one gulp.

She shrugged. "It pays the bills."

"Well, the night's young. We can make things a little more exciting," he points at the glass he pushed toward her.

Her stomach turned. *Does he expect me to take a random drink from a random man? Not even in the best circumstances.*

She lifted her faux-margarita to indicate she didn't need another drink. Drinking it down, she played along, and gave him a wink. He took the second glass of whiskey and guzzled it down, too.

"Careful with that stuff. Don't want to get too tipsy before we have fun, right?" She smiled innocently at him.

"Nah, I'm fine. I don't get drunk."

"Oh?"

He smirked and stood up. With his hand held out, he beckoned her to come with him. She stood and took his arm, all the while her plan played out in her head.

"Shall we take my car?" She smiled and batted her eyes as they walked to the bar.

"I took a cab, so your car works for me." Corporal Reyes paid his tab, and they started toward the front door.

She'd already known he'd taken a cab. It was a calculated move for her plan. Still leery about being tracked, she'd taken precautions. Utilizing contacts on the invisible internet site 'Silk Road Resurfaced,' she prepared herself with a fake ID, social security card, a credit card, a burner car, and enough wire to turn the inside of the car into a signal jamming Faraday cage.

When she bought it, the four door sedan was dropped off at a neutral location with no interaction with the seller. A package with the key and instructions to find it had been sent through a delivery service. Anonymity was important, and no one *truly* wanted to know anyone on Silk Road.

She led Antonio out to the street, and down a few blocks, where she'd been able to find parking. She knew full well that once he was considered missing, the FBI would be all over this area, so she kept her head down, and turned away from the buildings closest to her to avoid any CCTVs. They made small talk, but she purposely kept from asking about anything job-related, lest she look like she was actively probing him for information.

Approaching the nondescript car, she reached into her purse for the keys. Unlocking the doors with her key fob triggered the Faraday cage to come on, and she smirked while they climbed inside. Reyes buckled up and looked at her wantingly.

"We heading to your place?" he asked.

"I have a little place I like to go when I want some quiet time. It's down by the water." She winked at him to lead him on.

"Sounds perfect."

*I thought they were supposed to have increased intelligence.*

Getting through the busy streets and to the highway took longer than she'd liked. Reyes was still interested, and didn't question where she was heading because she kept him busy with flirting. They talked about menial things. At least, they were menial to her. Daily life, hobbies, what they considered fun. Of course most of hers was made up.

Finally, it dawned on him to question her when she pulled off the highway onto Goldsborough Drive, a well-lit but empty looking area.

"Where did you say we're heading?"

"Down to the Jersey port," she flashed him another smile in an attempt to disarm him again.

He slid his hand over and gripped her thigh. It made her skin crawl, but she played into it to keep his guard down. She let out a little moan, and he did it more.

Straight onto Port Terminal Boulevard, she slowed down to a building on the right hand side. The fence had warnings all over it, most put up by her. At the front there were many bay doors, but only one of them was accessible by a gate. She hopped out, opened the lock, and pulled the gate open so she could drive through. Reyes' brows were furrowed in question when she got back in the vehicle.

"What? Not up for a little excitement?" She egged him on while pulling her car into the bay.

"It's not that. This just seems like a strange place to take someone."

*Don't back out yet. I don't want to have to drag your body upstairs.*

"Maybe I shouldn't have brought you here." She frowns at him. "I can take you back to the pub."

Knowing he wasn't going to back down, she put the car in reverse and started to pull out. He put his hand on her leg again and squeezed.

"I wouldn't want you to have made this trip out here for nothing," he said.

She surmised that meant he was on board with the idea of danger, as long as he thought sex was part of the equation.

Parked inside the warehouse, which she'd also turned into a Faraday cage, she was confident he was completely off grid now. She shut the gate and the bay door before returning.

With her purse at her side, and the Taser ready to access, Morgan pulled out her cell phone and turned its flashlight mode on. She waved Reyes to a set of stairs leading up to an overseer's room. There were many things she'd done to the room in order to prepare it for holding him hostage, including a metal table with straps. He would soon find out.

He followed closely behind, grabbing her hips as she swayed them in his face. The door at the top creaked open, and she led him in. Dim light from across the Jersey bay seeped in through the dirty windows. Turning around, she grabbed his hand and pulled playfully, but he stopped dead in his tracks when he saw the table glimmering in the light.

She wasn't going to give him an opportunity. She didn't know what she was up against, or if the nanites really gave him the superhuman abilities she'd seen on the video. The Taser came out. She pointed at his chest, pulled the trigger, and the darts shot forward. They hit him dead center, and down he went.

She ignored the precautionary warning in the user's manual, the one which told her not to electrocute a person multiple times. If the nanites did exist, she was hoping they would keep him alive. Trigger. Drag. Trigger. Drag. She worked quickly to pull him in the moments he had no motor control.

*Don't die before I get what I need!*

The longest time she went without shocking him was to hoist him up onto the table and, even then, it was almost too long. Using the last of the charge, she had to work fast to throw the chains and shackles on to restrain him.

"Wha-what are you doing?" Reyes asked. "Damnit! What the hell?"

"I'm sorry, but I need your nanites."

"What the hell are you talking about?" Reyes struggled against the chains.

*What the hell am I talking about? Did I kidnap some innocent soldier? Were all the documents I read real?*

*Yes. They were. I saw them. I read them. How is he moving and talking after I used the Taser on him multiple times? They're there.*

"Let me go, you bitch!"

The deed was done, or at least part of it. She had him there, and now it was time to get answers. With minimal lighting, she grabbed a tray with the items necessary to draw blood. Morgan put on gloves, to avoid contamination, and grabbed the tourniquet to put on Reyes' arm. He struggled against her.

"Get away from me!"

"Shut up," she said while moving to prepare him.

"Stay away from me with that!" He struggles.

She was forced to find the Taser and pull the trigger again. There was enough juice to cause paralysis one last time, and she took the opportunity to put the tourniquet on and start a blood draw. The needle went in easy enough, and she plugged in the collection tube. Blood had begun to fill the vial, and she watched eagerly.

*

**Present day:**

Because of Morgan's resistance and ability to withhold information, he had no choice but to try the next technique. He viciously poured water on the towel covering her face. She struggled and screamed in between gasps of air and dry heaving.

The team assigned to reprogramming had made little progress, and they'd gone through a hundred mice already because of her kill command. *If we run out of mice, we'll have to test on infected people.*

"You can end this!" he yells in her face while practically drowning her. "You can make this stop. Give me what I want and you can rest."

Truman lets up, and Morgan gags and heaves.

"No more! Please, God, kill me!"

"Tell us where the key is!" he yells more.

"Arturo! He has the key!"

"We've checked all your contacts and found no Arturo! Who is he?"

"X. A. Four. V. H. Seven…"

"What is that? Is that a password?"

She doesn't respond. Coughing, she's struggling to breathe. *She's close. She has to be!* He shakes her violently.

"Keep talking, goddammit!"

She vomits and begins choking on it. He waves the soldier over and they unshackle her from the table. Doctor Tseng bursts into the room, slamming the door against the wall and the three of them turn her onto her side. Tseng clears her airway, and she wheezes and coughs.

"She can't take any more," Tseng scolds him.

"Shut the hell up!" he grabs the doctor by the collar of his coat and yells in his face. "Prepare to go again."

"No. That's enough!" He shoves Truman.

Truman comes back and punches Tseng in the jaw. He's already tense, but his body finds ways to tighten more.

"If you kill her, you'll never get what you need!" Tseng screams at him.

"You…you'll never get it." Morgan spits in renewed defiance. "I'll never help you."

He glares at her furiously. *How much farther can she be pushed? If she's still defiant after all that, can she be broken?*

Pulling his Glock 19 from its holster, he points it to her head.

"Cooperate or die!" He grits his teeth and bares them.

She mouth opens in a weak smirk. "Fu—"

*Click.* The gun fires. The bullet enters her skull and exits out the back, spattering the assisting soldier. His ears ring from the deafening sound, which has echoed off the closed room's walls. Her lifeless body falls backward onto the table and all hope of her helping them fix her mess is gone.

Truman turns the gun on the serviceman and fires two shots to his chest. Doctor Tseng tries to escape, but he puts two bullets in his back as he flees.

The president had already dismissed him, so he wasn't worried about his life as a decorated officer. No. This fight was now to move forward with curing the population, and then progressing with his goals for Project N.

*It has to be me. I can't trust that anyone else would understand the vision to bring humanity to its greatest.*

*

# Chapter 2:

**Three months ago:**

Within days of kidnapping Reyes, Morgan had liquidated her assets and turned the cash into cryptocurrency. Her former life as an InfoSec programmer, and her comfy life in a condo, was over. The less she was out in the public, the less chance she had of being caught. She had to buy another cheap car, since the one she'd used to kidnap him would likely be on every government hot sheet in the country. Resources came in the form of paying someone else to deliver to a random location at night, where she'd then go to pick it up.

It didn't take long to accumulate a few high end computers, several monitors, and other essentials she was sure she would need to begin reverse engineering TEAL's super soldier programming. What took the longest were special materials for building a *key*, an apparatus to interface with and re-program the blood cell sized robots.

First, God-Complex exploited a server vulnerability in TEAL's network and repurposed Morgan's exfiltration worm to grab blueprints for their version of their nanite docking bay. Then after studying them, she had to spend countless hours on the deep web tracking down prototypes of micro-circuitry, high end processors, learning how to make small amounts of carbon nanotubes, and creating her own USB-to-circuit connection.

This wasn't a trip to the computer store. Because of the unique application of such technology, she bought randomly, one or two pieces at a time, and from different sellers so her trail would be difficult to follow.

The key she'd developed allowed interface to a single nanite. It would attach to its docking slot to receive new commands, and then it would disseminate the instructions to its fellow nanites. It was incredibly simple to push out updates with software version numbers to keep them all straight.

She looked through a 1000x microscope into a closed petri dish of an electrical conductive gel. A group of incredibly small machines swarmed, forming her user name: Apocalypse M. It was something she'd programmed as a test, and just kept it that way.

It was one thing to hear rumors and see the idea on paper, but another completely to have the technology in hand. The government and TEAL had succeeded in pushing the transhumanism movement forward into a new, terrifying realm.

Amongst the functions which increased individual abilities, there was also the possibility of controlling brain function. The areas of code which increased mental capacity also had the ability to individually access the different regions of the brain, and emit their own electrical impulses to mimic the brain's neurons firing.

*The sheep will be true sheep. The government wants to create zombies? I'll give them zombies they can't control.*

Reyes grunted and jostled against his chains, bringing her back to reality for a moment. He threatened to break his wrists and ankles for the third time in his struggle to escape, but she'd installed a low amperage device which she could use as a giant Taser. She turned it on for a moment to stop him.

She sighed. What she was doing was a lonely existence, but she was in a race now with the government to push the nanites public. Sure, she had Reyes to talk to, but in her current experiment, he was a mindless drone. Before she'd taken away his higher brain functions, he attempted to persuade her to let him go. There were promises of money and that he'd never say a word about the kidnapping. In the end, she silenced him by commanding the nanites to inhibit his brain's speech center.

The new world she was in was madness. She knew what she was planning was no better than what the government had in mind. But she could control the narrative.

*Those who don't become infected will have no choice but to wake up and confront the government, and TEAL.*

The nanites were nearly ready. Taking cues from zombie movies, she'd reprogrammed them like a virus, which would take complete control of the host's brain. The only difference would be that, instead of consuming the flesh, they'd bite to infect and move on.

Sitting back in her chair, she chuckled and slurped some noodles. The chat box was open with God-Complex, and he was digging for information.

> God-Complex: Are you really going through with this? We have enough to damn this program, and any future iteration of this technology, forever. You could just leak the info.

> Apocalypse M: Leaked info hasn't done shit to make any real changes.

> God-Complex: What you're talking about is basically genocide.

> Apocalypse M: Except it's not. I'll have a cure prepared, and I'll release it when the US complies with whatever demands I come up with.

> God-Complex: What if I get infected? I don't want to have to wait for them to give in. Can you send me the cure? Just in case.

> Apocalypse M: No.

The key which held the cure would keep her alive if she was caught. If he had it, he could turn on her. Even though he helped her get to this point, she couldn't allow anyone access.

> God-Complex: What if you die or turn into a zombie?

> Apocalypse M: I won't die, and I won't get infected. I'm going to hide out after I let this guy go.

> God-Complex: Will you at least tell me when you're releasing it?

She clicked the X, giving him no answer. Staring at Reyes, she watched him in his zombified state, chomping his teeth at her. The next step would be to ensure the nanite virus was spreadable. In the programming, she'd tailored it so one hundred thousand nanites were transferred in a bite, and those would migrate to the new host's brain. After they took over, they'd reproduce.

She laughed, and though there was a tiny whisper in her head telling her she was deranged, she brushed it aside and set about finalizing the changes.

*

It was far from ideal, but she had to test the nanites somehow, and kidnapping another person was out of the question. The pressure mounted on her to make sure it worked as intended. At the Manhattan Animal Care Center, she paid to adopt a pit-terrier mix under her fake identity.

The dog was happy-go-lucky, and she felt a little bad bringing the animal into the experiment. After all, it wasn't animals ruining the world. But it was the only way to ensure she stayed hidden until she wanted to be known.

The nanites were programmed to work the same in animals with the caveat that, except for this trial, the human zombies wouldn't be programmed to attack animals to infect them.

On the drive back to the warehouse, she let the pup ride up front with her, giving him treats to keep him content. He stuck his nose out for fresh air when she rolled the window down for him. After infection, she would test his want to spread it to her, and for safety, she had purchased a muzzle and a sturdy chain. She couldn't allow him to bark or bite because even a drop of saliva meant potential transmission of the infected nanites.

In the warehouse, she parked, and shut the bay door. The dog, who she'd named Arturo after her favorite character in a 90s sci-fi series, leapt out of the vehicle as soon as the door was open. He was off to smell every inch of the musty building. She was okay letting him be for the moment, and unloaded the car of supplies.

Reyes greeted her from his table with grunting and gnashing his teeth. The chains were still intact. Next to the bed were eyebolts she'd screwed into the wall, where Arturo was going to be hooked up.

She'd purchased a full hazmat suit and programmed this round of nanites for delayed takeover. She wanted to be sure that in the event of her own infection, she would have time to use a *keyed nanite* to cancel it.

The supplies got put next to the desk where her protective gear was. While putting on her suit, she whistled for Arturo. The pup came bounding up the stairs and into the room. His tongue was out, and it appeared as though he was smiling.

"Come here, boy!" She patted her legs and spoke excitedly.

He wanted attention, and so he ran to her. She patted his head and gave his neck a few quick strokes. When she grabbed the muzzle, she expected resistance, but he took it's fitting like a champ. With her hazmat suit hood over her head, she led him to the eyebolt with the chain and locked him to the wall. He sat and waited.

The biggest challenge was going to be unhooking Reyes without being bitten, both now and when she released him to the public. Morgan grabbed her Taser, and with her free hand, unshackled his legs first. He kicked around, trying to stand. On the right side, she released his shackle, and he flung himself off the table to where Arturo was. Because of the close proximity, the dog was now the target. But he still couldn't quite reach. Arturo saw Reyes as an opportunity for attention.

She didn't want to watch, and so she turned her head as Arturo jumped up to greet him. He yelped in pain. In her peripheral vision she saw him run and cower at the end of his chain, out of Reyes' grasp. She felt horrible, but he would heal.

With Arturo now bitten, Morgan again became the center of Reyes' attention. He climbed back onto the table to crawl over, but the moment he was on it she flipped the switch to electrocute him, and he was incapacitated.

It didn't take her but a few moments to have him shackled again. Over on the side where Arturo was, she knelt down where the edge of his chain reached. She held her hand out to him to let him know it was alright. He inched over, looking back at Reyes with cautious eyes.

"Don't worry, boy," she called through the mask on her suit. "He won't hurt you again."

He was content for a moment to let her pet him with her rubberized hands. She saw the moment he changed. His eyes dilated, and he was quick to pounce. Because she had led him to the edge of his chain, he could do little more than jump at her and growl. The muzzle stayed in place, and the heavy duty chain was doing its job. Arturo was now her zombie-dog.

She used the Taser on Arturo, and drew some blood from his neck. Placing a drop on a slide, she slid it under the microscope. The nanites were there, replicating. Her experiment was a success, and now she had to undo it. Taking the key's probe, she put it onto the blood and waited for the prompt on her screen to tell her a nanite was connected. The code to disable the kill command and reverse the zombie programming was loaded and ready to inject into Arturo.

It took about five minutes for the single nanite to spread its code to the others, and his behavior returned to normal. He was once again the pup who wanted love and affection. Morgan let her guard down. She took off the hazmat suit and set Arturo free.

At her desk, she sat and pulled up a browser on the computer next to the one she used for programming. The browser asked if she wanted to restore her last session. She did and it brought up The Great New York State Fair's webpage. Pulling up their interactive map she set about virtually canvasing.

"What better place…?"

*

**Two months ago:**

The internet made her job easy. She figured out her point of entry, path, and exit all through maps, satellite images, and street views. The New York

Fair's website even had a button to show where the State Police zone would be located, giving her the ability to avoid it entirely.

Reyes grunted next to her, bound and gagged inside a generic rip-off of the Otto the Orange costume she'd turned into a walking Faraday cage. Dressing him up so his whole body was covered was the only way to get him in without his being recognized or drawing negative attention. Morgan primped herself in the visor mirror of her little beater car, fixing the blonde wig and oversized sunglasses to look just right. After all this preparation, she was going to make sure she wasn't caught.

Parked off State Fair Boulevard, across a small bridge, the walk was lengthier than she'd have liked, considering she was escorting a zombie. But she didn't want her getaway vehicle identified until long after she was gone. All she had to do was get him in in the gate without incident and make it about midway into the park before releasing him.

He wasn't compliant by any stretch of the imagination, but she'd made a modification to the nanites, one which sapped his strength for a limited time. She had another half hour to get in there and prepare to unleash him. On their way to the gate, every person they passed, he bumped into, no doubt trying to bite them. He was ready to begin his mission.

"What the hell's your problem?" a random bystander raises their voice.

She found herself apologizing every few seconds, and just hoping to get him in quickly. At the gate, she had to keep him wrangled by sticking her arm into the back side of the orange suit and grabbing the belt on his pants. When it was her turn, she fumbled in her pocket for the fifty dollar bill she'd prepared ahead of time. The woman squinted and scrunched her brows in question as the big orange faux-mascot kept trying to walk forward. While she handed the bill over, Morgan's arm was jerked hard. She pulled him back.

"Sorry, he's excited."

The woman said nothing and handed Morgan two passes and her change. She nodded and shoved Reyes through. Looking over her shoulder, she feared something would go wrong. Even with concealing his identity and blocking the GPS transmissions, everything felt too smooth.

Once out of the suit, the GPS would be picked up, and the government would correlate the zombie outbreak to their nanites. Then after the military swooped in, she planned to release a video to expose them. There wouldn't be any easy out for them. TEAL and those behind the scenes would have no option but to confess their involvement.

They reached a few concession stands, and she knew the timer was almost done. Within minutes, the nanite programming would return to normal and his super strength would return. Ducking behind a kid's mirror maze, she undid his bindings, and removed the gag through the back of the costume. He tried to bite her, but she was quick enough to pull her hand back.

She shoved him away and ran. It wasn't going to be the same as famous movies or television shows. There would be a crazed man running around, biting people. She expected law enforcement would find him quickly, but by the time they did, several more would *turn*, and the outbreak would begin.

Looking over her shoulder as she escaped, she watched Reyes rip the head off the faux-mascot and begin the mission.

*

"Sir! Corporal Antonio Reyes nanite-bio signature has just reappeared!" The tech looked over his shoulder at the commanding officer.

"Where?"

"Syracuse, New York. His nanite markers are pinging from the state fairgrounds."

"What the hell is he doing up there? How fast can we get the EH-US-11 unit on location?"

"Ten minutes."

"Mobilize them to extract Reyes."

"Yes, sir!" The tech begins typing furiously at his console and issuing commands.

General Truman was fuming. All he could think about was how much trouble this Marine was about to be in. He'd have him stripped of his nanites, then of his rank, and he'd then make him disappear.

*

Corporal Reyes was locked in his mind. There was nothing he could do to control himself since *that woman* had experimented with the nanites. All he knew was that he was craving to sink his teeth into the flesh of everyone nearby. He ripped himself halfway out of the bright orange costume, and he found his first target.

It was horrific. A little girl screamed as he bit deep into her forearm. The metallic taste of blood filled his mouth. A woman holding the girl's hand screamed also. She tried to rip the little girl from his grasp, but he was too strong. A man came to their aid and punched him square in the jaw. The monster within redirected to bite both of them also. First the woman in her neck, and then the man on his cheek. The fairgrounds erupted into chaos, and every single person was a target.

One after another, he pounced, tearing into flesh and moving on. He was covered with the blood of a dozen people by the time he heard law enforcement officers.

"Get down on the ground with your hands behind your head!"

Reyes whipped around to find himself twenty yards from two officers with their guns aimed squarely at him. If he could, he would have dropped right there, but the flesh hungry beast charged with inhuman speed. Their eyes widened, and the only thing they could do was pull their triggers. It's what he would have done.

They each double tapped, and four bullets entered his torso. The pain was brief because the nanites quickly set about pushing the bullets out and healing the wounds. Even with having been shot, it didn't slow him down, and he was too fast for them to get off another shot. He bit into one, and then the other, digging his teeth in wherever they were exposed. There was flesh between his teeth and blood in his mouth. He wanted to vomit so badly, but nothing came up.

*

Morgan wasn't far when the screaming and commotion started. Then there was gunfire. Out on the street, and halfway back to her car, people started pouring out. She ditched her wig and glasses over a fence and in some bushes to avoid being recognized.

It was only a few moments before she was in the car and speeding to the north exit of the field, and back onto the boulevard. Heading toward Highway 690, she checked her watch. 12:12 PM. *The second wave should be starting now.*

As she hit the onramp, a military chopper flew overhead. It was a much quicker response time than anticipated. The gas pedal hit the floor, and she was flying. Law enforcement would be concentrated on the fairgrounds, so she felt no need to limit herself until she had a good distance.

*

A military chopper came to hover a hundred yards from Reyes while he chased down an elderly woman and bit her shoulder.

People who had been bitten now attacked others. The masses didn't know what to do. Those who were trampled and fallen were the next wave to be bitten. That woman had made him the start of an outbreak which he could only identify as *zombies*.

Four fully armored soldiers rappelled from the chopper and disconnected their lines.

"Corporal Reyes! Stand down!" a woman yelled as the helicopter pulled up.

They were strategically spaced, rifles leveled at him. Without warning, Reyes pivoted on his heels and sprinted for the soldiers. They had no hesitation in pulling their triggers. He felt the hot lead enter all over, but he kept going.

He leapt up and tackled one of the men, clawing at the helmet and face guard to get it off. The other three soldiers tried to pull him off, but they were too slow.

"Get off me, you son of a bitch!" the man yelled.

Reyes ripped the mask off and bit him on the nose, severing it. Blood spurted out, and the last thing he saw was the muzzle of a rifle come to his forehead. *Bang!*

*

"What the fuck is going on?" Lance Corporal Garfield yelled.

"You mother… Son of a bitch!" Sergeant Charles Truman yelled out while shoving Reyes off of him and standing up. "What the fuck?"

More people rushed to attack the unit. They had a crazed look in their eyes and blood on their faces, like Reyes. Grunts and guttural growls filled the air.

"Stop!" Corporal Fitzgerald yelled at them.

It didn't deter them, and they closed fast. Sergeant Truman, the unit's commanding officer, was too busy holding his face to make any quick decisions. It had to be her. *This is how every zombie movie ever starts. If they're just crazy people, I'm going to hell for this!*

"Take them out!" she ordered.

She and two others opened fire to defend themselves. With ease, she, Lance Corporal Garfield, and Lance Corporal Ford took out the wave coming at them.

Truman's nose gushed. He tried cupping it, as if it would stop the bleeding. When it was safe, she grabbed a rag from her pack and put it to his face. She pressed hard, and then took Truman's hand and put it up to the towel.

"Hold that there until they kick in! Garfield, Ford, get Reyes in the chopper," she barked.

She turned and saw another coming at her, and she landed a headshot to stop them in their tracks.

"Wait for them to kick in? Find my goddamn nose, Fitz, and put it to my face so they heal it on there!" he screamed.

*His nose is probably still in Reyes' mouth.* She ignored his request and grabbed a flamethrower from the chopper. Garfield and Ford loaded Reyes' body into a body bag and tossed him aboard while she torched the ground where Reyes' blood and brain matter had spattered. The heat was intense, but she had strict orders to incinerate any and all remnants of nanite technology which could be left behind.

*Where have you been? We spend weeks looking for you and you show up half a state away.*

The screams of people nearby made her question what the hell was actually going on, but her orders were only to secure Reyes and return to the Airforce base at Hancock International. With the ground properly torched, she shut the flamethrower off, and the unit put the flames out. Back into the helicopter, they secured themselves and shut the door. The chopper took off and headed back the direction they came.

Turning her attention to Sergeant Truman, he'd found time to pry the bit of nose from Reyes' mouth. When Truman pulled the towel away there was no need for it. The nanites had completely reconstructed it, as if it were never gone. His face paled, and he looked like he might be sick to his stomach.

"Did you know they could do that?" he asked, and pointed at his new nose.

"No, sir," she responded.

"I was going to be pissed if they had to surgically reattach it!" He laughed. It made her smile, though only half-heartedly because of what they just had to do.

"Call it in," he commanded Fitz.

She picked up the headset and put it on. "This is Corporal Fitzgerald. Corporal Reyes is secured in a body bag. Reyes attacked Sergeant Truman. Scene scrubbed, but something bad is going on down there. Requesting ground support to contain. Over."

"Target acquisition confirmed. Return to the base. Over," came a command through the headset.

The pilot arced the chopper around. Below in the fairgrounds was a chaotic scene. More and more people were attacking others, and she felt she made the right decision when they were rushed. While it was a bit paranoid to think it was some sort of zombie outbreak, she had no other explanation.

"Command, confirm receipt of second part of message. There's an issue at the fairgrounds. Corporal Reyes attacked us, but it's not an isolated incident. It's like a crazed riot," she spoke into the headset again. "We may have a contagion outbreak. Requesting assistance for the ground. Over."

At these words, both Lance Corporals Garfield and Ford brushed their hands off on themselves in an attempt to wipe away any potential contagion.

"Let the local's handle it. Over."

"Negative, command. Possible contagion outbreak on the ground at the fairgrounds. Unknown if Corporal Reyes is Patient Zero. Requesting quarantine. Over."

"Return to the base. Over and out."

*Idiots! Romero would be proud that the idiocy portrayed in the movies actually happens!*

Before she could hang up the headset, she noticed Truman's head slump for a moment before springing back to life. Turning to his subordinate in the next seat, he lunged over and attacked Lance Corporal Ford. Ford freaked out and began screaming. Fitz knew what was coming next, and she sprang up and entered the cockpit and slammed the door shut. Locking it, she left Lance Corporal Garfield out there to fend for himself.

"Help! Fitz! Let me in!" Garfield yelled through the door. "Truman! Truman, what are you doing man? Back the hell up!"

She couldn't believe what was happening. Her half-joking idea of a zombie outbreak was turning out to be real. She grabbed the headset next to the pilot and began yelling into it.

"Mayday! Mayday! Confirmed contagion! Sergeant Truman was bitten by Corporal Reyes, and he is now attacking Lance Corporals Garfield and Ford! Confirm! Over!"

"Confirmed. Status? Over."

"Returning to the base. Side doors are shut. When we land, be ready to eliminate Truman, Garfield, and Ford to prevent the spread of the contagion! Over."

Her heart was in her throat. The pilot looked at her, his eyes wide. Now the commanding officer of the mission, she had to give clear direction.

"Return to the base! Do not deviate!"

A loud *bang* on the cockpit door startled her, and she directed her attention back to it. *Bang! Bang! Bang!* It was starting to buckle.

*What the hell? What the hell?*

She was at a loss for words. The only thing she could do was wedge herself against the door buckling inward. The pilot pushed the helicopter to its top speed, trying to make it back to base.

*

General Truman listened in and couldn't believe what he was hearing. *An outbreak? Of what?* He didn't truly care. All he knew was his son was aboard that helicopter, potentially infected with a disease the nanites couldn't target. He had to act fast.

"Get the CDC on the line," he ordered.

He was handed a phone, and he began delegating to the CDC exactly what was going to happen. His voice was so commanding, and his directions concise, they had no time to get a word in. Slamming the phone down, he dialed the commander of the Air Force base they were heading to.

"This is General Truman. Prepare for quarantine. Upon arrival of the helicopter to your base, take EH-US-11 unit, the pilot, and Corporal Reyes' body into holding for further analysis. Hazmat suits are required," he barked through a secured line.

Turning to an aide, he issued a command, "Get a jet ready."

*

Fitz was close to freaking out by the time the helicopter landed on the pad at Hancock. The door was bowing in, and despite holding it, she wouldn't be able keep it from collapsing. Hands from all three teammates reached in the gaps, and she popped the safety button on her sidearm holster, readying herself to shoot them if necessary.

She was relieved to see a dozen soldiers outside, weapons raised to take out whatever her teammates had become. There were a couple soldiers ready in full biohazard suits. Two of the soldiers outside held what looked like rocket launchers. One soldier crept up, rifle aimed at the side door to the helicopter. He opened the side door and backed away quickly. Her unit was distracted, forgetting about her and the pilot.

It didn't matter that Truman, Garfield, and Ford were now running full speed toward the unit, she wasn't letting the door go until she saw them apprehended. The rocket launcher fired and a large net was ejected onto the three of them. Caught, they struggled and clawed to try and find their way out. With them temporarily immobilized, she felt she could breathe a sigh of relief.

"Corporal Fitzgerald and Lieutenant Johnson, step out from the helicopter," came a voice over a bullhorn.

Fitz did as she was told and opened the door from the cockpit. The Lieutenant followed. Watching the men in biohazard suits, they struggled to apply restraints to the infected men. It was a surreal scene and caused her to completely miss the guns pointed at her, until someone yelled over the bullhorn again.

"Stop now or we'll fire!"

She stopped dead in her tracks.

"What the hell do you think you're doing?" she asked.

"Ma'am, you could be infected. Until we know more about what's going on, you and the lieutenant are going to need to be quarantined."

"Are you shitting me? I haven't been bitten!" Fitz fumed.

"What do you mean *quarantined*?" The lieutenant's voice quivered.

"We don't know what this is. If you're infected, you could start an outbreak."

"There's already an outbreak at the fairgrounds! Whatever the hell happened to them started there!"

"Ma'am, I'm sorry, but I have orders. If you fail to comply, we are authorized to shoot."

She was beside herself. *They can see damn well I'm not acting rabid!* The Lieutenant beside her twitched, and she wondered if he was going to be the real life movie cliché and try to run. And then they'd gun him down, and he'd be dead for nothing. She wasn't going to give him the chance to make the stupid decision.

Fitz put her hand on the Lieutenant's shoulder and whispered to him, "Relax. When they see we're not infected, they're going to let us go."

Putting her hands behind her head, she allowed herself to be bound, and followed the men in biohazard suits. There were two unmarked white vans waiting for them, and she was thankful when they separated her and Johnson from her teammates and Reyes' body. The windowless doors were shut, and it became pitch black inside. The van started, and they were off to wherever they were going to be held.

"What is going on?" Lieutenant Johnson was distraught.

"Zombies."

"That's just something you see on TV."

"They were bitten, then they went into a frenzied state trying to get to us. I'm not sure how else to explain it."

They became silent in the darkness, listening to the hum of the tires on the road as they sped to wherever they were going to be held.

*

She was already in Cicero. Her plan was to hop off the highway and drive around the north side of Oneida Lake. The smaller highway would be a good place to slow down and, hopefully, be off anyone's radar.

The radio blared the news as she sped along. The nanite outbreak was spreading fast. The voice on the radio spot, known as Jimmy Rock, was taking calls.

"Hey, you're on the radio with Jimmy Rock. What's your take on these people going all out and attacking others?"

"Bull—" a man started and was bleeped. "It's a hoax. You've seen those flash mob videos right? They're actors."

"Have you been listening to the news? The police and military are involved, trying to contain what apparently is being described as a full blown riot."

He played a dial tone and spoke again, "You're on the radio with Jimmy Rock. What do you make of this riot?"

"It's a nightmare. I-I didn't know who to call. 911 is busy! I don't know what to do. Help me!" a woman's voice whispered over the phone and barely came out audible. The volume increased, and dead air was heard for a few moments. "I can't move! They'll find me!"

"Ma'am, are you at the fairgrounds?"

"Yes!" she whispered frantically. "They...they shot my son! They shot him and he got back up!"

"Ma'am, stay calm. The police and military are working to clear the area."

"Oh God! No!"

Growls and grunting came through the radio as the woman was clearly being attacked. She screamed.

"Help me! H—"

Morgan turned it off. Infected innocents were part of the plan. Once the government complied, they'd get the key. No one was actually dying, because the nanites would regenerate them.

The video she planned to broadcast, shrouded behind a Guy Fawkes mask, would detail what the US government had been up to, and the hope was that she'd gain the entire world's attention.

Onto the smaller highway, she dropped down to the speed limit and kept a steady pace. Though she checked the mirror like a nervous wreck, she kept herself under control. Nothing would get her caught faster than drawing attention, either going too fast or too slow. With the nanite virus spreading, she just had to make it back to her warehouse, pack up, and hit 'Upload.'

*

General Truman boarded a small jet, readying to take off. The flight was going to take under an hour to get up to Syracuse. Between the reappearance of Corporal Reyes, the potential outbreak of an unknown contagion, and his son's infection, he wanted to have his boots on the ground up there now.

Even if his son wasn't involved, he had no choice but to get on the plane. The president wanted a status update as soon as he was there, to hopefully provide insight to the link between Reyes and this contagion. He had a hard time choking it down that Reyes was sick. *The nanites in his body should kill any infectious agent.* TEAL's nanites had created the perfect soldier, and with their technology, the chaotic world would soon be brought to order.

*We're so close to rolling this out. Why now? We need to get it under control so we can move forward with humanity's next step in evolution.*

He took a seat on the jet, and his personal aides, Bradford and Rosh, came to sit on either side of him. They pulled out their laptops to connect to the plane's Wi-Fi and began their work.

"I want a status report," he said.

"Yes, sir."

Rosh clacked away at her keyboard. The clicking noise of the keys drove Truman a little crazy, but he wouldn't allow himself to be ruled by emotion in this tense situation.

"Recap. What do we know about Corporal Reyes' disappearance and reappearance? Any connection?" Truman asked Bradford.

"He was on leave in New York city. Last seen and identified at a Midtown pub. He left with a woman, Caucasian, red hair, mid-thirties. Through facial recognition, we identified him a few blocks away when he got into a vehicle. The tracking on the nanites went dead at about 9:15 PM, caused by what the FBI believes was a signal jammer," Bradford recapped.

"After extensive hunting by the EH-US-11 unit and no success, he was classified as AWOL. This reemergence and emergency situation indicate his disappearance was probably not his intent. There are no current reports of how he got there, as law enforcement and the local military are too busy trying to regain control."

"Sir," Rosh chimed in, "Syracuse is in chaos right now. The local news has picked it up and are getting footage. Their current report is that a large number of crazed people are attacking others, and then the attacked joining in. It's like a zomb—"

"Don't finish that word," Truman interrupted. "I don't care what you think. Leave the movies to the movies. We're not going to spark mass panic spreading that idea. People are already going to be thinking it, let's not reinforce it."

Rosh turned her laptop so the three of them could see. The news crew was staying at a safe distance, flying overhead. The volume was muted, but the captions gave a clear depiction of what was going on: mass hysteria.

"What about fairground cameras?" he asked.

"We're working on getting all of the video we can, leading to, from, and inside the fairgrounds. Due to the chaos, it may take longer than normal," Bradford replied.

"I want to know everything about his entrance, who he was with, down to the color of their laces."

The news camera panned in as hordes were spewing across multiple highways. The crazed people were hit, and when cars stopped to check on them, they became the target of the horde.

He turned the volume up, and the report was gruesome.

"...stay indoors. It's chaos out here. People are attacking people. Local law enforcement and the military are out attempting to regain control, but their efforts so far are proving unsuccessful."

The camera zoomed in on one of the crazed people, who ran out onto the highway and is struck. Smartly, seeing what's going on, the vehicle's driver kept going. Panning away quickly, the camera operator caught a wider shot. Someone in the news station yelled out.

"They're getting back up!"

Redirected once more, the camera finds the wounded person, and they're back up on their feet as if nothing ever happened. No apparent broken bones, no visible lacerations. Truman's gut sinks at the thought that somehow Reyes has transmitted both a virus and nanites. The possibility of a sickening swarm of indestructible, crazed people was the farthest thing he thought he'd be dealing with today.

"What the hell is going on here?" The newscaster's calm broke, and he was visibly shaken. "I can't stay here. I have to go."

"Get the commanding officer up there on the line," Truman commanded, and felt a lump form in his throat.

The president hadn't taken the news well of one of his experimental soldiers going AWOL. There had been a full investigation, including international queries, to try to find him. It went as a negative mark against Truman, but now with Reyes' reappearance and whatever *this* was, the heat was about to be turned up tenfold.

"Sir?" Rosh spoke and held out a phone.

He took it and started speaking the moment it was up to his ear, "This is General Truman. I'm flying in from the Pentagon. We'll be landing at Hancock shortly. Have a vehicle and someone to brief me ready."

"Yes, sir!" came the voice from the other end.

He pressed the end call button and handed it back to Rosh.

*

They were in the vehicle but maybe fifteen minutes before they were pulling around sharply. The doors opened, and Fitz and Johnson were at gunpoint again. Led out to the emergency entrance of a hospital, she was absolutely in awe of how stupid everyone was acting. *It's like they've never watched a zombie horror movie, ever.*

"Let's go," barked a soldier in a biohazard suit.

Men and women in white doctor's coats barreled out with three gurneys for the *patients*, clearly alerted to the situation. Because she and Johnson weren't exhibiting violent signs, they were allowed to climb out on their own.

"Follow," commanded one of the soldiers.

They were led into a well-lit entryway and brought through the facility. Over her shoulder she saw her squad mates wrestled onto the gurneys. The staff were having a difficult time strapping them down. One strap went on, another snapped off due to the sheer force being applied. She was waiting for them to break free, but no screams were heard.

Led to an empty wing, she found this area lacking as a containment unit. The sliding doors were not reinforced in any way, and should one of her teammates escape, everyone would be in danger.

The doctor led her into a room, and Johnson into the next. The crazed Ford, Garfield, and Truman were wheeled by and stuck into the rooms a little farther beyond. The last to be hauled by was the deceased Reyes in his body bag. Soldiers were placed outside of every room, rifles at the ready.

The doctor who escorted her came to speak with the unit leader near Fitz's room.

"We can't keep these people here. We don't have the ability to properly quarantine. The ventilation has been shut off to this wing to prevent the spread of whatever this is," he said, "but if these people have a highly infectious disease, you're endangering other patients!"

"Not my call. I was ordered to bring them here. We need blood draws from all of them, and the deceased. Get me the supplies," the soldier in the biohazard suit directed.

The doctor ran off, calling nurses with him. Fitz's next step would be to comply and speak up about the danger. Her future would be determined by whether she could get out of here safely. When she approached her door, a rifle came to point at her head.

"Look, I'm normal. These people are turning within minutes of being bitten. If you keep me and Lieutenant Johnson in here, that leaves you short two people who can help."

"Sorry, Corporal, I have my orders. Need to clear you first."

"Then take my blood first, so I can get back to my duties!" she said, and rolled up her sleeve.

The doctor and nurses returned with enough supplies to draw from all of them. The hospital staff entered and began to set up, but a soldier in a biohazard suit came in and took over.

"Thank you, you can go."

"I—" the doctor started.

"This is classified. I can't allow you to handle any of their blood," the man in the suit interrupted and grabbed the supplies from the doctor.

Stunned, they stood there until they were waved off. The soldier wasn't gentle when he stuck the needle into her arm and connected the vial for the draw. As soon as it was out, Fitz's nanites healed the puncture.

He left, handed the contaminated medical supplies to another person in a biohazard suit, and directed them.

"When we're done, incinerate the contaminated supplies."

He labeled her blood with a sticker and placed it in a padded container. Fitz understood from this they weren't going to look at it immediately, and it meant she was stuck here.

Canvasing the room, the ceiling had removable panels she could get to. When the situation went sideways, and she knew it would, she would jump up and see if she could make an exit through them.

*

# Chapter 3:

General Truman's plane landed, and before they'd finished taxiing, he was at the door, waiting to exit. A contingent of soldiers saluted as he disembarked, and a sergeant greeted him.

"Sir, we have a chopper ready for you. The infected soldiers are quarantined at a nearby hospital," he stated while waving the general along.

He followed the sergeant toward a Blackhawk, its rotors already spinning. On board, they lifted off, and he put his headset on. The sergeant copied him.

"Give me an update," he commanded.

"The fairgrounds are out of control. The contagion is spreading faster than we can respond. Local law enforcement and soldiers are pulling back to the base to regroup. Calls for evacuations have already been sent out."

"Was Corporal Reyes' body contained?"

"Yes, sir. Staff Sergeant Johns is currently overseeing the operation, drawing blood samples."

"I want the infected prepped for transport, and I want to be on a cargo plane back to DC in the next hour."

"Yes, sir!"

The sergeant began communicating and coordinating as the helicopter neared the hospital. On the landing pad, Truman was met by a doctor, who was eager to bring him inside.

There was a steady stream of people exiting the building in evacuation. He couldn't ignore the fearful glances, but he was steady in both his gait and facial expression.

Down into a wing where soldiers and doctors in biohazard suits hurried about, one soldier stood at the ready, a small black case on a cart next to him. When his eyes met the general's, he saluted and greeted him.

"General Truman, the blood samples have been collected."

"Good. Get them and my soldiers out to the helicopter."

There was a scream down the hall and everyone stopped to look.

*

Corporal Reyes awoke in a dark place. The last thing he remembered was being shot in the head. He ripped open the fabric enclosing him and sat straight up. Nurses, doctors, and people in biohazard suits were moving around, but the moment he was seen one of them let out a bloodcurdling scream.

Still not in control, he leapt and attacked the nearest person, biting into them, and then moving on. Panicked hospital staff scrambled and soldiers shot at him, but he was too fast. He tore through clothes and suits, biting everyone he could.

*

Something had gone critically wrong, as Fitz anticipated. *There was no way this low level of quarantine was ever going to hold these infected.*

"General Truman!" she yelled as she threw open the hospital room door. "Get the hell out! Now!"

Soldiers were too busy aiming their guns down the hall to care about her breaking quarantine. The general took notice, though, and Fitz didn't have to say it twice. He grabbed the black case the vials of blood had been put in and made a beeline for the exit. Because she wasn't being watched, she ran, following him out.

Out on the helipad, General Truman jumped aboard the helicopter parked there. Fitz reached in and grabbed a rifle, pointing it at the door out to the pad.

He barked at the pilot, "Get us in the air! Now!"

The pilot did the pre-flight check and began the startup of the engine. Screams and gunfire were drowned out by the blades cutting the air. The door burst open, and a few people ran out onto the deck, followed by a revived Reyes.

She shot Reyes in the head once more, saving a couple people for a few minutes. They ran for the helicopter, but she took aim at them too. They stopped dead in their tracks. *Can't take the chance.*

With the engine full roar, she took a seat but kept her gun pointed, and they looked at her in disbelief. Only after the helicopter had taken off did she flip the safety latch and secure the gun. Fitz picked a headset up and waited for the general to put his on. He did, and she pressed the push-to-talk button.

"Sir! We have a major problem. The nanites in Corporal Reyes' body healed him from a headshot!"

"What the hell happened, Corporal?"

"He attacked Sergeant Truman. I delivered the kill shot to Reyes at point blank range. We loaded him up in a body bag, and the next thing I know, Sergeant Truman is attacking Garfield and Ford. With this contagion and the nanites, this just became a zombie shit storm!"

"With EH-US-11 out of commission, I'm going to reassign you to the EH-US-7 unit out of Maryland, and you'll assume command. I want your knowledge at the front of our defense plans, but do not call these zombies."

"General, the public is going to quickly make that assertion themselves."

"I want the media focused on evacuations rather than speculation. We need to slow the spread by taking away the fodder."

The general didn't seem shaken. He'd always come off as strong and a little pompous to her. Reading him, it almost felt like he was a little disconnected, despite his son being back at the hospital.

"Take me back to the jet I came in on," he ordered the pilot.

"Yes, sir!" came the reply.

Fitz stared out the door at the airport, and all hell had broken loose. People were out on the Tarmac trying to get on planes in the process of taking off. A group headed for the private jet the helicopter was landing next to. Several soldiers guarded the stairs up and were readying to turn people away.

She grabbed the rifle, an extra magazine, and then disembarked with the general. She flipped the safety latch, and she prepared to bring the gun up. A family of three reached the soldiers first.

"Sir, you need to go back the other way!" one of the soldiers called out.

General Truman headed for the stairs, and Fitz followed. Instead of climbing the stairs after him, she turned to her fellow soldiers.

"Please! Please let us on!" the father cried out, approaching to within a few feet of a soldier. "All of the other flights are booked or cancelled!"

"Sir! Do not come any closer or we will open fire!" The soldier brought his gun up to point at the man's head.

The man stuck his hand out in defense, while pulling his daughter to him. The wife stayed near, but still behind.

"I understand you're doing your job," he started, "but you don't want to kill innocent people, right?"

Fitz stepped up and put her hand on the muzzle of the soldier's rifle to push it down. If life had taught her anything, it was that scared humans were more prone to doing shitty things to one another when things were going south. She wanted to give some people hope.

"Sir, get on that plane," she directed the father.

"Ma'am, you don't have that authority," the soldier whose muzzle she was holding down protested.

"I do now. Stand down," Fitz snapped, and then nodded at the man. "Get on there, now."

"Thank you!" He had tears in his eyes as he led his family to the stairs.

Fitz followed them up. In the cabin, the man looked around, confused on where to sit. She directed them to some open seats. The general gave her a confused look.

Her moral compass was telling her to stay here and protect the country she swore to. Before the general could speak, she preempted him.

"These people will be riding with you back to DC. Sir, I understand your order, but I feel it would be best for me to be here on the front line, to help our troops *here* and assist with evacuations."

"Corporal, you don't have the authority to reassign yourself."

"Sir, then maybe you should consider me AWOL. I'm staying behind to save some people." Fitz wasn't going to back down from this. "When you get back to Washington, I need you to order a supply drop with as many flamethrowers and incendiary devices as you can send."

The general reached over to his side and pulled out a SAT phone. He handed it to her, and she knew she had the go-ahead.

Fitz saluted him, and he saluted back.

"Semper fi!" he said.

"Semper fi!" she returned.

"When I return to Washington, we will start working on finding out what this is. Until we understand it, and form a cure, under no circumstance are you to terminate Sergeant Truman."

If she had a child, she'd request the same thing. Cures never existed in movies or TV, but she was willing to give the general the benefit of the doubt.

"Yes, sir!" She saluted again and about-faced to leave.

Back on the ground, other people had taken notice of the private jet. The door was being closed, and they were running to get there before it took off. Unlike the family, these dozens of people posed a threat to the general's takeoff. Bringing her gun up, she leveled it at them. Her duty now was to protect his flight so he could make it back to DC.

The plane's engines roared to life and it began to taxi to the runway. People were determined to get out in front of it. There was no point in trying to yell at them over the whining of the jet, so with marksman skill she fired a round at the feet of a man. He jumped back, but others kept heading forward. The soldiers around her were left with no choice. They opened fire to stop the crowd.

*

She was trying to limit her speed, but the news had people flocking to the highways to evacuate, and so her foot pressed the gas to try and speed past as much of it as possible. The roads were becoming more and more congested, and at the rate people were fleeing, her original printed directions were likely to land her in stopped traffic. With perfect conditions, she'd have been back at the warehouse inside another three hours, but these weren't perfect conditions.

As she came to a halt on the highway, she had to weigh her options. Continue this course or pull off and plot a different route. Turning the radio back on, she pressed the 'Scan' button until she found the local news.

"...are urging anyone near Syracuse to stay indoors. If you are outside of that area and are planning to evacuate, please use caution. "

"The president has declared a state of emergency and is coordinating with FEMA, local law enforcement, the military, and the CDC to quarantine this."

*There's no way they'll be able to quarantine the area. They'd have to quarantine all of New York. If even one of them gets out, it will be impossible to stop.*

*I have to make sure. I have to get back to the warehouse and get the other sample of nanites. I'll create another patient zero, just so their resources are spread thin.*

Beyond getting to the warehouse, the biggest issue would be to create a second outbreak without getting caught. The precautions she'd taken to get to this point were extensive. There was no way for her to organize the same type of outbreak, and anything she did would risk exposure.

She veered off the road to a pull out and grabbed her road atlas. Mapping it out, she found she could follow Taconic State Parkway all the way down into Manhattan. It would hopefully get her close to home.

*

Truman landed back at the Ronald Reagan Washington National Airport. With the case with the vials of blood, his first stop would be at TEAL's regional office.

Bradford had called ahead, and a car was waiting for them. He, Bradford, and Rosh climbed into the glossy black SUV. When they were settled, the vehicle sped off. Driven only fifteen minutes away, they pulled up to an ordinary office building. There were no signs, no logos, and nothing to distinguish this office from any other.

The regional office of TEAL was left nondescript for the very reason of anonymity. Their only noteworthy feature was that inside the bulletproof glass, keycard locked door, you could see their plain white interior and a single receptionist. He dug in his inside jacket pocket and produced the keycard needed to gain entry. The receptionist greeted him cordially.

"General Truman, Doctor Gray is waiting for you."

Around the corner, there were closed doors to what he knew were empty offices. TEAL's program was too important and sensitive to house even basic staff on this floor. Alphaeus Lang had taken heavy precautions, putting everything on different levels of the facility, amongst other things.

He swiped his badge at the single working elevator amongst dummy shafts, and the doors opened. Inside, he had to provide a simultaneous retina and fingerprint scan before the elevator would even take an input of what floor to go to. He pressed the tenth floor button, and the elevator whirred to life.

When the door opened, Doctor Gray was there waiting for him. Truman handed him the case, and he took it with haste. The doctor led him into a general area where lab technicians in white coats were busy about their work. TEAL had multiple projects besides Project N, but this one was the most ambitious.

Gray set the case down and opened it to reveal the five vials from the soldiers. He put heavy latex gloves on and picked one up. He was careful in handling it as he examined the label. 'Sergeant Charles Truman' was the name on it. The doctor looked at Truman.

"Get on with it, Doctor. We need this blood analyzed immediately for a potential contagion the nanites can't eradicate."

"What's happening out there?" the doctor asked as he put the vial back, closed the case, and started off for a clean room.

"The AWOL soldier you were unable to track showed back up in Syracuse and began attacking people. While the military is handling that, we need to prepare some answers for the public."

"I'll see what I can do," the doctor replied and called two people over. "Beth, Mike. With me."

People in lab coats followed him to a decontamination chamber. One at a time, they were processed through, putting on full biohazard suits in the process. He stayed on this side of the glass to observe.

*

Doctor Gray pulled out Corporal Reyes' vial. He hoped Reyes was, in fact, patient zero. If the nanites had missed a contagion somehow, he was confident the team could correct the error to eradicate it. *Alphaeus will have to push the public release timeline forward if we can use the nanites as a cure.*

He, Mike, and Beth prepared the microscope to not only examine the nanites, but also check for any additional foreign bodies. Handing Beth the vial, she unscrewed the blue cap. He pulled out a sterile dropper and prepared a sample. Once it was placed into the microscope he sat at the desk and his fingers hit the keyboard with a flurry.

When the image of the blood sample came up, there was nothing abnormal about it.

"What are you seeing?" General Truman's voice came over an intercom.

Doctor Gray depressed a button to respond. "Nothing. There's no sign of any bacterial or viral agents. The blood cells are healthy, and the nanites are in working order."

"That's impossible. There has to be a reason for this spreading like a contagion."

"I don't know what to tell you. Perhaps it's something wrong in their brain matter? If not, this isn't biological."

"Corporal Reyes was AWOL for some time. Are the nanites malfunctioning?"

Pulling the sample from the microscope, he placed the slide into a custom port on the computer. Through the port, he interfaced the nanites so their code could be reviewed.

Once it was loaded, he stepped aside to let Beth take over. She was young, her fingers were faster, and she had been a key component to lab testing the nanites on mice.

He and Mike hovered over her while she scrolled through the code. She didn't need to say anything for him to immediately notice problems.

"General Truman, the code has been changed." He looked over to the glass and frowned.

"How the hell is that possible, Doctor?" he yelled. The doctor watched the veins pop out on his forehead.

"It's going to take time for us to find out. We had multiple layers of security, not to mention there was no other technology out there to even interface with the nanites."

"I think it's pretty goddamn obvious you have a leak somewhere!"

Doctor Gray headed to a phone on the wall and dialed the IT extension. It rang for half a second before it was answered.

"Hello. IT."

"This is Doctor Gray in the nanite lab. Have there been any security breaches into the system?"

"We've had a few outside pings on the servers recently, but our firewall did its job and kept out the unwanted."

"I don't think it did. 'Project N' has been compromised."

There was audible clacking on a keyboard in the background noise over the phone. He waited, impatiently, while the IT specialist searched. Minutes went by, and he watched the general pace about in the common area of the lab.

"No…look here…" the IT specialist spoke with someone on his end of the line.

"That can't be…" another person said.

"It is…something accessed several drives simultaneously…" the first person replied, and then spoke into the phone's receiver again, panicked, "Hello, Doctor Gray? It appears there was unauthorized access. We're going to investigate and get back to you."

There was a *click*. They'd hung up. He returned to the bench with the microscope and depressed the intercom button again.

"General, we may have been compromised. IT is investigating now."

This got his attention away from pacing, and he was at the window again in a matter of seconds.

"Are you shitting me right now?"

He was stupefied. For someone to have found a way to hack their nanites was completely unthinkable, and yet there was no other explanation.

"Sir?" Mike caught the doctor's attention.

The doctor looked over at the screen. Mike was running a report of differences between the original and the new code. Theirs had been gutted, modified, and replaced. A chill ran up his back when he saw a comment in the code.

```
/*You tried to play God. You lost control. This is my game
now. If you try to alter my code, the nanites will kill its
host. Wait for my demands.*/
```

The Doctor could feel the blood drain from his face, and he had to steady himself against the table.

*

It took her hours longer than she'd hoped to get back to the warehouse, not because the parkway was bad, but because the streets leading into and through Manhattan were jammed.

The moment she walked in the door upstairs, Arturo was there to greet her with a wagging tail. His food bowl was empty, his water halfway, and his messes were confined to potty-pads in the corner. She replenished his food and water and double-bagged the waste before settling in. Once in the computer chair, she got right to work on readying for her video upload.

She played it one last time, and when it was done, she knew very well she was going to be labeled a terrorist. Morgan anticipated TEAL and the government were probably figuring out their nanites had been hacked, and that they'd try to alter the code despite the warning she'd left for them.

Between her zombies and the government, she knew she was going to be running for the rest of her life. The only thing that would keep her alive would be the key. While her video compressed, she sought to finish a side project. A custom collar for Arturo with a small, waterproof hide-a-key box attached.

She took her nanite key, wound the cord nicely, and then tucked the whole thing into a static shielding bag. Once they key was inside the small box, she inserted a GPS tracker, and strapped the collar to his neck. She admired her handiwork.

*

Doctor Gray watched a mouse injected with the hacker's altered nanites attempt to shatter its ballistic glass prison. He gassed the sealed box with enough sleeping gas to kill a grown man. The nanites wouldn't allow the mouse to be killed, but they would take time to process the toxin out, and it would allow him to inject their own recoded nanites.

When it was asleep, the doctor vented the chamber, opened the top and grabbed it. Beth handed him a needle, and he injected it. The mouse began to wake, and to avoid being bitten through his thick gloves he dropped it back in and sealed the box.

The result was horrific. As their recoded nanites tried to overwrite the programming of the hacked ones, the mouse began to hemorrhage blood from its eyes, ears, and mouth. It wasn't fifteen seconds before it was dead, and the nanites weren't reviving it.

Doctor Gray picked up an audio recorder and spoke into it, "Subject fifteen has died through the same means as the others. Hemorrhaging from the eyes and ears first, and then complete body shutdown. As per previous attempts, we will likely see complete internal liquidation of the host and remnants of nanites."

He clicked the button to end the recording.

Somewhere, deep in the functions, this diabolical person had made good on their threat. They'd interwoven code to kill the host and cause the nanites to shred themselves down to the last one so regeneration was impossible.

He wasn't ready to give up yet. Mike and several others were still scanning line by line, looking for how to deconstruct this hacker's work. Every time the team made alterations meant another test of the nanites, but the night was turning into early morning, and he had already been up past the twenty-four hour mark.

"We need to get some rest," he said. "Incinerate the remains of the test subjects and take a few hours to catch some Z's."

General Truman had returned to the Pentagon, and Doctor Gray wanted good news to give when he got back, but things were not progressing at all.

He exited the clean room and headed down a floor to the lunch room. No one dared to change the TV in there from the news of the outbreak. A few workers sat and watched the coverage. No one had figured out yet that it wasn't a virus because the CDC, law enforcement, and military were keeping the public ignorant. Any samples taken were sent to TEAL's branches.

Thanks to the nanites enhancing body strength, these crazed people were able to run at speeds of thirty-plus miles an hour. No one was outrunning them. Reports were coming in that they weren't cannibalizing other people. Just biting and moving on. The news also detailed how they pillaged stores and ate all of the food, like locust.

He heated up leftovers and watched the TV. They showed a map of a current spread, as well as an elapsed time version to show the projected spread over the next few days, weeks, and even months. They had the entire continental US, large chunks of Canada, and parts of Mexico consumed within three months. If they didn't find a fix soon, they would have to relocate to the West Coast facilities.

*

"General Truman, this is unacceptable," President Ismail said, bringing her hands up to her mouth. "What is being done?"

The tension in the room was heavy. Even in times of war in the past, she'd never heard of the Situation Room being this full. Despite that Truman was in the *hot seat*, it was now everyone's responsibility to handle the outbreak.

"Madam President, I am working with TEAL to reverse the effects, and we've dedicated our best resources to track the hacker," Truman replied.

"Are there any leads? The sooner we have them in custody, the sooner we can figure out how to fix this," she said.

"No, Madam President. But as soon as I have anything, you will know." His face was red with embarrassment.

There was a brief pause in the conversation, but there was still a minor hum about the room as two watch teams worked together on gathering and organizing all information regarding the spread.

"If this outbreak is being driven by the nanites, can we initiate a high altitude EMP and disable them?" Secretary of Defense Bates asked.

The Situation Room erupted into a flurry of comments arguing for and against the idea.

One voice rang out over the others, "That's out of the question. Not only are you suggesting we launch a nuclear device above our own country and detonate, but we'd be sending a large chunk of the country, and Canada, back to the dark ages."

"I think you mean pre-industrial era," another corrected. "The dark ages were over a thousand years ago."

"Semantics! It's going to feel like the dark ages due to millions of people's reliance on electronics for daily life, including us."

"We don't know what would happen to these if we were to use an EMP," Truman spoke up again. "The person or persons responsible for this have programmed in a kill command. If the nanites are altered, the host dies. If we shut them down without a one hundred percent certainty, we could be sentencing millions of people to die."

President Ismail stood up and addressed the room. "Right now, a high-altitude EMP is the last resort. FEMA, all branches of the military, and the CDC are working on cordoning off as much as they can, but we need to call on our allies to help us contain this."

"Madam President, Canada has mobilized their military, splitting them between Niagara Falls and the St. Lawrence River. They're barricading bridges, and no one is being allowed into Canada, even their own," Vice President Abraham said.

The room erupted into chaos again.

"Are they content to sit up there on a high horse?" another official snapped. "People need a way out or this is going to spread!"

"They have to think of their own national security, too. We can't expect them to be at our beck and call."

"While we're working on cordoning off the outbreak zone, they're up there quarantining us!"

The president understood both sides, and even in the noise, she was able to think clearly.

"Get the Canadian prime minister on the phone," she commanded over the room.

*

# Chapter 4:

After a few hours of sleep, Morgan paced the warehouse, gathering all of the electronics in one area and dousing them in accelerants. Everything she wasn't taking with her was ready to burn with the abandoned building. All she had to do now was upload the video and set the crude timer to torch the building. By the time it was traced, and by the time the fire department showed up, she'd be well on her way. *Forensic data recovery is going to have a bad time.*

Arturo was loaded in the second car, along with necessities and fake identification. The only electronics she was taking were a second injection of infected nanites, a laptop she'd never connected to the internet, the hard drive with the incriminating documents, and the key safely hidden in Arturo's collar. There was no getting around the plates on the vehicle, though. She didn't have time to get another disposable car, so the risk of her plates being identified would increase. Her hope was that amidst the chaos, the government and law enforcement were going to be preoccupied.

The time came. It was all set. She logged onto a number of anonymous accounts she'd created and ran a bot to mass e-mail her video to as many news stations across the nation as possible. Another bot was tasked with uploading to every social media site and content streaming site. Even if one decided not to run it, another would. Eventually, it would be everywhere.

While the files uploaded, she made her way down to the car. Backing out, she initiated the timer for everything to go up in flames. Her best hope of escape was to hit the interstate highways and head south toward Florida.

It was a few minutes to the highway, and when she got there she hoped her video was now being seen and heard by millions of people all at once.

*

General Truman was resting behind the locked door of his office. There had been so little time to sleep with everything going on. He needed some time to process and had requested not to be disturbed. It didn't seem to stop someone from banging on his door, and he was intent on making them the target of his anger.

He ripped it open and began to yell, "What the hell do you—"

"Sir, turn on your TV," Bradford urged.

Scowling, he wanted to slam the door in his face, but indulged him. Grabbing the remote from his desk, he turned the wall-mounted TV on.

*

Fitz was running on fumes, heading toward the supply drop set up by General Truman. Her eyes were heavy, and she was sure she'd fallen asleep, despite trying desperately to keep her eyes open. Her body jolted, and she saw they were in a city, headed toward a stadium. *Rochester already?* They followed one of their Humvees they'd managed to meet up with after being separated. The Humvee led the way through the roads littered with vehicles and pushed them out of the way as needed.

Fidgeting with the dial on the radio, she hoped to catch any news broadcast of the local reports. It hit one station where a newscaster was frantic about a video released by a person claiming to be the mastermind terrorist behind this attack. Leaving it there, they began playing it.

*

The entire Situation Room was silent watching the video. No one dared breathe. President Ismail wanted to slap her own face in disbelief as she watched. It was a nightmare. General Truman had not only lost control of one of his enhanced soldiers, but someone had gone to great lengths to corrupt them.

*

The person on screen was masked with a cliché Guy Fawkes mask, synonymous with the Anonymous group. There was no background noise.

Nothing else existed within the frame except the person and a black curtain. A distorted voice came across.

"The United States Government has been creeping toward world domination. It seeks to control everyone through nanotechnology."

"What you're witnessing in New York is a sample of what they intended. This is not a virus in the traditional sense, but nanites programmed to take over a host's body."

Schematics were put up in the video of tiny machines with multiple legs so intricate it looked like something out of a sci-fi film. The voice continued while official government documents continued to roll.

"These nanites are the creation of TEAL Incorporated, who is funded by the US Department of Defense. The first and second phases were to create super soldiers. The machine's programming enhanced anyone injected with them, both mentally and physically.

"Meanwhile, the third and fourth phases were to begin US and worldwide public implementation respectively. It would be labeled as the cure to all disease, the perfect enhancement for the body in order to keep us healthy, fit, and extend lifespan.

"What you're seeing now shows that the hosts can be mind-controlled. The nanites can be reprogrammed to force people to do things against their will, anything the programmer wants. Once the program was public, every single person would become a slave."

One after another, official documents were shown on the screen, some harder to read than others. But there was enough there that anyone watching would have a hard time not believing what was being said.

"This *zombie* outbreak is temporary. I have reprogrammed them to infect as many people as possible in order to bring attention to this, and so the government can't bury this. Those infected can be cured with my key. It will unlock my repurposed nanites and allow everyone to revert to normal. All you have to do is get the US to come clean and make nanotechnology illegal."

A darkened map of North America showed up on screen with a red dot appearing on Syracuse. A clock ticked in fast forward, and the red dot grew to spread, showing projections. In less than two months the United States, the Eastern half of Canada, and parts of Mexico would be overrun.

"To any foreign governments: if you use nukes or EMPs, you could lose the key, and then everyone becomes a zombie. So don't. To everyone else: the clock's ticking."

The video ended abruptly.

*

The audio ended, and the newscaster fumbled for words. Fitz's stomach knotted up, and she felt ill. They'd sat parked dead center in the stadium where the supplies had been dropped, listening intently. She clicked the radio off, and as she did, the SAT phone rang loudly, causing everyone in the car to jump, except her. She answered it.

"Yes, sir?" She knew it was the general.

"Have you seen it?"

"I heard it."

"Did you make it to the supply drop?"

"Just a few minutes ago. We can't stay long. The horde can run upwards of thirty miles per hour. Orders, sir?"

"You have authorization to survive by any means necessary. I'm spreading out the EH-US units to where the military is working to cordon off the northeastern US. Your destination is near Cleveland, Ohio. A few of our units are already there. Head to Cleveland and report in."

"Yes, sir!" she replied and ended the call.

She wanted to fight back. But there was little way to do that right now except for building a cordon.

Out into the crisp air, she and the other soldiers made their way to the crates. Inside were flamethrowers and riot gear. But there was now a moral question of whether the flamethrowers should be used at all.

*If people can be saved, we should use these only as a last resort.*

Fitz picked up pieces of riot gear and inspected it briefly.

*It may not be bite-proof, but at least it will give a little more protection than uniforms.*

"Ma'am?" a soldier asked.

"Suit up and load up!" she ordered.

With it revealed they were up against people infected by corrupted nanites, she understood the odds were not in their favor. Bullet wounds to the head wouldn't kill them permanently, and they'd be stronger than the men and women she was now commanding. The idea of drawing her own blood, nanites and all, and injecting the soldiers came to mind. She'd be giving them classified materials, but it would increase the group's odds of being overcome…and General Truman had given her the *OK* to survive by any means necessary.

When they were geared up, and the weapons were secured in the Humvee, Fitz stood in the middle of the vehicles.

"Fall in!" she belted.

Pulling a knife from her belt, she watched as her group came to her. She understood some of the soldiers might shy away from the very technology causing people to attack and spread a corrupt version like a plague, but she needed a new unit.

"What you heard on the radio was true. There are people with enhancements in the US military, thanks to nanotechnology."

This piqued everyone's attention.

"I was in one of those units, and in me, there are trillions of nanites working to keep me in peak physical and mental condition." She paused to point at the soldiers. "If we're going to stay ahead of these zombies, you're going to need them, too."

She held up her knife and sliced her hand open, giving people no time to react. The shock was audible at the cut and the blood. Someone even retched. But she knew their attention was entirely on her as they watched her blood pull back into her body and the wound heal up.

There was no hesitation from one serviceman. Without flinching, he held out his right hand and Fitz ran the blade over it. Blood pooled. She cut her hand again and shook his hand. Both wounds healed up. The other soldiers lined up, and were ready and willing.

"What about us?" a civilian asked.

"I'm sorry, but this is classified material."

"Classified? Is that why there's a zombie apocalypse bearing down on us?" One man was outraged. "It seems like you, your commanding officer, and the president are all morons! You're helping end humanity!"

"I understand your objection. If you don't want to stay with us, that's your choice, but if you want to make it to the safe zone it would be in your best interest to shut your mouth and keep up."

She was blunt, and she didn't care. The man scoffed at her and returned to his car.

"We're heading west. Destination is Cleveland. The infected won't have spread that far yet, and they're mobilizing there," Fitz informed.

Everyone returned to their vehicles, and she showed both her driver and navigator the coordinates of the next destination.

"Head west."

"Yes, ma'am," they both responded.

*

She kept her speed regulated, and worried about authorities identifying her once the video of the area was put out. Her plate number would be on every radio, TV, and electronic highway board.

There were two options as far as she was concerned. Steal a license plate, or steal a car. It would be a gamble either way, but she hoped with either one of those options she would go unnoticed. Pulling off the packed highway, she headed for a nearby neighborhood. In the cozy cookie cutter development, she looked for any car left abandoned.

People were out, packing and looking to leave before the zombies reached this area. *Maybe I can catch a ride?*

She parked, grabbed her bag, and let Arturo out of the car. He tugged on his leash, trying to pull her along, but she steadied him and walked toward a woman loading up into a mini-van.

"Excuse me!" Morgan called out.

The woman saw her while placing some food into the back of the van.

"Hi," she put on her sweetest voice. "I really need some help. My car is having troubles, and I'm afraid it won't make it much farther. Are you headed south?"

"Sure, hop in. We're heading for Atlanta," the woman was cordial.

She was caught off guard, expecting a *no room* response. Morgan didn't hesitate.

"Thank you!" She was truly excited about getting away with this, and being able to start a second infection.

She and Arturo headed to the open side door. Inside was a young boy and girl, maybe six years old each. They were already strapped into the seats behind the driver and passenger seats. The little girl saw the dog and squealed in delight.

"Doggy! Doggy!"

Morgan went from feeling excited to awkward. She carefully led Arturo in, and to the back seat of the van. The little girl brushed her hand over Arturo's back as they passed by, and she giggled.

"It's soft!"

The mother hopped in and started the van.

"You could have sat up here," the woman said while looking over her shoulder to back out of the driveway.

"Oh, thank you. But Arturo here gets a little nervous without me."

"No worries. I'm Theresa, and these two munchkins are Tommy and Terry."

Theresa turned back to face the road and focused on getting them out of the neighborhood.

"I'm Morgan." *Stupid. Why'd you give your real name?* "And this is Arturo. Thanks so much for letting us catch a ride."

"No problem."

"Hi!" The little girl waved and reached her hand back to pet Arturo again. "I'm Tommy! Are you a good boy?"

"Honey, turn around and face forward. It's not safe for you to be turned like that while I'm driving," Theresa was firm, but not scolding.

"Okay," Tommy was dejected.

She let Arturo's leash go a little bit. As much as she just sent the world to hell, she wasn't a complete monster. Tommy giggled and pet him.

It was a moment of peace, something she wouldn't pass up, because it wasn't going to come again any time soon. She closed her eyes but listened intently to the road. Theresa turned up the radio, and she was glad to hear quick tempo music. Not hearing the news put her mind at ease.

"Hey, when you need to stop for gas, let me know. I've got some cash and I'll fill your tank," Morgan offered.

"Okay. I had just filled up, so it'll probably be a little while."

"I'm going to rest my eyes. I've been traveling for a bit, and I'm a little fatigued."

There was no response, and Morgan assumed Theresa saw her eyes closed and wasn't going to bother her.

*

The general's phone had been ringing off the hook since the video, and there were half a dozen officials ready to string him up. He had promised the president answers, and when Rosh took a call from his longtime friend, and

FBI Director, Gerald Crawford, he hoped to have new information he could relay up the chain.

"Norm," Director Crawford greeted. "I'm at TEAL, working with their information security team."

"Have you found anything?" the general asked.

"We've made progress. A hacker by the username God-Complex dinks around on a deep web site, Silk Road Resurfaced," he replied. "We think we're close to tracking his home location. We've narrowed it down to western Massachusetts."

"Good work, Gerald. How long do you think it will take to track him precisely?"

"Not too much longer."

Truman wanted this hacker in his hands, and he desperately wanted that key.

"Update me the moment you have a location."

"Will do."

He hung up his phone and sighed. He hoped the capture of this arrogant hacker would be the end of their hunt, but he knew if this was actually supported by the Anonymous group, this could be just one operative.

He picked up his phone again and dialed President Ismail to give her the news.

*

When the call came in, they had fifteen minutes to prepare and take off. Choppers carried three dozen soldiers toward Springfield, Massachusetts, sent to apprehend a suspected terrorist.

Two blocks from the house identified as the suspect's, they dropped to the ground, and the three units separated to surround it. The neighborhood had all but evacuated, leading to locating the culprit faster. Everyone had earpieces in for coordination, and Master Sergeant Gorski utilized it to command.

"We've been ordered here to apprehend the criminal believed responsible for this attack! Lethal force is *not* authorized for this mission!"

He was met with a, "Yes, sir," from the commanders of the units.

Gorski led his unit to the front door using hand signals. Looking in a window, he saw zero movement. Trying the doorknob, he found it locked.

"Front door locked," he whispered into his com.

"Back door locked," came a response.

"Enter on three," Gorski commanded. "One…two…three!"

The house was breeched, and he led the charge into the house, rifle raised. They cleared room after room, on both the first and second floors. There was no one in the house.

*

Apocalypse M had given him no warning when they were releasing their monstrosity. He half-wondered if they were actually going through with it, or if it was all big talk. When his phone alerted him to mass hysteria at the New York State Fairgrounds, he knew it had to be them. He just didn't realize how close they'd been to one another the whole time.

Alerted online by an Anonymous member that he might become the target of a raid, he left the safety of his home. As a calculated red herring, he purposely kept a burner laptop running with a script to ping Silk Road Resurfaced, so that if his activity was being tracked, they'd continue to think he was home.

*They really did it... All those people now unwittingly a part of Apocalypse M's plan. What did I do? I've helped a domestic terrorist...*

Because Apocalypse M was crazy enough to act on their plan without a heads up, safeguarding his mother was now much harder. For all of the talk he did on the internet, and the harassment hacking, he had a hard time grasping the reality that he helped set into motion. His mother, and others, were in danger.

As he grew closer to Pittsfield to pick up his mother, he pulled up the video feed from his home cameras to see what was happening inside. It was invaded. He sent a command to shut off his router.

*

Master Sergeant Gorski contacted command, "House is clear. No sign of the suspect."

"The house isn't empty," General Truman said confidently. "The connection from that location just went silent. They know you're there."

"Fan out! Toss everything!" Gorski yelled. "Tear down the walls!"

The soldiers ransacked the house, going as far as throwing things out onto the lawn. They found several micro-cameras, and a handful of electronics, including a router and computer, but no operator.

An hour passed, and the house was a disaster. The walls were destroyed and floorboards were coming up. Though there was no basement listed for the house, he was positive they'd find the culprit.

When the near complete destruction of the home resulted in nothing, Gorski was infuriated. He had no choice but to call it and pack up. He left a small group of three in the neighborhood to see if anyone came back, but he was sure they'd been outsmarted.

*

Reese hoped to reach his mother's living facility in time, and then take her to his hideout in the Tolland State Forest, where they'd be safe. The roads were mostly open, due to everyone going the other way, but he didn't feel he was going fast enough. He phoned the assisted living facility, but there was no answer. He tried again.

"C'mon. Pick up!" he said, and slapped his hand on the steering wheel. "They better not have just left her there..."

He got the facility's voicemail.

"This is Reese Gordon. I'm trying to get ahold of anyone to make sure my mother is okay. I'm on my way to pick her up. Please call me back."

The Interstate was slowing down, and it took far longer to get to a side highway up into Pittsfield than he'd hoped. When at the off ramp, he was quick to turn. It was far less crowded, and his foot pressed the gas pedal hard. He dialed the assisted living facility, but again got the voicemail.

He threw his phone against the passenger door in anger, and drove aggressively to get to the facility.

*

General Truman had to yet again answer a failure to President Ismail. On a secure line, she became irate with him.

"General, this is unacceptable. How did the suspect avoid your team?"

"Madam President, we aren't sure. It's under investigation, and we're still looking for them. I've left a small team staked out there in case the person returns."

"I'm exhausted from all the running in circles, General. Lives hang in the balance in the worst possible scenario of ransomware, and I'm having to hold foreign powers from taking drastic steps against our country."

"Madam President, I understand the gravity of the situation. We're also pursuing a warehouse fire we believe was where the video was uploaded from, and a second base of operation."

"There might be more than one terrorist?"

"Director Crawford and I agree that this was a coordinated effort."

"For God's sake." The president sighs, loudly. "We have literally every country breathing down our necks over this. I'm bringing in technical specialists from the United Kingdom, Japan, and China to aide TEAL with reverse engineering the terrorist's coding."

"China, ma'am?"

"Yes, China. I believe they'll be a worthwhile ally in our endeavors to undo this."

"Ma'am, I think—"

"I don't care what you think. We're going to cooperate with other countries, and in return we'll allow them access to the nanotechnology."

President Ismail paused, and Truman wasn't sure if he should interject any more.

"General Truman, the next time we speak, I want positive forward movement in finding the terrorists."

"Yes, President."

She hung up, and he was immediately back on the phone with Director Crawford.

"Norm," Director Crawford answered.

"Gerald, any leads on the warehouse."

"Pieces so far, but they're coming together. The blurry face from the night your Marine disappeared seem to match handfuls of video from areas surrounding the New Jersey port. Still working on getting a clear enough shot to run through facial recognition."

"What about a vehicle?"

"We got the plates. It's stolen. Registered to an elderly man who has no ties to that area. He didn't even know it was missing. We have a program running to scan New York highways and other roads we can get access to."

"Let me know as soon as you have anything."

"You'll be my first call."

They hung up. He wanted to continue, but he was exhausted. Getting up from his desk, he exited the office space and headed over to Rosh.

"Forward all my calls to my cell, and then take some time to rest up. I'm heading out."

"Yes, sir." Rosh smiled sympathetically.

Rosh and Bradford had been alternating, taking care of the menial stuff so he could focus on the bigger picture.

He felt eyes on him as he passed by, but he held himself together as he made his way out of the building.

*

Reese's heart sank when he got close to Pittsfield. Forced to slow, and then stop, he noted crashed vehicles; fiberglass, metal, and glass were everywhere.

There were people farther up ahead, but they moved in a horde-like manner away from the wreckage. His heart thumped hard.

He dared not try to push past the accident, because if the group on the road were zombies, he'd likely get himself turned. His map showed he could backtrack to a side road to get to where he needed. He hoped the way was clear and free of the infected.

He U-turned in the middle of the street and sped past others just now coming to the accident. He thought about rolling down his window and warning them, but he couldn't risk wasting time. He picked up speed to seventy-five and made it to Holmes Road in short time. He spun his car around and began driving recklessly through a residential area.

In the heart of Pittsfield, there was chaos. People tried desperately to evade attacks by fast-moving, extremely agile zombies. He watched the infected tackle and bite. Those on foot, or going slow enough in their cars, were perfect bait and allowed him to avoid the zombies.

He sped through red lights, nearly ran people over, and swerved around vehicles. His heart beat faster, seeing the number of nanite zombies was growing at an incredible rate. The hope of reaching his mother in time looked grim, but he had to try.

Outside the assisted living facility, his heart sunk. Glass was shattered. Doors were caved in. There were some elderly people in the yard, but they moved with incredible speed. His mother was there amongst the infected. The group noticed his car, and they turned to intercept.

"Damnit!"

He threw it in reverse and looked behind him only to see he was blocked in by more infected. Gunning the car in reverse, he ran over several people and didn't stop until he was back to the street. The zombies returned to their feet and gave chase.

He sped away and pushed through other residential areas. Neighborhoods which hadn't been hit would now be overrun because of the zombies that followed him.

Anger burned in him, because he wasn't able to save his mother in time. He wanted to contact Apocalypse M, and threaten them into giving up the key, but they wouldn't respond well to that.

"If I turn myself in, I could offer to help find them and the key," he rationalized out loud. "They might punish me as a scapegoat. I could cop to stealing the files, and plead ignorance to the plan, and hope they buy it. Maybe they'll show leniency."

Hearing his own voice was no comfort, but he had to fill the void or he might burst into angry tears.

"Damnit. I should have done more to convince them to send me a copy of the key."

He may have watched one too many action films, but the number of what-ifs running through his head right now made him want to be the double agent and catch Apocalypse M. Either way, the next step would be to get to his safe location, connect to the deep web, and reach out.

*

Fitz tried to get some rest, but most of the time was spent in a half-sleep, and any dreams she had were horrific. They weren't about anyone in particular, and they blended a little bit of reality with fiction. Things were bloodier in her dreams, and pop culture's idea of zombies seeped in.

Her mind cleared as military helicopters chattered overhead, lifting cargo containers into place to build a wall. It stretched from north to south, and four containers high. They'd successfully stayed ahead of the horde and reached the cordon. The opening left in the wall was only large enough to fit one vehicle through at a time, which made it slow going.

Being so close, she felt safe enough to hop out and take a breath.

"Keep moving forward," she instructed the sergeant driving. "I'll meet you inside."

"Yes, ma'am," he answered, and she was out of the vehicle.

Walking toward the checkpoint, she kept a brisk pace and took in the chilled air sweeping from the north. She approached the soldiers stopping vehicles and checking them for infected. Fitz saluted as they noticed her.

"Corporal Fitzgerald and company reporting in. Where's your commanding officer?"

One soldier stopped to salute her. "We have a temporary command center down the highway, off to the left."

"Thanks. Keep up the good work."

Fitz nodded and passed through. She walked along, and about halfway to the outpost, her vehicle pulled up alongside her. Instead of getting in, she jumped on the side step and held the mirror.

At the tent, she hopped off and signaled for the Humvees to park. They were safe, for now, but the infected were coming, and there was no telling if the wall of shipping containers would be enough to hold them off.

She ducked into the command and reported to the highest-ranking officer she could find, a master sergeant. Presenting herself, she saluted. Though he was amidst planning and coordinating, he took a moment to notice her and nod.

"Corporal Ella Fitzgerald, EH-US-11 unit, reporting for duty," she announced.

"At ease, Corporal. General Truman filled me in on what happened to your unit."

"Yes, sir." She put her arms behind her back.

"Give me a status update."

She recapped the endeavors, and though it appeared as though he wasn't paying attention through all of his planning, when she was done, he looked her dead in the eyes.

"Congratulations on surviving this far, but we're just beginning. The president has issued martial law and given orders to isolate the entire northeastern US."

"I sense a *but*," Fitz observed.

"Closing it off is also closing them in. The best we can do is hope that this terrorist didn't program these things to be smarter than us."

"I've seen them firsthand. They're aggressive and fast, but I don't know how smart they are. They might break through glass and doors, but I don't know about metal. People may be safe inside the cordon."

"I sure as hell hope so."

"Assuming the terrorist was telling the truth about having some sort of cure, General Truman's likely to reassign us to finding it."

"Possibly. Until then, your assignment is to help build a wall. Report to EH-US-19. They're in charge of building the south end."

"Yes, sir. I've brought some other soldiers along with me and given them nanites. I'd like them temporarily assigned to the EH-US-11 unit."

"Send them in to report. I'll pass their whereabouts along."

Fitz nodded, saluted, and excused herself. Outside, the soldiers who were with her waited, conversing and speculating about the nanites. She approached, and they took notice.

"Attention!" she commanded, and all eyes were on her. "I've coopted you into the EH-US-11 unit, and I'm your new commanding officer. Check in inside the tent here, and then return to me!"

"Yes, ma'am," they replied and saluted.

They did as instructed, and when they reported back, she spoke.

"Before you ask, let me give you some info. The EH program stands for Enhanced Human. There are fifty EH-US units, one for each state. There are also international ones, but we'll save that for another time.

"With the nanites, your entire body has been enhanced, and while you were protecting your country before, you're now the front line. You can survive most fatal wounds, but avoid bombs, fire, and hazardous chemicals. Now, let's move out. We've got work to do!"

"Yes, ma'am!"

*

Reese had done a fair amount of angry swearing, but none of it made him feel better. He was almost to his hideout, and as soon as he got there, he would activate his network and try and contact Apocalypse M. If they wouldn't provide him with his own key, he would turn to whichever bureau was trying to capture him.

*They can't let this consume everything. They've made their point.*

Pulling onto a hidden dirt road, he followed it slowly for a half-hour. At a small cabin, built halfway into a hill and covered with moss for camouflage, he was safe. It was an illegal building within a protected forest, but it was vital for it to be off the grid. Electrical lines were snaked up a nearby tree, and they connected to solar panels, and an antenna, which were precariously attached toward the top. It was high enough that passersby wouldn't see it from the ground.

He parked abruptly and was out of his vehicle before it settled. The sun was setting, and it was about to get a lot colder in the already shaded area. He needed to get the space heater going first.

Inside, he flipped the light switch, which powered a single LED light. It was enough to illuminate the whole hideout. On the far wall was enough canned food to last weeks, and next to it was the heater. He pulled it to the center of the room and turned it on. While the cabin was heating up, he removed the protective covering from his electronics and fired up his computers.

In short time, he accessed his network and looked for any presence of Apocalypse M in the typical sites. There was no indication they'd been active since they released their video. He opened his encrypted messenger and typed.

> God-Complex: OK. You've made your point. Send me a key, or a cure to undo this. My mother was infected, and I need to cure her.

Sent. But he couldn't be sure they'd ever access the message. Or if they'd give him what he requested. While he waited, he scoured the deep web and looked at any new bits of information regarding the infection. The reactions were mixed, everything from praise to condemnation of Apocalypse M. Despite the demand that the US declassify the program, and start making such technology illegal, there were no signs they were doing either.

*What if they were infected? Damn it!*

He sat, waiting for them to respond. The forest had become pitch black, and the night was dragging on. It seemed either he was being ignored or they weren't getting his messages. He couldn't take it any longer.

"Son of a bitch!" he whispered harshly at the monitor.

He clicked away and began reaching out on various active threads, asking if they'd had contact with Apocalypse M.

*

"We've got a hit!" a FBI analyst called Director Crawford over. "Same username of the guy whose house was raided."

Director Crawford and TEAL InfoSec analysts rushed over. Crawford had been preparing his team to pack up and relocate back to the Pentagon, since getting what they needed from the breech of TEAL's servers.

"He's asking around for someone with the user name Apocalypse M," the analyst stated. "What do you want me to do?"

"I'll take over."

The director and the analyst switched places, and he composed a direct message to God-Complex.

> AggressiveTorrent: Who is Apocalypse M?

God-Complex: Who are you?

AggressiveTorrent: Not your friend. But not your enemy either. Who is it that you're looking for?

God-Complex: They have something I need.

AggressiveTorrent: Maybe I can help. What do you need?

God-Complex: A key.

AggressiveTorrent: A key? Get locked out of your house?

God-Complex: Who *are* you?

AggressiveTorrent: What did you do to the nanites?

God-Complex: I didn't do anything to them.

AggressiveTorrent: Your friend with the key did?

*

"Shit! Is this another hacker or the government?"

He paced about the cabin, debating on if he should turn himself in.

"It's fine. If it's the government, I can convince them I didn't know what they were doing, that I just stole the documents for Apocalypse M."

AggressiveTorrent: Hello?

Reese sat back at the computer.

God-Complex: They weren't my friend.

AggressiveTorrent: Is Apocalypse M the one who altered the nanites? Or did you? Who else was working with Apocalypse M?

With this line of questioning, he was sure that it was a government agency he was talking to. He had to keep his involvement close to his chest.

God-Complex: It wasn't me. I didn't know anything about this until they unleashed this abomination on the public.

AggressiveTorrent: You hacked into a US contractor's servers and took highly sensitive documents, and you didn't know what they were going to be used for?

God-Complex: God, no. My mother's been infected!

AggressiveTorrent: Who is your mother? Maybe we can do something for her.

Despite proxies and bouncing his connection, he was sure they would eventually trace him, even with being in the woods. Now seemed like the right time to broker a deal.

God-Complex: I don't know where Apocalypse M is. They haven't contacted me, but put in writing that you'll pick my mother up and keep her safe, and I'll try to help you find them.

*

Director Crawford glanced at his team, and the lead analyst was working hard at locating this hacker.

"Their pinging all over the place. I don't know how much longer it's going to take to track them," the analyst told the director.

He had a choice to make. He could offer the deal now and pick them up, or possibly draw it out and find them anyway. The only issue was if they chose to disconnect and go into hiding.

AggressiveTorrent: Alright. You have a deal. We'll pick up your mother and keep her safe until Apocalypse M gives us the key.

*

He was torn. Should he let them find him, or run?

*If I can position myself, maybe I can assist with the investigation. Maybe mediate between them and Apocalypse M so both sides get what they want?*

83

He typed his coordinates into the message box and sent the encrypted message to AggressiveTorrent.

*

Truman rested in his car after eating. The radio blared constant news updates. The infected were well beyond New York's borders now.

He turned down the volume and closed his eyes. He wasn't sure how much time had passed, but his phone ringing startled him. Dusk had come and gone, and he sat alone in the dark. It took him a moment to gather himself. He picked up the phone and recognized the number.

"Gerald," he greeted groggily.

"Norm, we've convinced the hacker who broke into TEAL's servers to turn themselves in. They claim to have only passed the files on, but might be able to get ahold of the real culprit."

"I want them in DC, ASAP."

"He's being picked up now, and if all goes well, he'll be on a plane to us soon."

"Good work. I'll meet you at the Reagan airport."

*

# Chapter 5:

Truman pulled into a parking garage at Reagan airport and stewed. He was ready to wring this guy out, but he needed to feel for what he knew first.

He drove to where Gerald waited for him, parked, and exited his vehicle.

"He'll be landing within the hour," Gerald informed.

"Easy pickup?"

"He put up no fight," he replied.

They entered the airport and headed to the terminal where the plane would be landing. The airport had been taken over by the military in order to keep it operational, but not for the public. All flights, except for those which had government clearance, were grounded. This made it particularly easy to navigate the normally bustling hub.

"One branch of the Anonymous group has claimed responsibility for this," Gerald shared. "The Cyber Division is narrowing it down. The NSA has given us full access to their archives, and they're running keyword searches hoping to find any trail."

"Any hits?"

"Not many. There's been some chatter about someone searching for a number of prototype electronics. My gut is telling me this wasn't a large group effort. So far, the only ties we have are the woman in the video, and the guy we're bringing in."

They stopped in front of a large bay of windows and watched for the plane. Truman let Gerald breathe a moment before he continued prodding.

"Anything on the woman?"

"The warehouse was mostly a bust. The high end equipment she'd acquired had their serial numbers removed. The car Reyes was seen getting into the night he disappeared was there, but the fire made sure there was no DNA evidence to find, and that the hard drives were unreadable. She did her homework on arson."

Gerald sighed and headed to the door out to the docking ramp.

"Was it the same car used in Syracuse?"

"No. We were able to recover video of a woman escorting Corporal Reyes in, both of them in disguise. She's seen exiting again not ten minutes later, and a vehicle sped away as the outbreak was happening. We lost track of her as she headed north, but we have an APB out on it."

"North?"

"The timeline suggests she headed north to escape, then doubled back to the warehouse to release the video and set everything on fire."

"She probably continued south," the general proposed.

"It's likely. She could be headed right to us."

"I'm hoping her accomplice might give us something to find her."

*

Reese checked out the window. They descended onto the runway. His heart jumped into his throat. Behind a computer screen, he was invincible. But here, now, he was vulnerable. He'd read a number of the leaks put out on WikiLeaks, and across the deep web, and the idea of the government's enhanced interrogation techniques scared the hell out of him.

The airplane came to a halt at a terminal. Rather than pull up to the loading bridge, it stopped short. Two men exited through a nearby door and proceeded out onto the ramp. His heart beat harder.

The soldiers on board escorted him from the plane and into the custody of the two very official looking men. One he could tell was a high ranking officer in the military, and the other wore a suit and tie.

"Reese Gordon, you're going to tell us exactly what you know or you'll never see the light of day again," the officer barked.

"I want to help. I didn't know this was going to happen when I passed those files on," he tried not to show any emotion.

They took him, the key to his handcuffs, and a bag with one of his laptops inside from the soldiers who had escorted him. The man in the suit stepped away and made a phone call. He returned and looked to the man in uniform.

"I know how my involvement looks, but I didn't create this zombie apocalypse."

"Don't use those words. It's an assault on my intelligence," the officer snapped. "In fact, from now on, choose your words wisely in everything you say."

"I want to help—" he tried again.

"If you wanted to help, you should have been a patriot and turned the terrorist in before this happened. As far as I'm concerned, you're just as culpable." He was harsh.

Reese shut up. *Damn it!*

A helicopter came in overhead and landed a hundred feet from the plane. The motor never even shut off. He was led to it, thrown in, and they were airborne. They gained enough altitude to clear the buildings, but not much higher. They were soon nearing one of the most recognizable buildings in the United States; the Pentagon.

The helicopter landed on the helipad, and it was a long walk into the building. Security met them halfway, and they were escorted to a checkpoint. The man in the suit produced a badge, and security took it from him and swiped it through a card reader.

"Good day, Director Crawford." The guard nodded and handed him back the badge.

The officer produced his identification, and the guard did the same with his card.

"Welcome back, General Truman."

He nodded, and they entered the building. Director Crawford pulled him along, following the general. Reese had never wanted to visit the Pentagon, but now he was there, it piqued his curiosity. While being led, he took the time to look. People were hustling and rushing around.

They reached an elevator. The general swiped his badge, and it opened. Once inside, he provided a fingerprint scan, and then pressed a blank button under the 'B2' button. They descended, and when the electronic sign passed 'B2,' it also went blank. The door opened, and they exited into an underground, semi-open office space with standalone rooms spaced out through the basement level. Chills rolled down his spine.

He was led into one of the rooms, and General Truman chained his handcuffs to the table. He and Director Crawford both stepped out.

*Shit! I'm going to die down here.*

It was quiet. He couldn't tell if there was anyone out past the frosted glass windows. He shifted nervously in his seat and looked over his shoulder, waiting for them to come back. He sat for what seemed like a half-hour and wondered if they were coming back.

They both re-entered the room, and in a TV investigator fashion, the general slapped down a thick manila folder with papers inside. General Truman opened it, flipped it around, and shoved it in front of him.

"Do you know this woman?" he asked.

Reese didn't have to look long. It was no one he'd seen before. He shook his head.

"I don't recognize her. Is this the person?"

"Whom did you have contact with about Project N?" Director Crawford took his turn.

"There were a few people on some deep web forums who were looking for answers when the super soldier video leaked. We all conversed and theorized about what it was. One person seemed more obsessed than the rest of us."

"Did you initiate the contact with them, or did they contact you?"

"I chatted with a few people about it on neutral grounds, but one person contacted me personally. Their username's Apocalypse M.

The general flipped to another picture. It was the same woman, but with a disguise on, outside what appeared to be a fairground. She was with someone in an orange mascot-like suit.

"Is this Apocalypse M?" Truman asked.

"I don't know. I don't even know if Apocalypse M is a man or woman."

Crawford set down another file. There was a list of high priced equipment and electronics.

"Did you acquire any of these for them?" Crawford asked.

He hadn't acquired anything except the plans, but he browsed the list and recognized a few items he did outsource for. Apocalypse M didn't get them from him, but they might as well have.

"No. I didn't get any of these for them, but I did set Apocalypse M up with contacts for some of these items."

"I want their information," Truman demanded.

"I know exactly as much about them as I do Apocalypse M. See that's the thing about the deep web, most people on there are anonymous for a reason."

"Anonymous the group, or anonymous in general?" Crawford asked.

"Either, or both. I can give you usernames, but I'm sure that people have put two and two together about this whole situation and have gone underground."

Director Crawford provided a pen and a scrap of paper for Reese, and he scribbled down a slew of usernames. Crawford took the paper and headed for the door.

"I'm going to pass these to my team and see if we can come up with anything, or anyone else," the director told the general, and then left.

General Truman tapped the picture, right on the person in the orange suit.

"Did they ever mention they were working with anyone else directly?"

"No."

"I want you to contact them." Truman seemed sure that he had the ability.

"I tried, before I let you know where I was. They didn't respond."

"You're going to try again."

The general wasn't going to take no for an answer.

*

Morgan woke, and when she looked, Theresa was in line to get gas. She'd worked her way into the fourth position on a pump, while behind them the lines stretched farther than she could see.

"Where are we?" she asked groggily.

"Outskirts of Aberdeen in Maryland. We're still north of Baltimore."

*Baltimore...that would make a good place to start a second wave.*

"You're making good time," Morgan complimented.

"We'd be making better time if we could get through this line."

She moved up to the side doors. Both Tommy and Terry were asleep. The innocence of the children wasn't lost on her, but her mission was of far greater importance. The government would have to cave when she started the second wave.

"I'm going to step out and use the bathroom. Might grab some food."

"Okay." Theresa smiled and nodded.

Morgan was quiet to open the door next to Tommy and slip out. Arturo followed. The crisp air was a shock, and the cold put a little extra spring in her step to get to the bathroom. When she'd finished, and Arturo had done his business, she tied him to a pole and went inside to grab supplies.

At the counter the cashier stood with a shotgun laid out. The shelves weren't as empty as she'd thought they'd be. She got food for everyone, and passing through another aisle, she found camping supplies. She eyeballed the lighter fluid and some matches. *Just in case?* Grabbing them, she brought everything up to the register and laid it all out.

The cashier took the first item, a can of Pringles, and scanned it. It rang up as fifteen dollars. She choked on her saliva. A bag of jerky was forty-five.

"That's not what the price said on the stand," Morgan protested.

"Prices have gone up."

"That's bullshit. You can't price gouge in the event of a disaster."

"Sue me. Either you want this stuff or not, but if you don't pay me you're not walking out of here with any of it," he said, and eyed the shotgun.

Pissed, she had to acknowledge this was a direct result of her actions. The total ran up to four hundred seventy seven and some change. She glared and handed over five hundred. The man gave her change and bagged up her food. Taking it, she left and returned to get Arturo. He wagged his tail happily as she untied him, and led the way back to the pumps.

Theresa had made it to the pump and was filling up. Thinking of the price on the food, Morgan took a peek at the pump. The man was charging thirty dollars a gallon, and Theresa was muttering.

"I have the cash," Morgan offered again.

"I already put my credit card in. Son of a bitch, scalping people," she kept her voice down while swearing.

"Should have seen the food bill," she said and held up a couple grocery bags.

Theresa shook her head. "It's fine. I'll just call the credit card company and claim it as fraud. Screw them."

Morgan got back inside and Theresa entered in shortly after.

"Do you need me to help with the driving?" Morgan offered.

"Maybe in a few hours. I can probably get us to Baltimore."

She sat back, and Arturo rested his head in her lap. Theresa got underway, and they were back on a packed highway to the next big metropolitan area.

Her phone buzzed. She pulled it out to find she'd missed some e-mails from a dummy account, set up to funnel messages from the deep web to her phone. It bounced across half a dozen countries, and through several levels of security, before reaching a generic e-mail address. Only a few people had the ability to contact her, and she was sure of who it was.

She opened the first one.

> God-Complex: Ok. You've made your point. Send me a key, or a cure, or whatever to undo this. My mother was infected and I need to cure her.

*He'll get it when everyone else does.*

She hit the delete button, and the e-mail disappeared. Opening the second one, it was him again.

> God-Complex: Where the hell are you? My house was hit. I had already left, but you didn't give me any warning. I didn't have an opportunity to safeguard my mother.

*Idiot.*

Delete. A third one came up.

> God-Complex: I'm safe, for now, but I need to talk to you.

She pounded out a response to be sent back through the same secure networks.

> Apocalypse M: A little busy.

Sent. It wasn't a few moments before another one came back.

> God-Complex: Look, I just want to meet up. Can you provide one antidote nanite?

> Apocalypse M: Not until the government caves, and last I heard, they weren't cooperating.

> God-Complex: Then maybe I can stick with you until they do. If you're headed north, we could meet up.

He was being pushy, and it was irritating her. It was too much for him to ask her to break her anonymity.

> Apocalypse M: Where are you?

> God-Complex: Safe. I could keep you safe, too.

> Apocalypse M: Then stay safe and just wait this out.

> God-Complex: What if you get turned? You can hang out in my hideout in Massachusetts.

> Apocalypse M: I'm nowhere near you. We're done talking.

She deleted all of the messages, and then deleted the e-mail account. She'd already been in contact for too long, and though each message took a different path along the virtual networks, she wasn't sure of the exact capability of him tracking her. He was good, and she couldn't take the chance.

Because of God-Complex's requests, she wondered how safe she was. Arturo held the key to everything, and if he was with her in the event of confrontation or capture, her plan could be over before her goals were achieved. She looked up at Theresa and the kids, and it seemed like a good option. The GPS tracker in his hide-a-key on his collar would allow her to find them again later.

"Hey, Theresa," Morgan opened and waited for acknowledgement.

"Yeah?"

"I'm going to get out at Baltimore. I have something I need to take care of."

"Are you sure?"

"Yes, but I have a favor to ask."

She gazed out the window at landscape going by slowly.

"Hmm?"

She refocused her attention on Theresa.

"Can you take Arturo with you? I'll leave you money to get him whatever, and then I can meet back up with you wherever you end up."

"My kids would love that, but how will you find us?"

"You have an address and phone number where you'll be?" Morgan asked, knowing full well she'd be relying on the GPS in the collar.

The traffic was going slow enough that Theresa was able to scribble on a shred of paper. She crouch-walked to the front and took it from her, then returned to her seat. She glanced at it and stuffed it in her pocket.

*

Truman had watched Reese's conversation with Apocalypse M intently, hoping to catch any tells or pertinent information, which might lead them to their suspect. Reese had been telling them the truth, at least in the aspect that he didn't have anything they could use to break the programming of the infected nanites.

Gerald returned with new documents and held them out to Truman. He closed the laptop, moved it out of Reese's reach, and laid the papers out.

"We have a name to match our suspect to. Her name is Morgan White."

There was Morgan's life on paper. Graduated college with degrees in computer science and programming, top of her class. No criminal record. No protests on record. No ties to radical political parties. She'd gained a job with tech giant Revel working in their IT and InfoSec departments. Her photo ID with Revel was the cleanest picture they had of her, and it was definitely the same woman from the video footage.

*Son of a bitch.*

"Apocalypse M. M for Morgan?" Truman assumed.

"It's likely. I've already passed her picture on, and we'll have her name and face plastered all over the place soon."

"It's chaos out there. Can we mass force information to cell phones without crashing the networks?"

"That's NSA territory, but I can make a few calls and see what can be done. The biggest hurdle to that is the cell network, which is already taxed to the maximum. It's a miracle they're not having mass outages yet."

He looked at Reese and scowled. He didn't want to put his hope in one of the co-conspirators of this terrorist attack, but if they were going to find Morgan and force her to give up the key, it wouldn't hurt to blast her profile across the deep web.

He was glad he would finally be able to provide the president with some positive news and movement toward cleaning up this mess. She'd give him any resources he needed to apprehend their terrorist, but he already had the best.

*The EH units may be currently occupied, but that can easily be remedied.*

"What can I do?" Reese asked.

Before he could think of something, Gerald spoke up.

"What *can* you do?" he asked.

"I'm a hacker, and I have connections. I'll try to help find Morgan," Reese said, a hint of desperation in his voice.

"You don't think *we* can get to the deep web, Mr. Gordon?"

"I'm saying give me time, and a chance. I'll do whatever's necessary to find her."

"For your mother?" Gerald questioned his motive.

"For all of us."

Truman looked to Gerald, and they exchanged glances.

"He's under your jurisdiction for cybercrimes, Director Crawford," he offered.

Gerald nodded and unlatched the handcuffs from the table. Truman picked up the papers and computer, and they exited the interrogation room. He led the way back to the elevator, and Gerald gave Reese a rundown of what was to come while they walked.

"I'm going to assign one of my agents to oversee you. You'll tell them everything you're doing, while you're doing it, and how it's supposed to be helping us find the terrorist. If you do anything counterproductive, to alert her, or that's not on task, I'm going to bring you back down here, and when this is over, you'll be charged for cybercrimes and terrorism as an accomplice."

"Okay," Reese said. "Can I eat first, though?"

"I'll see what's available."

They reached the elevator, and he went through the motions to open it and get them heading back to the surface. On the first floor, he pulled his phone out and dialed the president's direct line.

Walking in the opposite direction of Gerald and Reese, he got the quiet necessary to talk with her. It rang once, and she picked up.

"This is President Ismail."

"Madam President, we've identified the terrorist, and we're initiating a search now."

"It's about time, General. What do we know?"

The general gave her a full update but reserved the detail that Reese was now working for them to find Morgan.

"This is good, General, but it's not enough. The majority of the north east is gone and Canada's borders are about to be overrun. I don't care what it takes, get it under control."

"Yes, ma'am."

She hung up on him. It pissed him off. She could be shrewder than he, and it was hard for him to choke down.

He returned to his office and picked up his SAT phone.

*

Fitz heard the ringing come from her hip, and she grabbed the phone. She answered and put the receiver to her ear.

"Corporal Fitzgerald speaking."

"It's Truman. We've made a breakthrough in tracking the terrorist. I'm commissioning you, and EH-US-10 to return to DC and be ready for deployment when we have a location."

"Yes, sir. If I may?"

"Go ahead."

"I've already commissioned a new EH-US-11 unit. In order to survive, I've given nanites to soldiers I escaped with. No need to take EH-US-10 from setting up the barriers."

"Understood. Collect your unit and head for…" the general paused and she could hear his keyboard clacking as he typed. "Cleveland Hopkins International. I'm arranging a flight now."

"Acknowledged. We'll be there as soon as possible."

"Godspeed."

Fitz hung up and watched her unit move a shipping container to the next open position. They'd made significant progress, but she knew that all too soon the nanite zombies would catch up.

She made her way to them, and before she even called them to attention, they finished what they were doing and lined up.

"Alright team, we're on our way out. We've received a high priority mission, which may lead to the terrorist who started this. We leave now."

"Yes, ma'am!"

There were more than her original unit, seven in total including her. She had a little bit of everything in her new unit, everyone with various different skills, and from different branches of the military. There wasn't the comradery she had with her previous squad mates, but they cooperated well.

Fitz led the way to their Humvee. Due to the limited seating, those who couldn't get in, climbed on. Sergeant Adams was in the driver seat and Private Welch took passenger. Welch had previously directed them here, and he took up that mantle again.

"Destination?" he asked.

"Cleveland Hopkins International Airport. Plot a course around major population areas."

"Yes, ma'am."

"Cut it with the *ma'am*. Call me Fitz."

Adams started the vehicle, and Welch plotted their course. They were going to have to leave the security of the wall, but Fitz hadn't yet seen or heard of the zombies reaching the blockade. They had stretched it north, along highway 91, from Wickliffe to Eastlake, and then cut over to the shoreline of Lake Erie in anticipation they'd come from that direction first. But she knew it wouldn't be long before they found their way south, and maybe around the shipping containers.

Adams sped them away from safety, following Welch's directions. Fitz prayed for somewhat clear roads. Being transferred back to the East Coast, they'd soon likely be in the thick of the zombies. For now, she wanted to let her mind rest a bit. She closed her eyes and listened to the sound of the tires on the road.

Every once in a while, she'd take a peek at their surroundings. Highway 480 was a mess. If not for the crawling at five miles per hour, it would be a parking lot. Some cars had been abandoned on the sides of the highway, but they weren't the cause of the traffic as far as she could tell.

Opportunistic lawbreakers were taking opportunities to break into abandoned cars, but it wasn't enough. They started breaking windows on still occupied vehicles. She wanted to get out and beat some sense into them, but the mission at hand was more important. Adams appeared to have the same thought and glanced back at her.

"Keep going. Push through vehicles if you have to," she commanded.

He nodded and revved the engine. Lieutenant Victoria Smith picked up the loudspeaker microphone and stuck her head out the top of the Humvee.

"Get off the highway! Return your homes or get inside a secure building!" Smith bellowed into the mic. "You'll be safer indoors!"

Some on foot stopped to look at her but quickly continued on. It seemed pointless, but Fitz figured it was a matter of Smith feeling like she was being productive.

"You there, in front of us, move out of the way!" she commanded through the speaker.

The vehicle moved as much as it could, and so did the next one in front of it, but there were plenty more which didn't budge. Adams looked at Fitz again with a frown.

"Official government business! Move out of the way!" Smith yelled.

Adams revved his engine and a few more moved, but not enough. He eased off the brake and began shoving through the lines. It was slow going, but it was better than being stopped. People began yelling at them. Soon, the Humvee was swarmed with angry people. The soldiers readied their weapons.

"This is your fault!"

"What the hell are you doing here? Shouldn't you be fighting those things?"

"I'm going to sue the government for all it has!"

"Who the hell do you think you are?"

"Get off the highway! Get inside and barricade the doors!" Smith tried again. "The infected will be here soon!"

The crowd started shaking the Humvee. She knew it was only a matter of time before they tipped them over, and she couldn't let that happen. Fitz grabbed the mic from Smith.

"You are impeding the capture of the terrorist who has endangered the country! If you do not disperse now, you will be labeled as a co-conspirator and you will be shot!"

This stunned the crowd. She hoped it sent wild images through their minds that maybe the terrorist was here somewhere and their lives were in imminent danger if they didn't cooperate.

The group took a moment, but they dispersed. In front of them, the traffic started parting again, and though there was still not much room, Adams would be able to make it through only bumping a few cars.

"Adams," Fitz said and pointed to the opening. "I don't care who is in the way. Ram them."

"Yes, ma'am."

She repeated her message to all in front of them, and they continued toward the airport. She reflected on the morality of "sacrifice a few to save the many," which got played out both in movies and in real life. It was a cliché she couldn't get away from because as a soldier, sacrifice was necessary.

They were passing the junction to Highway 77 when a voice came in over the radio.

"Attention all military personnel. Hostile incursion into Ohio. ETA: ninety minutes to reach the wall at Highway 271."

It took them a half-hour more to get to the airport, despite normal air traffic having ceased when martial law was implemented. No one seemed to care they were supposed to be inside. Stuck getting to the loading zones, they were at least close enough to walk.

"Everyone out!" Fitz ordered. "Grab all of the weapons and head for the terminal!"

Her unit followed orders. Before leaving, she picked up the mic and poked her head out toward the traffic behind her.

"Return to your homes!" she warned. "They've breached Ohio borders and are headed toward the military cordon!"

It caused a bit of a panic, but it was all she could do to protect these people for now. She grabbed her gear and jogged to catch up to her unit.

She dialed General Truman on the SAT phone. It rang, but there was no answer. Trying again got the same response.

"Damnit, where are we supposed to be going?" Fitz muttered.

She took the lead of her unit and led them into the airport. There were many civilians looking to get a flight out, only to be denied. Announcements over the PA system that all flights were canceled, and every line on the boards reflected that. People were irate, wanting to get as far away from here as possible, and she wouldn't be surprised if an uprising started. *Not that it would get them anywhere.*

She led her unit up to security, and they didn't bother to question her. The metal detectors sounded, but she didn't look back. She tried to contact the general again and got through.

"General Truman speaking."

"Sir, EH-US-11 has arrived at Cleveland Hopkins. Directions?"

"Head to gate B6, and exit onto the ramp. Your jet is waiting to bring you to DC. I'll meet you at Reagan airport."

"Yes, sir."

He hung up. She led EH-US-11 to the terminal, and it was there with soldiers waiting for her unit. They saluted, and she returned it before bounding up the stairs.

They were seated, and the jet was taxied for takeoff.

"Rest up," she ordered the unit. "There's a lot to do ahead."

*

Truman re-entered the Pentagon with an entourage of TEAL scientists, a dozen government employees, and a handful of Marines. Nobody was empty handed, bringing in electronics and equipment. He sought to bring TEAL and the government's teams together. He worked with Gerald to create a small team from the FBI's Cyber Crimes division, and managed to talk Lang into leaving a core group and enough equipment to continue working here. He hoped they might discover a way to disable Morgan's kill command, in case they weren't able to catch up with her.

He led them to the elevator, which went to the unlabeled basement level. Due to its small size, several trips had to be made. He left the groups to set up, and met up with Gerald to get a status update on their terrorist. On ground level, Truman dialed his friend. The phone rang, and he heard a ring in the hallway.

"Director Crawford speaking," Gerald's voice echoed. His voice came from down the hall before he heard it over the phone.

Truman looked for him and spotted him coming, with Reese and another. He hung up and moved toward Gerald.

"Norm," he greeted.

He nodded. "Anything?"

"Some. Based on about when the fire was set, we started reviewing footage from highway cameras. We've got her leaving New Jersey in the vehicle from Syracuse, heading south towards Philly."

"She might hit our side of the cordon then?"

"If she hasn't already been infected, it's likely. We're trying to narrow down the search window before dispatching anyone."

"I have EH-US-11 on their way to handle it once we locate her."

"Sounds good. We also have news outlets running with her info, so the nation is our eyes and ears. Some tips are coming in with potential sightings, but with the chaos, I'm not expecting any solid leads yet."

"Let's bring Mr. Gordon down below also," Truman said. "I still think he knows more than he's letting on, and if he's around TEAL's equipment, he might slip up and say something incriminating."

"Sure."

Gerald retrieved Reese, and the agent he'd been working with, and they descended to the basement. The once semi-empty temporary holding area was now a command center for thwarting the end of the United States.

They commandeered a pair of computers and stuck Reese in one seat while the agent took the other. Together, they conversed, and some of the technobabble was a little beyond Truman, but he understood enough.

"What we have on Morgan isn't enough. There are some within Anonymous who have already doxed her and started releasing information," Reese mentioned.

"I'm contacting the Dragon's Head Anonymous group," the FBI agent added. They should be able to push what we have, including video, to all phones. The phones that can receive photos and video will get those, too. It'll be systematic, sending to every phone number at the same time."

"That would be useful. Do they have that access, though?" Director Crawford asked.

"The US has been holding onto cell service vulnerabilities for just a circumstance," the agent replied.

The agent clacked on the keyboard, and Truman tracked what they were doing; uploading a file onto a dark web cloud. They typed out a quick message on a forum, which gave the instructions of what to do and the link to the shared files.

"And now they have them. They'll be able to broadcast her info across US, Canadian, and Mexican services."

Truman rested his hand on the agent's shoulder and leaned into to his ear. He kept his voice low.

"Is this going to open us up to more Anonymous attacks?"

"Maybe, but we don't have much choice. They have a better ability to push that much data at once. Their network is greater due to a hive-like virus we know is sitting dormant on a number of personal computers."

"What about the cell services? Won't that shut down the system?" Reese asked.

"Yes, but it'll be temporary. It shouldn't take long for the satellites to catch up and for normal service to resume," the analyst said with confidence.

Every phone in the command center began chiming, buzzing, and making noises. The general grabbed up his phone and it showed a message waiting. Looking at the text, there were a few attachments: Morgan's driver's license photo, video of her entering the fairgrounds incognito, and a blunt message.

> Wanted: Morgan Ophelia White for starting a zombie apocalypse. Hair color: Amber. Eye color: Blue. Height: 5'6". Weight: 117. Age: 35. May be wearing a disguise. If found, capture ALIVE and call the FBI: 202-324-3000.

Truman grumbled about their wording, but he couldn't be choosy right now. He just hoped they'd be successful.

*

Morgan's burner phone buzzed and, oddly, Theresa's chimed at the same time. She picked up her phone and felt the blood drain completely from her face. Her info was plastered all over the screen, along with her license photo and footage of her bringing Corporal Reyes into the fairgrounds. They'd figured her out.

She looked up at Theresa. She was driving and not paying attention to her phone. The original plan of leaving Arturo with her was out. Once Theresa saw her phone and identified her, she'd lose her chance of creating a second wave. In fact, Theresa would inform the authorities of her location, what she was wearing, and that she had a dog.

She didn't like it, because Theresa had been nice enough to pick her up with no questions asked, but she couldn't leave a witness. She pulled out the capped syringe from her bag and hid it against her leg. Up past the kids, who were waking up, she crept toward Theresa. Her bag was on her shoulder, and Arturo's leash was in her hands. She was ready.

"Hey, can you do me a favor? I just received a text and my plans changed. I need you to let me out here," she did her best to keep her voice steady.

"Are you sure? It'll be quite a walk to reach Baltimore."

"Yeah, I'm sure."

She pulled over to the side of the highway, onto the shoulder. As she parked, she turned to Morgan and smiled. It made what she was about to do even harder on her, but it was her only chance. Morgan pulled the latch on the door to open it, and then reached up to Theresa to hug her.

"Thank you for the ride," she said as she pulled Theresa in, hiding the syringe behind Theresa's back.

"It's no problem. If you need a place to go after, just come to the address I gave you."

"I'm so sorry," she said, and meant it. "It's only temporary."

Before she could do anything, Morgan poked her with the needle and depressed the plunger completely. Theresa shoved her.

"What the fuck?" Theresa screamed.

Morgan jumped out, pulling Arturo's leash hard. Theresa got out of her vehicle and came around the passenger side, but she was already running toward a business area.

"What the hell did you do?" she continued screaming. "What did you do?"

She kept her head down and didn't look back. It wouldn't be long before Theresa turned. Theresa continued yelling and screaming, but Morgan hoped she wouldn't leave the kids alone. She tore through a parking lot as fast as her legs would carry her.

It was done. The second wave would begin shortly. Being so close to Baltimore, this new wave would tear through Washington DC in short time. She had to stay ahead of the ripple and out of the grasp of any would-be captors.

There was a mall nearby. She wondered if it was operating as normal, or if it was closed. It was a gamble, but if it was mostly empty, it would be a good place to steal a change of clothes and food. She came close to the parking lot, and saw no one was coming or going.

Car horns blared behind her, signaling the start. She had to move, now. Running again, she headed for a department store, the closest entrance to her. The doors were locked and all of the lights were off inside.

A Macy's had an exit door propped open, and she slipped inside. With the door closed behind her, it instantly became dark. She fumbled with the dim light of her phone.

Finding new clothes, she changed into them: jeans, and a hoodie to hide her hair. The clothes weren't enough, though. She needed more. At the store's makeup section, she set up her phone as a light and began applying anything she thought might conceal her identity.

*With that much info on me, they might already know I have Arturo. I need to set him free, and track him down later.*

She reached into her bag and grabbed out some jerky, then dropped some near his feet while she finished her makeup. He practically inhaled it, and whimpered for more.

Finished, she headed toward the front of the store. The gate was down and locked, leaving her no way into the mall without breaking the lock. There wasn't much at her disposal to even try, but it was that, or go out the same door she came in and face the second wave.

Kicking it just made it rattle. A search with her phone's light revealed a fire extinguisher, and she remembered hearing what she thought was an urban legend about being able to break locks if they were cold.

*Could it get it cold enough?*

She secured Arturo in a safe location, and then retrieved the fire extinguisher. It was CO2, the type she needed. It took some mental preparation of going over the steps she'd take to make sure she optimized her attempt. Positioning herself, she readied to spray, and thought better of it.

"I need gloves," she mumbled.

After searching the makeup areas, she came up with rubber gloves. They weren't the best, but they'd provide some protection.

Now ready, she pointed the nozzle at the lock, and pulled the handle. The spray startled her a little, but she kept the hose pointed where it needed. The cold was bouncing back and hitting her knuckles. Even with the gloves protecting her, it began to hurt, but she wasn't about to stop and lose the opportunity. Ice crystals formed on the lock. When she felt it was likely cold enough, she used the end of the fire extinguisher as a hammer.

It took several blows, but the lock's metal gave way. She smashed it until there was a hole, and she was able to actuate the locking mechanism with her fingers. She raised the gate enough to slip under, bringing the fire extinguisher, her bag, and Arturo with her.

In the empty common area, she remembered a movie about zombies and a mall. It didn't turn out so well for those people, but then again, she was alone, not subjected to idiotic behaviors of other people.

At the other side of the mall, there was a common entrance, which was locked up. It didn't deter her. The fire extinguisher's cold blast frosted the window, and when the bottle was depleted she threw it at the glass. It shattered, and she escaped.

Out into the open air, she made a run for it, with Arturo happy to keep pace. They made it to a neighborhood, and while people were rushing around, trying to escape the city, she hid next to a house and dug into her bag.

"Alright, boy, we're going to split up for a while," she said while dumping the entire contents of the jerky package on the ground for him.

He began scarfing it down, and she unhooked his leash. She took one last look at the hide-a-key box on his neck to make sure it was secure, and then ran while he was distracted. Her goal now was to get as far away from here as possible. Both north and south were out of the question, and to the west would be overrun soon. She had to head east in hopes of finding a boat.

*

"What the hell do you mean they've already made it to Baltimore?" Truman was beside himself.

"There's a wave of them taking over just outside of the city, and it's spreading fast!"

*All of a sudden they're in Maryland? There's only one way that's possible!*

"She's there! It's a second wave!" he yelled out to the entire crew. "Get your asses in gear to gather as much footage from the area that you can!"

He picked up his SAT phone and dialed EH-US-11. Fitzgerald answered.

"Yes, sir?"

"How long until your boots hit the ground?"

"Ten minutes."

"Good, I'm going to have a chopper waiting with all the resources you'll need. The terrorist has created a new wave north of Baltimore, and she couldn't have gotten far."

"Sir, yes, sir!"

He hung up, angrier than ever. He grabbed his cell phone and dialed the president.

"This better be good news."

"Madam President, we have the terrorist's general location. There's a good chance we'll have her in custody soon. I have EH-US-11 heading to the area now."

"It's about time, General. I expect an update as soon as you have information."

"There's a problem, though. The terrorist has created another wave, this time near Baltimore. The wave will reach DC before we can finish the cordon."

"General, if they reach DC and you don't have the cure, you can consider yourself dismissed," President Ismail threatened.

He knew it wasn't just a promise to dismiss him. The president would make sure he felt the full brunt of the blame because it was *his* program.

"Yes, President." It was all he could say.

She hung up, and he made additional phone calls to make sure everything was ready for EH-US-11 to pursue and secure their suspect safely. Thoughts of self- preservation crept in, ready to do anything necessary for his survival, and to retain his control.

*

The airplane's door opened and stairs were rolled up. A Blackhawk waited, blades spinning.

"Alright! Move, move!" Fitz yelled while signaling with her hands.

The unit bounded down the stairs and leapt into the helicopter. There was a master sergeant waiting for them, and he handed her a file. Everyone strapped in, and they lifted off. Glancing through the file, she committed the information and images to memory, and then passed it to a teammate.

As they looked it over, she familiarized herself with the area. They were coming up on another shipping container wall, cutting Baltimore off from Washington DC. *With the new infection, there's no way the cordon can succeed.*

The chopper sped along, following the highway, and they were soon over Baltimore. Just a bit past the city, she could see the leading edge of the zombie wave below. It overtook everything, spreading like a wildfire. And like a wildfire, there was a void where it all started. The second ground zero. Fitz grabbed up a headset and turned to speak with the pilot.

She pointed where the pilot could see, and bellowed through the noise of the blades, "Bring us down there!"

The area was mostly vacant, minus a few lingering zombies. Fitz signaled her unit, and instructed them to get headshots. They all acknowledged, and they took positions at the open doors. The zombies that came to surround the helicopter were gunned down.

A group of cars was piled on the highway, and next to them was a car parked on the side of the road. When the helicopter was low enough, she jumped out and surveyed. Lieutenant Smith, Ensign Naki, Private Welch, and Sergeant Allen followed, and she signaled them to check the wreck.

Fitz brought her rifle up, ready to fire at anything that moved. Heading toward the car parked on the shoulder, the sight was horrific. Two blood covered children, strapped into their booster seats, clawing to get out. They were clearly infected, but there was no sign of the parents. There was, however, a needle cap on the driver's seat.

Movement off the highway caught her attention. A group of zombies wandered toward a parking lot. *That's the way I would have run if I'd just infected someone.*

"Back in!" Fitz yelled, and waved to her troops who were fending off a new wave of zombies.

They retreated and entered the helicopter. She put her headset on, pointed, and directed the pilot.

"That way!"

He lifted up and arced toward some buildings. Past them there were zombies running around, and beyond was a heard of them headed for a mall. Fitz pointed, and he headed for the massive building. The roof was mostly covered with solar panels, and there wasn't any real access point to the mall from the roof she could see. *This is it. This is where she'd have run.*

"Gotcha, bitch," Fitz declared under her breath.

*

Over her shoulder, a military chopper hovered in the distance, but even a few miles away was too close for comfort. *They must be looking for me.*

Taking some creative shortcuts, Morgan avoided major streets and populated areas as much as possible. Running through a neighborhood, many people were out trying to pack up and flee. She couldn't take the chance of asking for help and being recognized. This time, theft was her only option.

A man hastily brought things out to their car, and she waited until he went back inside to sneak over and check the ignition. The keys were there.

Before he could come back out and stop her, she jumped in, started the little two door, and sped off. In the rearview mirror, she saw the man come out and start chasing. Gassing it, there was no way he'd catch up.

*

One of the mall store's had a loading bay with walls and a gate, and they were lucky enough to find the gate closed. The zombies were blocked from getting to the rollup doors into the building. She pointed it out, and the pilot dropped down enough for them to jump out.

She grabbed a hand radio, tuned it to the helicopter's frequency, and gestured for her unit to exit. EH-US-11 rappelled out, and they secured the perimeter of the interior of the loading bay.

Fitz radioed the pilot, and instructed them. "Land somewhere safe and await pickup instructions"

"Yes, ma'am!"

She led the way to the rollup door, and pulled on it. It was locked.

"Everyone, put your fingers under and pull up."

They did as they were instructed. When they all pulled together, creaking and popping was heard. It warped outward some, and the lock gave way. The door rolled up enough for her to poke her rifle flashlight into the dark interior. Over her shoulder, she beckoned Ensign Naki over.

"Naki, watch our six," Fitz whispered, and he nodded.

Inside the loading area, the unit lit their flashlights, and cleared the warehouse-like room. Safe, she signaled Naki to close the rollup door behind them.

From the backroom to the main store, Sergeant Moss and Private Welch held the doors open while Captain Frederickson and Sergeant Allen advanced through and cleared their sides. She and Smith cleared their front, and behind, Naki kept their tail safe.

With no signs of life, she led the way toward the mall's interior, only to be stopped by a locked roll up gate. She motioned for them to listen for noises. There was a slight commotion down a ways. Shooting the lock might alert whomever it was, be it the terrorist or zombies, but there was no other choice.

"Take out the lock," Fitz ordered.

Welch was closest, and so everyone backed up while he fired at it. Metal warped, and the lock shattered. The unit rolled the gate up and cleared the area outside the store. The noise was coming from their right, and she signaled to move toward it.

Approaching a corner between a jeweler's and a Starbucks, they eased up, and Fitz poked her head around. There was daylight, and zombies who sauntered about.

*Shit!*

Her unit huddled, and she whispered.

"We have a dozen hostiles around the corner. Fan out, cover each other, land headshots. Morgan White may be amongst them, so keep an eye out for her."

There were nods of acknowledgement, and they readied themselves. Fitz waved her hand and gave the order. As the unit's leader, she put herself out first. In her peripheral, she watched the unit stagger themselves.

She raised her rifle and let the first bullet fly. It tore through a man's skull, and the zombie dropped. The zombies' attentions were drawn, and they ran at high speed toward the unit. Rifle shots echoed through the open space, and within a few moments, the area was clear. More poured in through broken glass at the mall entrance, but they stood no chance against EH-US-11. Proceeding forward, they each took turns gunning down the zombies now flowing in at a steady pace.

"Check for Morgan!" Fitz hollered while glancing down at the first few zombies. "Naki, check wallets of anyone that looks like her!"

They continued, taking out every one that came through. The horde slowed to a trickle, then to one and two at a time, then none.

"None of them are her!" he called out.

She looked over her shoulder and directed, "Frederickson, take Moss and clear the ground level. Smith, take Welch and clear the second level."

They left to complete their tasks. Fitz waved for Naki and Allen to join her at the side of the common area.

"You ever played Resident Evil on hard?" she asked.

"Yeah," Allen answered. Naki shook his head.

"They're going to respawn. Don't let your guard down."

"Are you shitting me?" Allen asked.

"The nanites have made them immortal. They'll heal from headshots."

Ensign Naki became nervous and pointed his gun at the bodies. Fitz was glad he was being diligent about it. The one thing about working with other soldiers that she loved is they understood threats better than a civilian ever could.

Ten minutes passed. A few additional zombies found their way in through the broken glass, only to be felled just steps inside. She hoped to have good news to give General Truman soon.

She heard the first grumbling from one of them returning to life, and as soon as it started to get up, Allen used a knife and put it down again. More followed, but thankfully, while they were regenerating from the mortal wounds, they were significantly slower, appearing to be disoriented. The three of them gunned down the poor souls a second time.

Her people returned, absent Morgan White.

"Report," Fitz requested.

"There's clear sign that *someone* was here. Looks like they broke in through Macy's," Frederickson replied.

"Second level cleared. No signs of life, no break-ins," Smith added.

She felt it in her gut, they'd just missed their terrorist. There was no proof it was Morgan who was here, but with the car nearby, and the spread pattern, she couldn't shake the feeling. There was no giving up.

"Move out," she waved toward the broken glass. "I'll radio for our ride."

They fell into formation, and Fitz grabbed the radio from her hip.

"This is Corporal Fitzgerald requesting pickup. Over."

"Acknowledged. Extraction point? Over."

They exited into a nearly empty parking lot with a few zombies milling about. Her unit took care of them while she continued her conversation.

"North parking lot. Over."

"Acknowledged. Over and out."

Fitz heard the motor start up on the helicopter from somewhere close. It appeared overhead, and the pilot descended. The unit loaded on, and she put a headset on.

"I want to canvas this area. I'm certain the terrorist is close."

"Yes, ma'am!"

The pilot circled, and they were now looking for a needle in a needle stack.

*

"General?" Reese spoke up.

"What is it?" Truman responded roughly.

"We've been scanning the area with your satellites, and I've found something out of place." He paused and wondered if it was important enough to point out.

The general came to look over his shoulder, and the FBI agent leaned in from their seat. *If this is a good lead, the general might ease up on me.*

"Spit it out. Time is critical," he snapped.

"Here, look." Reese pointed at the screen where a real time map of the second infection point was displayed. "I've been tracking your unit out there. I've had some guys working with me on looking for odd behaviors, outside of the zombies."

He panned the map to the north.

"I've also been looking at traffic, and while everyone is trying to go anywhere but north, there's one person heading north right now. Who in their right mind would head from one infected area to another?"

"It could be anyone," the FBI agent assigned to him tried to play Devil's Advocate. "There could be one person thinking they can outrun it because no one else is heading that way."

"Are there any traffic cams out on that road?" Truman asked.

"Yes, but they're not high enough quality to determine if it's Morgan White or not," the agent replied.

"Try anyway," he commanded. "The least we could do is determine if the driver is female."

"Understood."

They worked on it, and pulled up every camera the driver would pass. It took a few minutes, but the car passed the first one at high speed. They all leaned into the screen, trying to get a better look. It was hard to tell.

"Keep an eye on that car. I'll be right back," Truman said, and headed to the elevator.

*

The pilot had circled the area several times. There was one instance Naki thought he saw a zombie who fit Morgan's description, but upon descent, they could see it wasn't her.

Her SAT phone rang, and she answered.

"This is Corporal Fitzgerald," she yelled into the phone over the noise of the helicopter.

"I'm sending you information. I want you to investigate a vehicle headed north."

Her regular phone buzzed, and she looked at it. There was information on a car heading north on Highway 95.

"Yes, sir! We're on our way!"

Truman hung up, and she instructed the pilot. He veered hard to port and began following the highway below.

*

Morgan was looking for a good route to head toward Rumsey Island. The map on her phone showed docks there, and if there were, maybe a boat she could board. That was until she saw a helicopter heading her way. She was the only one heading north on the highway right now, and in case it was police, she slowed down to the speed limit.

After only a moment, she knew it wasn't law enforcement. It was military.

"Shit. Shit!"

She kept her pace, and the helicopter gained on her quickly. There wasn't much she could do. There weren't any exits coming up.

*

"There!" Fitz pointed and yelled into her headset. "Bring it down in front of the car!"

The pilot obeyed and sped up to get well in front. The car sped up too.

They pushed forward a bit more, and the pilot overcame the vehicle. He dropped it right onto the highway, and she waved for her unit to get out. The seven of them readied their rifles and leveled it at the car, which was speeding toward their location.

*

Morgan had two choices: press the gas pedal and hope they don't shoot, or hit the brakes and throw it in reverse. If she martyred herself, she couldn't be sure her plan would succeed. If they captured her, she'd probably never see the light of day again.

She slammed the brakes as a soldier fired her rifle at the windshield. The bullet ripped through the cab of the car, barely missing her. She stopped a hundred yards from the soldiers ready to gun her down. The woman in the front of their unit motioned for her to get out.

Morgan sat there with her hands on the steering wheel for a moment before turning the car off. She was thankful for grabbing the lighter fluid and matches, but could she really torch her only way of finding Arturo?

*Burning it would be better than letting them run a decryption program and finding the GPS service. If I survive, I'll have to find him another way later.*

With minimal movements, she dug the lighter fluid and matches out of the bag and sprayed it all over the passenger seat. She dumped the whole canister. The soldiers were getting impatient, and they started encroaching. Morgan threw it in reverse and put another few hundred yards between them.

She lit a match and tossed it on the bag. Flames burst up, singing her arm hair. Getting out with her hands in the air, she surrendered while the bag and seat burned. There was panic in the unit leader's eyes, and it was likely they knew evidence was being destroyed.

"Get in there and get whatever's burning!"

It was too late. The fire had already engulfed the interior of the car. Morgan stepped away and got down on her knees with her hands behind her head and watched the car burn while the soldiers reached into the fire and attempted to retrieve the contents.

She wasn't surprised when the soldiers came out with third degree burns and healed up. Their efforts were useless, though, as the bag and its contents were completely torched. Naki brought over a bag from the helicopter to put it all in.

"What the hell did you burn?" The unit leader came over and pointed her rifle at her forehead.

Morgan said nothing.

"Get her in the chopper!" the woman yelled and pulled out a large phone.

The soldiers forced her to her feet and dragged her to the helicopter. She glanced over her shoulder and saw the woman making a call.

*

"General Truman, it was her, and she's in custody," came Corporal Fitzgerald's voice over the phone. It was loud enough the people in the vicinity of Truman began cheering.

He shot stern glances to shut the group up, and Fitzgerald continued.

"Unfortunately, sir, I think she destroyed evidence. We're bringing her in now. We'll see you shortly."

"Understood. Good work, Corporal."

"Thank you, sir."

He sighed and hung up. Even if Morgan had destroyed evidence, she would quickly find out how far he'd go to obtain the answers he needed, and to secure her key.

*

# Chapter 6:

President Ismail was relieved they had the terrorist in custody, but that didn't stop the infected from approaching.

Her staff shuffled her, her husband, and their children out of the White House doors and onto a helicopter bound for Air Force One. The rest of her cabinet would be on their way behind her, but it felt like she was running from the problem. The idea that the president and highest-ranking government officials were getting flights out, but no one else could, made her sick to her stomach. It felt like she was abandoning her people.

Their helicopter landed at Ronald Reagan airport, and they boarded Air Force One. Her cabinet and immediate staff joined them within minutes, and the plane taxied to take off.

She kissed her children and husband, and left them in their seats to head to the plane's conference room. Vice President Abraham approached and spoke with a soft voice.

"Aisha, we're ready to do another press conference from the plane," he said.

"Thanks, Rich. I'll be ready shortly."

Once they were in the air, everyone set about finalizing preparations for the broadcast. A camera was pointed down to the head of the table, where there was a small podium. Near the cameras were several screens, which lit up and connected them to news sources.

President Ismail stood and tugged on her jacket to straighten it out. She nodded and waited for her cue, a red light, to start. She took a deep, cleansing breath, and they began.

"My fellow Americans, and fellow nations of the world, it is with a heavy heart that I must announce a second terror attack has occurred just north of Baltimore. However, we also can take a breath, as this led to the terrorist being caught. We will soon have their cure to reverse this attack.

"Anyone who is seeing or hearing this, stay put. If you're in any of the affected areas, lock your doors and don't make any noises that might draw attention. If you are in a military safe zone, stay there. This will be over soon. We must show resolve in the face of the fear and anger we all feel for being put in such a vulnerable position. We will prevail over this."

It was short, but she was sure it would hit home and soothe some people's anxieties.

"Madam President, John Rancor, CNN. Can you comment on the video that the alleged terrorist put out?"

"At this time, what I can say about it is files and property were stolen in order to push a narrative. Their ideology of anarchy is illustrated by their use of the Guy Fawkes mask."

"What about the claim of super soldiers, and this nanotechnology eventually being pushed out to the public?"

"Nanotechnology was approved and put into development prior to my presidency, and I only recently learned of the program myself. As to its public usage, the repercussions of nanotechnology is one hundred percent clear right now. A person has taken them and turned them into a non-biological virus, and on top of acquiring the terrorist's *key*, we're working on methods to combat this new form of ransomware."

"President Ismail, Andrea Ludvig, Fox News. What happens to those who are infected?"

"Right now, we have no solid answers. Once we have the terrorist's key in hand, we believe we'll be able to use it as a retro virus and cure those infected. The hope is they'll return to normal and be able to resume normal life."

"Do you have a contingency plan?"

"Yes, but I'm unable to give any details at the moment. Should the need arise, we will inform the public." She cringed at the thought of employing nukes over the states for the EMP effects. "Thank you all for your time. When we have more information, we will share it."

The red light went off, and she breathed a sigh of relief. She stood and grabbed a cup of water from a nearby coffee bar to cure her dry throat. Vice President Abraham approached.

"Well said," he offered.

"Thanks," she said and lowered her voice to keep her next statement between the two of them, "We have to discuss what happens after this is contained."

*

Dusk neared. Truman waited at the Pentagon's helipad, and watched the helicopter carrying Morgan White come in. He expected her to try anything to get away, including jump to her death before they landed. They touched down, and Corporal Fitzgerald had a firm grip on her. She had no chance to escape.

Fitzgerald marched Morgan over to him, a bag slung over her shoulder. While keeping the terrorist close, she saluted the general. He returned the salute.

"Well done, Corporal," he spoke loudly while the helicopter's engine was winding down. "The nation, and the world, are in your debt."

"It was a team effort, sir. I just hope her attempt to burn her electronics was in vain."

"There might be hope yet. If you pulled them out in time, we may be able to salvage something."

"Orders, sir?"

"It's only a matter of time before the infected make it here. Do you think you could devise a way to draw them to one area to buy us more time to get the cure?"

"They respond to sound, and the sight of other humans. It's plausible that we could set up decoys and stations on the cordon wall to attract them."

"Good. You and EH-US-11 are to report to Master Sergeant Thomas at the wall north of here."

"They're going to get you anyway," Morgan snapped.

Fitzgerald balled a fist, and though Truman felt the same, he intervened.

"Dismissed!" he barked at her.

"Sir, yes, sir!" She handed Morgan over.

Master Sergeant Gorski had exited the helicopter and come up behind Fitzgerald. Truman handed Morgan off to him, and he took the bag from the corporal. They turned to leave, and the helicopter's rotors spun up again.

He smiled a little. This terror attack felt like it had been going on forever now, and he was glad to see they were now on the cusp of a turning point. They would be back on the path to curing the world's diseases, while ushering in a new era for humanity.

Gorski led Morgan into the Pentagon, and to the elevator that would take them to the hidden level. Truman didn't care what she saw, because even when he got what he wanted, she'd never see daylight again.

The elevator descended, and then *dinged*. When the doors opened, and they stepped out, silence fell over the room. All eyes were on their terrorist.

"Now that we have the terrorist, split into two teams. One to find a fix that won't kill the hosts, and the other to recover information from this," Truman instructed, and held up the bag containing the remnants of Morgan's belongings.

"Wow. Is this the biggest party you could throw for me?" Morgan sneered.

"Shut up," Truman snapped and yanked her from Gorski.

As he led Morgan through, she yelled so everyone could hear.

"I wasn't lying. If you do what I instructed, I'll give you the key! This technology should be illegal!"

Not a single person spoke up. Truman pushed her harder toward a set of secured double doors. It took a keycard and his biometrics to get through. Inside them was another set, which required the same clearances, creating a buffer between their makeshift command center and an area far more sinister. A place only a handful of officials knew existed right under their work spaces.

Most people thought Guantanamo Bay was where they held and tortured most terrorists. Even through years of classified document leaks in the recent past, the American populace never had any proof there was a detention center right under the Pentagon.

In the secured hall, a soldier saluted the general. Shoving Morgan along, he deposited her inside the first door on the left, a room with a chair, which was centered and bolted to the floor. Sitting her down, he grabbed a chain from the floor and strung it up over her handcuffs.

"You're going to tell me everything, one way or another," Truman threatened.

"I'm not going to tell you shit, unless you do what I demanded," she retorted.

"You'll answer me soon enough. I'll return after you've had some time to think about the situation you're in."

He did an about face, exited the room, and closed the door behind him. He ushered the soldier over, and when they approached and saluted, he directed them.

"Ignore anything you hear from her. Don't open the door. Don't respond to her."

"Sir, yes, sir!" he responded.

The soldier took his place, and Truman headed back to the command center.

*

Reese had been assigned to TEAL's small team. His reputation of being the one who hacked them preceded him, and their team lead, Beth, had opposed allowing him to help on multiple grounds. In the end, because of his assistance with capturing Morgan White, Director Crawford overruled her.

"General Truman," he called out and waved him over. "We've been looking through the infected nanite coding. Some parts are solid, some are rushed."

"What does that mean for us?" the general addressed Beth.

"It's going to take time to find out," Beth responded. "But if she got sloppy, we might find a way to work new code in without triggering the kill commands. I'm going to need a lot of mice for tests."

"We'll get you more," he offered.

"Has she divulged anything helpful?" she asked.

"Not yet. She needs time to stew. Keep working and keep me apprised of any progress."

"OK." Beth nodded.

When General Truman walked away, he struck up conversation with her, even though the FBI was still watching over him.

"When you created these, did you ever think that there would be vulnerabilities?"

"Of course, we did," she said in a condescending tone. "What we didn't anticipate were some *assholes* stealing sensitive documents, reverse engineering a nanite dock, and then perverting our work!"

"What about the general population? The plan to control the masses once everyone had nanites?" he asked and came off defensive.

"Paranoid delusions. There was no plan to control anyone. Alphaeus is a humanitarian, trying to better the world not destroy it," she snapped back. "The nanites are the next step in human advancement, the transhumanism movement."

"But wouldn't that open up the possibility of control to whoever's in charge? What if it was conform or die?" he prodded her, irritated at her arrogance.

Beth looked at him, and she was dead serious. "This isn't a *movie*. The government *isn't* out to get you, and the world isn't as dark as you think. TEAL's goal is unity and enlightenment."

That's not what the documents indicated. What he'd seen clearly identified a new order of humanity. It hit him like a truck, and he peeked over his shoulder at General Truman. The implementation of the nanites as a new social order were signed by *him. Does she believe Morgan doctored documents? Or has she even seen them?*

He huffed, and returned his attention to his screen to compare differences in original and zombie code. Despite his contribution to the situation they were in, he believed Morgan's findings, and determined he was in a unique position to possibly open TEAL's eyes.

Though hostile, she helped point him in the right directions quite a bit. He located a new behavior function, which appeared to control when an infected person would seek out real food, eat, and then return to infecting.

He began tweaking the code, which told the zombies when to eat, and decreased the time so they would do so more frequently. Beth saw him working on it and peeked over at his screen.

"Eat more, slow them down?" she asked.

"It's basic, and we'd have no way of mass distributing them, but it's something," he answered. "I can't tell if it will trigger the kill command yet."

"Only one way to find out. Compile it and try it out."

He finished, bringing the time between meals to every second, hoping to create a loop in the programming and cause the infected to turn in circles.

She took over, and he watched as she began a fresh compiling on an uninfected nanite. With the complexity of the code, it would take an estimated hour before it was ready. While he waited, he grabbed one of the rations brought down, and ate.

When it was finished, Beth got up and went to the computer where the newly reprogrammed nanite was. He followed and watched her prepare her instruments to inject it into a mouse.

She brought the needle to one of a few ballistic glass boxes, and inside was a mouse desperately trying to attack anyone. At the bottom of the cage was chicken-wire, and when Beth hit a button, it shocked the creature. While it was stunned, she opened the box and injected it.

With the top closed, they waited to see. It would be almost instantaneous if their new code was going to trigger the kill command. The mouse recovered from the shock, and tried attacking them through the glass. The glass held.

Nothing horrible happened to it. After a moment, it circled, sniffing. While it was distracted, Beth was quick to drop some pellets in. The mouse pounced on the food. After it had eaten it turned to the glass again and began attacking again, except only a moment later it was sniffing and looking for more food.

"What happens if we put more food in?" Reese asked. "If it's full, will it still eat?"

"Let's find out," she said and dropped another handful in.

The mouse gorged. It ate every last pellet. The cycle repeated and she threw more food in. It was apparent there was a problem. It ate, but it was moving slower. Its body was bloated to the point Reese was sure it was going to pop. Instead of exploding, its stomach continued to expand as it ate and slowly tore open. He had to look away as the mouse's intestines began spilling out, and the nanites did everything they could to repair the damage.

"We could still use this," Beth whispered. In his peripheral vision, he could see she was transfixed.

She flipped the switch to shock it, and dialed it up to max. The mouse squeaked, and the smell of burning flesh nauseated him even more. He left the area and heaved into a nearby trash can. Despite being sick at the sight and smell, he still wanted to know the outcome. When he was finished, he returned and the sight was ghastly. The nanites had tried to repair the damage, but began creating new enclosures and growths around the wounds. It nearly doubled the mouse's size and severely disfigured its body.

"This serves as proof that there are areas in the code we can alter and not trigger death," Beth was matter of fact about it. "This may provide a temporary relief, but it's not the answer. We need to get back to work."

Reese nodded, and when he turned back to the work area, all eyes were on them. The pressure to succeed was heavy, but there was a ray of hope they could do this.

*

Fitz and her unit had checked in with the master sergeant on the cordon wall, and jumped right into working. Sleep and eating were in rotations, and they were scheduled far and few between. As of the last information relay from the end of the wall, they'd been successful in keeping the zombies away from the edge of the cordon, where the building continued unhindered.

Most of her time was spent standing on the top of the shipping containers they'd stacked, banging on them and letting the zombies see them. Many hundreds of infected had gathered, and they threw themselves against the metal containers unsuccessfully. There were heavy munitions on the wall, but they were there as a last resort.

She was on duty with Sergeant Allen. Though they were busy randomly banging the containers and drawing zombies, it was still relatively uneventful. The zombies weren't coordinated with each other, except they somehow knew the others were already infected, and they didn't need to bite them. Curiously, Fitz noticed that, though most of the time the zombies spent was at the wall trying to infect, some would wander off, appearing to search behind them.

"Why do you think they're doing that?" She pointed at some heading toward a nearby neighborhood.

"What?" Allen replied. "Wandering?"

"Yeah."

"Malfunction maybe?"

Her curiosity nagged. She'd seen most zombie movies there were, and there was never a reason for zombies to wander off randomly when there was fresh *meat* in front of them.

Pulling the SAT phone, she noticed the battery was low. She could make a call to General Truman and report the behavior, but it would risk the phone dying on her. She needed to find a place to recharge it.

After hours of banging, her arms were sore. When she checked the phone again, her designated shift was over. She nodded at Allen, and set her rebar down. On the back side of the wall, she descended to the ground on an extension ladder, and headed to their makeshift camp a hundred yards away.

*God forbid, but this is usually when something stupid happens in the movies. Some asshole rams a car into a blockade and lets zombies through; zombies find a way to climb the wall; the virus mutates to be airborne.*

She dared not look back at Allen, just in case. It was a movie sin. It was dumb to think tropes would find their way into real life, but she wasn't going to chance it. She kept walking.

Light poured from the operations tent. Every time she'd passed the opening, there were no less than six people constantly at work, making sure things were flowing. But much like up near Cleveland, they were having to take the shipping containers farther and farther out. It didn't matter that they were pulling all the containers they could from here to Florida, they'd eventually run low. And then zombies from the north would make it past.

She wanted to find a charging cable for the phone, but fatigue was hitting her hard. She retreated to where pup tents had been set up and climbed in an empty one.

*

Truman greeted Doctor Tseng at the Pentagon's entrance and brought him inside. He was followed by a small contingent of soldiers carting in additional supplies. More rations, more mice, and more equipment.

"Doctor." Truman nodded at him.

"General Truman, what's this about? I was getting ready to head south, and the next thing I know I'm being carted off in front of my wife and daughter." The doctor crossed his arms and scowled.

"Your medical services are required, and you're the only one with enough clearance I could get ahold of," he was curt. "I'll brief you when we're inside."

Down in the command center, he led Tseng to the secured doors, with Master Sergeant Gorski following behind with a cart of medical instruments and supplies. Prying eyes watched.

In the secured hallway, Truman led them to an empty room, and Gorski stored the medical equipment there.

"Okay? Now what?" the doctor asked.

"We have the terrorist who started this outbreak, and we're going to use some enhanced techniques. Your job is to keep her alive," Truman said.

Tseng raised his voice, "You pulled me away from my family so you can torture someone?"

"Unlike every other terrorist attack in the history of the world, we have an opportunity to reverse the effects," he snapped. "So you're damn right I'm going to get answers, no matter the cost."

"This is idiotic. I won't help you." Tseng turned to leave.

Truman glanced at the serviceman who'd been guarding Morgan, and he came to block Tseng's path. The doctor faced Truman, his cheeks reddening.

"Let me out."

"You can leave once I've got what I need." He turned to leave the room. "If we hurry, we might even be able to get you back to your family before the infected reach the Pentagon."

He led the way to Morgan's room. It had been a day since she'd been brought in, and he hoped the lack of food had made her malleable.

*

Fitz woke with a start, and a nightmare lingered about actual flesh eating zombies. She looked around as if she were surrounded. It was quiet.

It took a moment, but she realized the sun was high overhead. She'd overslept. She tore out of the tent. *Why didn't they come get me?*

She reported to the command center and found a familiar face; Master Sergeant Thomas. When he noticed her, she saluted. He saluted back.

"Sir, I apologize, but I overslept my shift," she spoke, panicked. "It won't happen again."

"Calm down, Corporal. Your shift was covered by your squad mate, Captain Frederickson. He said you'd been running yourself ragged since the outbreak. You were at ground zero, right?"

"Yes, sir. The original EH-US-11, was tasked with retrieving the AWOL Corporal Reyes."

"Well, get some grub and take it easy for a few. You're taking over Captain Frederickson's shift at fourteen-hundred."

"Yes, sir!" She saluted and pulled her SAT phone from her belt. "Do you have the right cable to charge this? It's my direct line to General Truman."

"Sure, leave it here, and we'll get it back to you when it's charged up."

"Thank you." She set it down on their planning table and saluted again.

"Dismissed!" he ordered.

Fitz headed out and to the mess hall tent, where she grabbed a double portion of reconstituted eggs, dried fruit, and some Tabasco sauce. It was half-gone before she even sat down, and she was done eating within a few minutes.

There was still an hour and a half before her shift on the wall, but she couldn't help herself. Back into the command tent, she grabbed binoculars, and overheard officers discussing readying an air response to cut down on the numbers.

At the top of the wall, she found the increase of infected was significant. Frederickson was there, busy banging, but he took a moment to acknowledge her.

She looked through the binoculars. "Thanks."

"No big deal. You were going to run yourself into the ground, nanites be damned. Need our C.O. in top shape."

"I guess so. Doesn't matter that the terrorist is caught. It feels like we're still far from victory. Suppose they get her key, or reverse engineer her code without triggering death, they still have to find a way to spread it."

"Probably. That's above my pay grade, though. We'll do our best to keep these things at bay until then."

"Mmm." She grunted and nodded.

*

President Ismail had made and taken a dozen phone calls during the flight. Her current call was to the owner of La Casa Pacifica, Nixon's *Western White House,* to thank him. The owner had obliged a request to use the mansion as their base of operations until the East Coast was back under control.

The phone calls were put on hold when Air Force One landed so they could be transferred into vehicles. Then they resumed, and though she'd just spoken to him, Canada's Prime Minister, Jacob Murphy, called again.

"Prime Minister, I'm afraid we don't have any new information since we spoke forty-five minutes ago," President Ismail answered.

"Aisha, our borders have been breached. The rivers and blockades on the bridges could only do so much. We need more than your assurance that this will be fixed soon!"

"I don't know what to tell you, Jacob. The terrorist is in custody, but as of the last I spoke with the general I left in charge there, she's being uncooperative."

"Just do what the terrorist wants."

"I can't do that. The US doesn't give into terrorist demands. It would set an incredibly dangerous precedent. Beyond that, declassifying this program could lead to additional unwanted parties gaining access to this experimental technology."

"You'd sacrifice North America because of the high and mighty ideals of your country. Give us something!"

"We've been bringing in experts from other countries to work with Alphaeus Lang's team on the West Coast, and you're welcome to send programmers to join them."

"We will. But if this can't be resolved soon, we're going to have to call on our other allies to make the hard decisions."

That was a threat. Canada didn't have their own weapons of mass destruction, but the UK and France did. Whether he was thinking about an EMP or an actual nuclear strike, the words rang loud and clear.

She lowered her voice, "We each swore to protect our respective nations, and what you might *think* is the answer could endanger lives. We have people working on this, and there's currently no need for drastic measures."

"Currently? Your inability to consider additional options might be the doom of our nations. We'll be approaching the UN to discuss alternate containment measures."

He abruptly hung up, and it pissed her off. She dialed General Truman and waited impatiently as it rang, intent on passing her anger on. The line connected.

"President Ismail, have you made it safely?" he asked.

"Yes. Canada's seeking an ally and UN approval to launch a strike at us. You need to have something for me, now."

"We have made some headway in changing code without killing the host, but my team hasn't perfected it yet. We're also still working to recover data from the hardware White burned, and she's resisting questioning about the key."

"General, this is on you. Your incompetence in the handling of this program, and the Marines under your command, will be your legacy. When this is over, I will be forced to have you dishonorably discharged as a result of this disaster."

"President—"

"Don't talk. I don't want to hear it. Work faster."

She hung up on him. It felt like the world was imploding. A hand gripped her thigh. When she looked up, it was her son. He smiled at her.

"Mom, it'll be okay," he said.

It was a heartfelt attempt to reassure her. She gave her son a fake smile.

"You're right. It will be," she replied.

*

It was a couple hours into Fitz's shift when she noticed a new, larger wave of zombies approaching from the north. Like the white lines on the sea, they built slowly, but increased in speed to create an enormous wave. They covered the horizon.

"Zombie horde incoming!" she belted out. "Get the commanding officer!"

They were coming fast, running at breakneck speed. At that pace, they would be there in a matter of minutes, colliding with the already large group spread out along the wall. *If they all start pushing at once, or they start climbing each other, the wall won't hold.*

The C.O. jumped up onto the wall.

"What's going on?" he asked.

She handed him the binoculars, and the moment he put them up, he pulled them down.

"I am authorizing the use of the extra munitions caches! We have a finite supply, so make it count!" the commanding officer yelled to everyone in range. He looked back to Fitz. "I'm going down to radio everyone else on the wall, and to prepare for potential breech. Keep it held down here, Corporal."

"Yes, sir!" she replied and saluted.

He saluted and headed back down to the ground. He was gone, and more soldiers climbed up the wall. Fitz put herself into the command mindset and belted out for everyone to hear.

"All right! Here's what I want to see! Flamethrowers, rocket launchers, and automatic weapons alternating in that order down the wall! Automatic weapons and rocket launchers: your job is to thin the horde so they don't all get to the wall at the same time and push it over! Flamethrowers: your job is to mitigate any pushing on the wall! Make your ammo count!"

While soldiers passed on the information and took positions, helicopters whirred to life behind her. When the horde was close enough, the first rockets were launched. The explosions were felt, reverberating the metal containers.

The area quickly became a war zone. Helicopters flew over, and the sounds of automatic fire filled the air. Their machine guns mowed down hundreds of zombies, but many of the shots weren't headshots. Fitz joined the attack. She picked up an M4A1, took aim, and fired.

The front lines of the horde fell, but it was clear they didn't have enough firepower to take out the tens of thousands coming at them. And then the fallen began getting back up.

A half-dozen A-10's screamed by the wall, their famous *brrrrrrt* overcoming all other noise. They had enough firepower to thin the herd, but they were limited to flybys.

Major groups of zombies healed, and they began running at the wall again. The A-10's arced back, and the helicopters fired until they were out of bullets. A tsunami of infected built up, and the base of the containers she was on shook. She was safe, but a container a few hundred yards away had been hit harder. The stack wobbled, and the group of zombies continued pushing, causing greater instability.

"Go! Secure that area now!" Fitz yelled and ran toward the unstable container.

She added her weight to the back of the container to keep it from falling over, and several others joined her. It stabilized some, but the zombies kept pushing against the bottom. Soldiers focused their flamethrowers at the base of the one nearing the tipping point, and the awful smell of burning flesh filled the air.

She turned and located a convoy, which was prepped to leave with more containers. *The only way to keep the zombies out is to push back that section.* Jumping down, she ran for a heavy forklift and fired it up. Spinning around, she angled for one of the convoy trucks and slammed the forks under the container on it.

Being gentle or slow was out of the question. She had to get it there in time. The top was starting to teeter again, held only because of being wedged in. The bottom was pushed in more, from the sheer weight of bodies against it, and if it moved any more there'd be a giant doorway for the zombies. She blew the horn and yelled at the soldiers on the top.

"Get the hell off, now!"

They scattered to the sides, and she used her container as a ram. It shoved the bottom one back in line with the others, but dislodged the two on top. They tumbled to the other side of the wall.

"Damn it all to hell!"

Pressing the gas pedal, she hastened the forklift in bringing the new container up, and shoved it in the hole in the wall.

"Keep them out!" she yelled.

The soldiers focus-fired the zombies trying to climb up and over while she pulled the forks out, and sped to turn around. Reaching the next truck, she lined the forks up and slammed them into place. The container came up, but it was too late. The zombies were climbing over.

She wasn't about to give up. With the gas pedal to the floor, it barreled along. Any zombie that got in the way, she ran over. There weren't enough to overwhelm her, but they kept coming and wouldn't stop unless she got the container in place.

Her fellow soldiers covered her, taking out zombies trying to get to her as she brought the container over. It wasn't enough. They continued to climb over the top of the wall. There were too many of them for the soldiers to deal with, and she wasn't going to be the difference. It was now about survival, but not just hers.

Pulling the forklift up to the wall, where soldiers were trying to fend off zombies, she moved slowly and yelled.

"Get on!"

There were some *thumps* and soldiers dropped to her level to give cover fire. She pressed the gas pedal and moved farther down the wall, away from where the zombies were climbing up and over. More soldiers jumped on, including Lieutenant Smith and Ensign Naki from her squad, and she now had a shield of them covering her on the forklift while she saved others. When the forklift was full, soldiers would rotate off and continue to cover.

Most of the zombies were busy overwhelming the camp. The helicopters fled, as they couldn't land and pick up more ammunition. The A-10's tried to give some cover, but it wasn't helping. The situation was unsalvageable.

The forklift wasn't fast enough, nor did it provide any real protection. They needed military vehicles. She parked and brought her rifle up to defend herself.

"Everyone off! Take turns alternating fire! Cover one another! Head for the armored vehicles!" she ordered.

They did as they were told. With enough distance from the breech, they had time to take out groupings of the zombies. It was enough to keep them safe for the moment. They moved steadily toward a parking lot of military vehicles, some with heavy weapons on top.

The group made it without incident, and a couple clambered to occupy the machine guns. Casings began falling and clanking before Fitz could even jump into the driver seat. She waited until they were at max capacity and floored it.

"Damnit!" She slammed a closed fist on the steering wheel.

On the highway, she headed the only way she could go without doubling back into zombies, directly for DC.

"Get on that radio and see if anyone can get in contact with General Truman. He needs to inform the president that we've lost the wall," she barked at Naki.

He nodded and did as he was told.

*

"President, we have a problem," Secretary of Defense Bates barged into the living room she was using as her temporary Oval Office.

"What?"

"Russia is showing signs of pointing missiles in the direction of the United States. We're getting confirmed satellite images from our allies. We believe they have live warheads on them."

"What the hell do they think they're doing?" President Ismail fumed.

"They're taking advantage of our disarray," he answered her rhetorical question.

"I want our defense systems ready to shoot down any incoming attack, whether it's Russia, or one of our allies. We're not going to let the world bully us while there's still hope of finding the terrorist's key."

"Yes, President," the secretary of defense replied and nodded.

He left, and she ushered everyone else out of the room. She'd put on a strong face to the world, to her cabinet, to her family. But she needed a moment to let out a controlled burst of emotion.

She grabbed a pillow from one of the couches, put her face into it, and screamed as loud as she could. It was likely she could be heard if a person was standing right outside of the doors into the room, but it couldn't be helped. That was all she would let out right now, a single, angry scream.

After she placed the pillow back on the couch, she put her game face back on. The country still needed her to lead. Picking up the phone, she dialed General Truman. It wasn't the general who answered, though.

"This is Master Sergeant Gorski," came the man on the other end.

"This is President Ismail. Where is General Truman?"

"He's currently busy, ma'am."

"Put him on the phone, now," she was firm.

"Yes, ma'am!"

It was a few moments of silence, and then there was knocking on a door at the other end of the line.

"Sir, phone call for you," the master sergeant spoke.

"I'm busy," Truman barked.

"Sir, POTUS is on the line."

General Truman said something, but it was unintelligible. A door slammed, and he addressed her.

"Madam President, I am in the middle of interrogating Morgan White—"

The president cut him off.

"General, I've received a memo that Canada is seeking allies to use high altitude warheads to blanket eastern North America, and now Russia is pointing missiles at us. Give me answers."

"Madam President," his tone was aggravated, and it agitated her. "White is on the verge of talking, and the data recovery team is still working on her torched hard drive. She's been spouting gibberish, but mentioned a name, Arturo. As far as we can tell she has no relatives or any professional contacts with that name."

"Truman, I want—"

"General Truman," she heard Master Sergeant Gorski on the other end of the line. "Master Sergeant Thomas is on your SAT phone and demanding to talk to you."

"One moment, President," he said, interrupting their conversation.

Silence.

"Is there any chance of recovery?" Truman asked.

She waited, wondering what that meant.

"What about the Cleveland wall?" He paused. "Understood. Order all units to fall back. Retreat and head west."

Her anxiety level rose higher, and she didn't have to wait long for her fear to be confirmed. General Truman returned to her phone call.

"Madam President, the cordon has failed. Cleveland is gone, and DC will be overrun shortly."

"General Truman, you are relieved of your duties. Put Director Crawford on the phone."

"Madam President, we're close! I just need a little more time with Morgan."

"General Truman, give your phone to Director Crawford, immediately."

*

He hung up on her and turned the phones off. Master Sergeant Gorski stood there with a knowing look.

"She doesn't understand. I intend to defy her order and keep going until I have answers. Are you with me, soldier?"

"Sir, yes, sir."

"Good. Keep it quiet. We have to do some damage control before she takes this from us by force."

He needed to cut all communication with the outside while they continued to work. He'd cure the East Coast and prove that nanites could still play a part in building a better world.

He ushered Gorski to follow. They returned to the main room from the secured hall, and he headed to Crawford, who was working with his team.

"Let me see your phone," Truman spoke roughly to his friend.

"Why? What's going on?"

"Everyone, I have grave news." He turned to the room and led in loudly so he would have undivided attention. "The president has just informed me we're at risk of an EMP attack on the East Coast from our allies, and Russia is pointing weapons of mass destruction at the West Coast. If that wasn't enough, the cordon failed and there will be infected in DC in short time.

"If we're going to succeed in averting World War III, we need to focus. No more distractions. I need all cell phones brought to me, and we're to function on *intranet* only. The nation's counting on you!"

The silence was deafening. He took Gerald's phone, turned it off, and set it down on a desk. The room, though hesitant, complied by turning over their phones.

"Any luck on the hard drive?" Truman asked Gerald.

"They recovered some. There were some searches of animal shelters on her browser. The down side is they're all in New York or New Jersey, so we couldn't get in contact with anyone there if we wanted to."

"Hmm...she mentioned a name; Arturo. Could be an animal she experimented on first?"

"Could be that the key we're looking for is an animal with cured nanites?"

Truman rubbed his chin.

"It's possible. For the moment, we need to make sure we have enough supplies to continue on. I'm going to send half a dozen soldiers topside while we still have the opportunity. The infected will be overhead soon enough."

While he gave orders to the unit, he couldn't get his mind off Morgan. She'd resisted hunger, sleep deprivation, sensory overload, and repeated striking. He needed more answers. The next step was waterboarding.

*

**Present Day:**

Truman slams the door shut. On the other side, Morgan, Doctor Tseng, and a serviceman lay dead. There was no recovering from that, as none of them had nanites.

It didn't matter. He'll do whatever it took to cure the infected, and because the president turned against him, move forward with his vision of Project N and force the next step in human evolution. He'll be the leader humanity deserves.

Blood spots dot his uniform, and while Crawford would chalk it up to enhanced interrogation techniques, it wouldn't do well for the others to see him like this.

*I'm sure I still have time to change upstairs.*

He heads back through the secured doors to the command center, concealing the red spots with his jacket. *I'll need to keep up a façade that I'm still questioning Morgan.* Gerald eyes him as he heads to the elevator, but he's preoccupied with assisting the teams.

Truman is back on the first floor with in a few moments, and it's eerily quiet. He makes the trip to his office quick, and upon his descent back to the bowels of the Pentagon, he starts forming a new plan in his head.

*If I'm going to bring humanity to the next level, I need to keep the project in my hands. But I can't trust Beth or her team to do what I need. Reese, though, I can manipulate and plant ideas in his head.*

He walks up to Reese and hovers over him, watching his movements.

"What are you working on?" he asks.

"Just trying to understand the kill command's depth. It's complicated, and has redundant branches into so many areas. It pretends to be overwritten when an uninfected nanite docks with new code. But then the kill command is restored through some backup measure and begins telling all the other nanites to kill the host."

"Ok. Well, take a break for a minute."

Reese tilts his head to the side, and raises his eyebrows in question. Truman ignores it and brings him to the side of the room.

"I know what I did was wrong, but if you just let me—"

"Stop talking," Truman interrupts. "You're actually the person I can count on the most right now. While we all have loved ones out there, your dedication to your mother tells me you're actually the most motivated."

The corners of Reese's mouth downturn, and Truman assumes he's experiencing grief.

"We need to talk about your future," Truman says quietly. "There's no denying that nanites are out in the world now. Even when we cure the infected, there are going to be millions of enhanced humans who will need guidance and leadership.

"Unfortunately, the president has forsaken us and our efforts," he lies. "Only Director Crawford and I know. And now you."

"Why me?" Reese asks. "What did the president say?"

"Even if we succeed, we'll be held completely responsible despite this being Morgan's fault. That includes you. The country is in chaos, and our lives could be in *danger*," he keeps it vague on purpose.

"What do you want from me?"

"TEAL's efforts were to slowly move the transhumanism movement forward. We can keep that alive *and* cure people. But we need new protection in the system. If Morgan has taught us anything, it's that the nanites are vulnerable. I need you to start thinking about additional security."

"What about the people from TEAL? Beth?"

"You can key her in, except for being declared a loss by the president. Let her know we need added security. Use Morgan's idea of tying the new protocols into everything so it can't be tampered with by outside people."

"We haven't even been successful at circumventing the kill command. What am I supposed to do this on?"

"You're a skilled programmer and hacker. You'll think of something." He pats Reese's shoulder confidently.

He looks unsure, but he hasn't declined to help.

"Go on, head back to Beth. I'm expecting good things out of *your* team."

He nods, and Truman hopes he bought in.

*

*What is he playing at?* Reese walks back to his desk.

He sits and stares at the code on his computer. It's not even a few moments before Beth notices and interjects herself.

"Are you stuck, again?" She scoffs.

"No, thinking about a request General Truman just made," he says and looks at her.

"What request?"

"He thinks we should work in upgrading the nanites security using Morgan's idea of tying into everything."

"That's not going to help the people who are currently zombies." She squints. "Why'd he come to you?"

"I have no idea."

*Trying to rewrite the infected nanites results in the death of the host. Maybe…maybe we're going about this wrong.*

"I haven't had any luck finding where the kill command keeps repopulating from, yet. But what if overwriting the nanites is the wrong idea? Can we program new nanites to dismantle infected ones?"

Beth stares at him, blank faced for a moment, and he begins to wonder if he actually said his idea out loud. Before he speaks again, she answers.

"Wage nanite war in people's bodies?"

She leans in, clearly intrigued.

"Yeah. Program our nanites—"

"*My* nanites," she interrupts.

She's not smiling, or otherwise consciously showing excitement, but she's a little more alert. He imagines the wheels turning in her head, and he feels a sliver of satisfaction.

"Could it work?" he asks.

"I haven't seen anything in the code that would make me think otherwise. They'd have to be faster at dismantling than the infected nanites running their repair programs. Ours will need defense against recoding, too."

"Do you think this will trigger the kill command?"

"They're not sentient. They won't know they're under attack, just that something is mechanically wrong."

She turns back to her computer and pulls up the schematics and code for the original nanites. Using the mouse to draw, she begins designing a shield over the nanite's connection port. And then scribbles it out.

"No. Shit. Too many additional parts."

Erasing her crude sketch, she redesigns the nanite to no longer accept manual inputs, and changes a small area on its body. He watches with anticipation. She stops, and waves the couple other TEAL employees over.

"Look," she says, and shows them her idea. "This is what we need the nanite to look like. Get to redesigning the body so it's structurally sound, and I'll work on the code."

They nod, and the work commences. Reese is left out, and has to ask.

"What are you planning?"

"Adapting the transceiver. We hadn't implemented a way for us to transmit to them from outside. Every new upgrade was manually input to avoid potential wireless packet loss. But with any cure we create, we'll need a way to tell them to self-destruct once their job is done," she speaks hastily while coding. "The population can't have nanites yet, not permanently."

It's a lot to think about, and no doubt ethics committees had already been formed to discuss implications of nanotechnology in society.

As Beth codes, he watches over her shoulder and attempts to learn from her. They now had hope without Morgan's elusive key.

*

President Ismail is running herself ragged trying to avert World War III. Despite cooperating with other nations by allowing some of their best programmers to work with Alphaeus Lang, Russia has begun positioning their naval fleets in the Pacific international waters. China has followed them, at her request, with the promise to enter first rights agreements to share the nanotechnology with them. To add yet another problem, her phone call with the United Kingdom's Prime Minister isn't going as she hoped.

"I've been in contact with Lang at TEAL. In addition to trying to reverse the terrorist's programming, they're working on building a small scale EMP to test on mice. If you detonate an EMP before we know what happens to the host, you may be sentencing millions of people to die," she argues.

"President, the Canadian Prime Minister is right. If North America falls to this threat, South America will be next. If they somehow jump from Alaska to Russia, the entire world will be lost," Prime Minister Mills replies.

"And if you detonate an EMP over our continent you'd leave us crippled and open to attack!" She's borderline yelling at this point. "Can you protect us from Russia?"

"We understand you are in a tough place, President Ismail, but we have to think about the whole of the world. Your country is threatening everywhere else, albeit unwillingly."

"I'm putting you on notice. If you attack us, I will regard it as an act of war, and we *will* respond accordingly," she threatens, hoping it forces them to rethink their position.

An aide bursts into the empty room and interrupts.

"Ma'am, Russia has launched six ICBMs capable of carrying a nuclear payload."

"Time's up," she blurts into the phone and hangs up.

Pushing past the aide, she passes through the house to the command room, where a dozen analysts are furiously working. Secretary of Defense Bates is hovering over the shoulders of Department of Defense analysts.

She comes in behind and watches as a real time map of the US shows where missiles are being launched from.

"Targets?" she asks.

"Hard to tell yet. Their high trajectory indicates the Midwest and East Coast."

"Are *we* safe?"

"For the moment."

"Counter?" the president looks to Secretary Bates.

"We anticipated this and maneuvered naval ships to the area. Laser-mounted drones are in the air, and on an intercept course. Any the drones fail to destroy will be targeted by our missile defense system," he replies.

"Prepare a response strike. Target the Kremlin, and military installations," she commands.

"Nuclear, ma'am?" Secretary Bates asks.

The idea that she would be the second president in US history to use a weapon of mass destruction causes her to shudder. She shakes her head.

"Attempt to cripple their government infrastructure only. I anticipate they'll shoot our missiles down, as we are theirs. Then issue a warning that if they try again, the next volley will be with a nuclear payload."

"Yes, Madam President."

*

# Chapter 7:

Beth injects their first batch of *deconstruction* nanites into a stunned zombie-mouse. She closes the lid quickly, and it recovers. It bashes its head trying to get at them, but stops dead in its tracks after about ten seconds. It sits there for a few moments, and Reese wonders if it died. The lack of hemorrhaging from eyes and ears gives him hope.

The silence behind him has become awkward, and he looks. The whole room is watching and waiting with them. Looking back to Beth, she bends down and taps on the glass in attempt to illicit a response. Another thirty seconds passes, and its nose twitches. It looks around and moves about its box, docile once again.

"I need all of your attention!" General Truman bellows from across the room.

Everyone turns, except for Beth, who is still observing.

"The world above us has gone to hell. I've received word we've entered World War III. Missiles have been launched, and foreign naval fleets are bearing down on the West Coast. We're on our own here.

"I want all efforts doubled to finish the cure. We may need to use the cured as an army to fight off invaders."

Their success should have brought about applause and cheering, but the news they were going to war destroyed that idea. He sighs and looks to Beth. She shakes her head in dismay. Truman approaches.

"How close are you to finishing?" he asks.

"We've only just tested the first batch. Next I need to see if the antenna is working to receive shutdown codes," Beth says.

"Can they receive other instructions as well?"

She scowls at Truman.

"In theory." She's curt with him. "The coding, which tells the nanites they can receive new information, was adapted from their physical docking protocols, but I won't know until I run several tests."

He crosses his arms and glowers.

"Do what you can to expedite the process. Have you thought of a deployment system to the infected?"

"We're *working* on it, and the more you interrupt, the slower it goes."

The veins pop out on Truman's forehead, and Reese is sure he wants to wring her neck for talking to him like that.

"We're pressed for time, short on supplies, and the horde is well on top of us now," Truman replies, restraining his anger as much as possible.

Beth pushes past him without further response, and Reese tries to follow. The general grabs his arm roughly and pulls him aside again.

"How does the antenna work?"

"It a transceiver so that at least in short range we'll be able to transmit a command for the nanites to shut down permanently. It can also broadcast that shutdown code to anyone else who has the same nanites nearby."

"We need to limit who has access to being able to transmit to the nanites. I want you to put security in place so only you, Beth, and I can add new programming to the nanites."

Reese's stomach is unsettled, and anxiety creeps in. While the general's idea of preventing another terrorist intrusion into the nanites was valid, limiting the number of people to only a few could also mean they're just as vulnerable to being abused.

"General, I think maybe we should add a few more people to the list. We don't want a small group responsible for this. What about Director Crawford, and the other TEAL employees?"

"Director Crawford, yes. The others, not yet. I think between the four of us that should be enough for now," Truman says. "Like before, let Beth know, but don't tell anyone else about the new security protocols."

"Okay." He nods.

*There's something not right. He was quick to accommodate.*

General Truman heads for the secured doors, and Reese breathes a sigh of relief.

Back in his seat, Beth stops what she's doing and turns to him.

"What the hell did he want this time?"

He lowers his voice, and looks over his shoulder. "More security layers. He wants access restricted to you, me, him, and Director Crawford for the moment."

"I don't like that. Too much power in the hands of powerful men."

"I agree. For now, we should go along with it, and make sure there's a way to grant more accesses in the future."

She turns back to her computer, and her fingers bang on the keyboard methodically. He was nowhere near her level of ability, but he'd been trying to keep up anyway. He begins working on the limited access security function.

"What if we programmed the nanites to reverse infect the person who bites them?" she blurts, not breaking eye contact with her screen.

He isn't sure if she's thinking out loud, or if she meant for him to answer.

She continues, "It should work. We'd need our own patient zero, and we'd be subjecting most of the people who've been bitten to being bitten again. Once the zombies notice there's an uninfected near them they'll be swarmed, and we'll be torturing them."

She looks over his shoulder, at what he's working on, and she practically shoves him out of the way to take over.

"What—" he barely has a word out, and Beth cuts him off.

"Adding fingerprint security to your permissions function. Work with the team to start building a fingerprint scanner. I don't know if we have everything, but if we don't I'm sure we could rob some components from the walls here."

"Okay," Reese replies and nods.

*

President Ismail sits in a meeting with key members of her cabinet, plotting their next strategic moves. Both they and Russia had destroyed each other's missiles in the atmosphere, which was a relief. But the conflict isn't over.

Tensions rise higher as Russia refuses to back off, inching their flotilla closer to the West Coast. China's fleet was right on their heels, ready to intervene if necessary, but it was only because of their agreement. Adding insult to injury, the UN passed the first round of resolutions to use three high altitude nuclear devices to blanket all of North America with an EMP.

"It's clear. Russia is planning a land invasion," Secretary Bates speaks.

"We don't have enough forces along the West Coast to keep an invasion from happening," Secretary of State Holden speaks up.

"That's why we're relying on China." President Ismail folds her hands and props her chin on them. "Having the Chinese army here will help us in more ways than one. Deter Russia, keep our citizens safe, and use them as leverage to force the UN to push back the EMP resolution."

"That's a terrible idea. If we let China's army in, we may never see them leave," Vice President Abraham interjects.

"I'm aware of that, but what other choices do we have?"

The cabinet members become silent. *The EU and UN are going to be angry, but we need to buy more time for Lang's team over here.*

*

He and Beth stand near their cured mouse's box ready to test their Gen-II nanites.

She injects the mouse with the Gen-II, waits for them to spread, and then tests the shutdown command through a crude interface on her computer. She takes a blood sample to ensure the transceiver received the code. It doesn't take her but a few moments to analyze it under the microscope before turning to the waiting group.

"It's a success."

The room erupts into cheers, and they all begin congratulating each other, including Reese. His hand is shook more times in a few minutes than he can remember ever having received in the past. Of course, he can't help but smile, but it was actually Beth and the TEAL team's achievement.

Truman is there with a somber face. Despite his imposed communications silence on everyone else, he'd been on a phone call as they were testing. From his frown it was clear there was something wrong.

"Our work is not over yet. We still have to distribute the cure. But there's more. The president has not *just* lost the West Coast, but has in fact given up America's sovereignty to China. They are allowing foreign troops onto our soil to come and *kill* those who we now know can be cured. Once Chinese soldiers make landfall, we will lose this country to them! America will fall if we don't act!"

"I'm going to speak to the president and let her know—" Director Crawford speaks up, but he's cut off.

"I just spoke with her. She stated that until we can cure the east, her duty is to protect the uninfected in the west," Truman says, and sighs.

"I'm sorry, I know this was supposed to be a moment of relief and joy," he continues. "You've all accomplished so much, but we now have a duty to cure as many people as we can, because Chinese forces are coming to kill anyone on this side of the US. We need to fight back, to save American lives!"

The elated mood is dead. Crawford pulls Truman away, and they talk quietly. Reese can't hear what's being said, but their discussion seems heated due to animated hand gestures on both sides.

He puts his hands in his pockets. Beth's jaw is clenched again, and he wants to give her reassuring words. He has none though.

"So what now?" he asks.

She looks at him.

She whispers so only he can hear, "I don't trust Truman. He's the kind of man who will do anything to stay in control. I need to verify what he's saying."

"What are you going to do?" he whispers back.

"I think Crawford is questioning him, too. We should try to get my phone from the pile." She eyes the general.

"Okay. I'll keep my eyes open for an opportunity. Maybe I can cause a distraction for you?" he says. "What do we do in the meantime?"

"Pretend to be with General Truman. We still have to cure everyone."

*

Truman is hot under the collar. Though Gerald is a longtime friend, he can't allow him to get in the way of the bigger plan; transhumanism. Spinning true events to his advantage was an opportunity to stay in control.

"Gerald, the *president* has labeled us a loss, and I can't help but think she's compromised. Why else would she let Chinese troops on our soil?"

"There has to be an explanation."

"There is. The explanation is not only to deter Russia from invading, but to keep the uninfected safe, no matter the cost. She's putting American lives at risk, despite our having made headway in a cure!"

"What are you going to do? What *can* we do?"

"We have to mount a defense. We have to draft everyone we cure into an army to repel the invaders!"

"If they're here helping us, they're not invaders!"

"Not yet they aren't. But look at history. We've helped other countries by sending our troops to take care of other's problems, and now there are US bases all over the globe. Who's to say China won't do the same?"

"You're being too cynical, Norm!"

"Look, I don't like this idea either. Propose another, viable option, and we can consider it. But we need to accept the idea that the president and her cabinet are *not* acting in the best interest of all American citizens now, but for their self-preservation."

Gerald is silent. He's sure he has his friend on his side, for now. With their conversation finished, they address the room together.

"Now that we have a functioning cure, and it's tested, we need to try it and check for any lasting trauma or brain damage," Gerald says.

Truman takes over.

"We'll be sending soldiers up to the surface to cure an individual and bring them down here. Beth, prepare some Gen-II nanites."

She nods and prepares a syringe. Capping it, she hands it off to Truman, who promptly turns to his contingent of soldiers.

"Master Sergeant Gorski," Truman bellows.

"Sir!" the master sergeant steps up and salutes.

"You and three others will head to the surface and administer the cure, and return with them."

"Yes, sir!"

General Truman hands off the syringe and a two-way radio. Gorski points at three from his unit, and they follow him. Truman inputs his biometrics to call the elevator and sends them up. After a few moments, Gorski's voice comes across his two-way.

"We're at ground level," he whispers. "Upper level is quiet. Heading to the nearest exit to survey. Will assess and relay."

"Understood. Godspeed," Truman responds.

He turns to the remaining half-dozen soldiers.

"I want everyone in front of the doors and prepared to shoot if an infected makes it down here."

They acknowledge and form a semi-circle around the elevator. Truman joins and pulls his sidearm. It's about ten minutes before Gorski calls over the radio.

"This is Gorski! Bring the elevator down!"

He brings them back and takes a distanced position. The doors open, and the four soldiers exit out into the room. Inside the elevator is a woman collapsed on the floor. If it weren't for her sobbing, he might think she was dead.

"Master Sergeant?" Truman questions.

"She was infected. The cure has been administered, and she has returned to a docile state."

"Good work." He walks past him and claps him on the shoulder. He heads for the woman. "Ma'am, can you tell me your name?"

She's unresponsive. Truman kneels by her.

"What is your name?"

She mumbles. He leans closer to hear her.

"Wh...where is...my daughter?"

"I'm afraid I don't know. Can you tell me what you remember?"

"*Everything.*"

"Everything?"

"I remember everything!"

The woman begins to have a meltdown, crying hysterically. He attempts to assist her in standing, and she freaks out.

"What have you done to me?" She shoves him with inhuman strength.

He stumbles backward into the soldiers. He's caught, and guns are aimed at her. She cowers, and Truman reaches up to pull the nearest gun down.

"Stand down," he orders.

The soldiers return to relaxed positions, and he tries again. He steps forward and extends his hand for her to take.

"We'll find your daughter. We've created a cure, but it's going to take time to distribute it."

Where she's from, and how long she's been infected, are just a couple of the questions burning in Truman's mind. The state of her appearance leads him to believe she's been infected for a significant amount of time.

"Where are we?" she asks.

"We're hidden inside of the Pentagon. You're safe here."

"My daughter, her name is Penny Freeman. Please help me find her."

"We will."

*

Fitz isn't sure what to think about the state of the world right now. Zombies. Missiles. Possible EMPs. Foreign troops on their soil. Her knuckles whiten as she grips the steering wheel harder.

Through Master Sergeant Thomas, Secretary Bates relayed new orders to meet up with foreign troops making landfall on the West Coast. Allowing China in felt like a complete betrayal, but despite her doubts, she was a Marine, and she would hold together and carry out the orders she was given.

She was making great time racing along at eighty-five miles per hour, minimizing stops to only when absolutely needed. They were well ahead of the zombie wave. Even so, they still had about twenty hours before they would reach their new base of operations, San Francisco.

*

Reese was returning from the bathroom when he noticed General Truman and Director Crawford occupied with the cured woman. A quick survey of the room, and he sees everyone else is busy with preparations to return to the surface. *An opportunity...*

Slinking over to the table Truman had put all of the phones, he searches through them, hoping to find the right one. There are dozens of them, ranging in all different models and sizes. *If I turn on any of the screens I risk unwanted attention.* He grabs one at random and hides it in his pocket.

Making his way back to his desk, he clears his throat in hopes to gain Beth's attention. She doesn't notice.

"Beth," he whispers.

She looks, and he pulls the phone part way out of his pocket. He expected happiness, or shock. She snatches it and hides it under her desk. Fiddling with it, she checks to see if she can get in, but it has a passcode.

"Whose is this?" she asks.

"I have no idea."

She rolls her eyes, but plugs it into her computer and begins fiddling with files. Hiding the phone in between her legs to hide the light, she gets into a folder on her desktop and runs a program. A window pops up, and a string of code starts running. To avoid detection, she switches back to coding the nanites and continues working. He follows her lead and makes himself look busy.

*

Truman offers a glass of water to Veronica. Taking it, she drinks hastily.

"I want you to know that the terrorist who has done this was apprehended. This is almost over," he tells her. "Where were you when you were infected?"

"Harrisburg. We were trying to head south. There was an accident that backed traffic up. We got out and ran. My daughter, I have to find her."

"My son is out there too, infected. Don't worry, we'll find her and cure her," he speaks reassuringly.

"She's sixteen. We were going to pick out a dress for a dance...I..." Veronica begins to cry again.

He wants information about the experience of infection, but he has to pretend to care. To keep her from breaking down into hysterics, he continues the conversation.

"Do you have a picture of her?"

Veronica looks up and pats her jean pockets. Pulling out a phone, she tries to turn it on, but nothing happens. The screen is shattered, but the body looks intact. Truman holds his hand out for it.

"I'll have one of my men charge it up for you," he says.

"Thank you."

She hands it to him, and he pockets it with no intention of giving it back.

"I'm afraid for the time being, you'll have to get used to this room. It's not the homiest, but it's safe from up there while we work on distributing the cure. Can you tell me what it was like while you weren't in control?"

"It was horrifying. Penny and I, we were running, and I was tackled from behind. At first I thought someone just knocked into me, but then they were on top of me. I tried kicking them off, but they overpowered me and bit my wrist. Then they attacked my daughter. She was trying to help me. He bit her and ran away.

"I don't remember how long it was, minutes, but my limbs started moving on their own. I couldn't control them. Then it was my whole body. I wasn't in control of my actions. I started running toward people, and then biting them. They cried, and I could taste their blood in my mouth."

Veronica looks down and becomes quiet, fidgeting with her fingernails. He thinks about the best time to begin reverse-infecting the population, and growing his army. Standing up, he walks over to the other side of the table and puts his hand on Veronica's shoulder.

"Master Sergeant." He looks to Gorski. "Get her some food and more water."

He nods and heads to their stockpile.

"I know you've been through a lot already, but the reality is that the terrorist opened up a laundry list of problems. The president has turned the West Coast over to China, and essentially defected from her own country. They're readying to kill everyone who is infected."

He has Veronica's undivided attention.

"It will take them some time to reach the east, but they're advancing this way. It's my duty now to raise an army to regain the sovereignty of the USA. As we start reversing the infection, we're going to need them to join up and fight against an oppressive regime. Can I count on you for your help?"

"I... What do you want from me?"

"Nothing right now. But we'll be calling on the cured to help fight back foreign invaders in the near future. We'll need everyone."

She's silent, and for the time, it's okay with him that she hasn't responded. He's planted the seed in order to manipulate her later. *In the end, she'll answer the call to save her nation, one way or another. They all will.*

*

Fitz awakes to honking.

"Where are we?" she asks.

"Just outside Hayward, California," Naki responds, driving past stopped vehicles on the highway.

They approach heavy spotlights, and a blockade. The lights point into their cab and a voice yells over a loudspeaker.

"Stop your vehicles!" they order.

Naki looks to her for guidance. She shakes her head and picks up the microphone for her own loud speaker.

"My name is Corporal Ella Fitzgerald, and I'm the acting commanding officer of EH-US-11 of the Marine Corps," she replies. "We have orders to report."

"Step out!"

Fitz gets on the radio and calls back to her convoy.

"Do as they say. Step out and identify yourselves to them. Have your IDs ready," she directs.

They exit and present themselves for inspection. A wave of soldiers approach with guns aimed at them. Fitz holds her hands out.

"Name and rank!" they address her as she's out in front.

"Corporal Ella Fitzgerald, Marine, EH-US-11 unit."

"Who is your commanding officer?"

"The Secretary of Defense. Get him on the phone."

"Are any of you infected?"

She isn't sure whether it's an honest question or if they have to ask for security purposes. *They haven't seen them yet out here, so all they've heard so far is reports coming from the east.* She errs on the side of caution and answers promptly.

"There are no infected among us. If you'll put me through to Secretary Bates, I'll provide a full report to him."

"You have to be cleared through medical. If you're deemed clean, you'll be debriefed. Until then, you're all remanded to custody!" He looks over his shoulder to soldiers behind him. "Bring their vehicles in and reallocate any weapons you find!"

Her group is walked in, past the blinding lights, and she felt like she was entering a POW camp.

This operation isn't anything like what they had at the wall. They're ill-prepared for the zombies. Civilians come in behind them, and they're herded toward tents on the right. Her group is led to tents on the left, and the distinction is clear; military or civilian.

Fitz is the first of her troop into the medical tent. There's a plain chair for her to sit on, and a person in a doctor's coat there waiting.

"Take a seat, please." The doctor is polite, waving his hand to the chair.

She sits, and he cleans her arm at the crease of her elbow. Warily, she eyes him and waits. He opens sterile equipment and takes a vial of her blood.

"That's classified material, *doctor*," she says.

"I'm aware. Your blood is being sent to TEAL's team on site for analysis."

The doctor doesn't bother to put a cotton swab on the puncture site. He watches the pinhole in her skin close up. Bagging her vial of blood, he fills out paperwork.

"Name?"

"Ella Fitzgerald"

"Active military?"

"Yes. Marines, EH-US-11 unit."

He copies her info onto the paperwork, removes a tear-away barcode, and hands it to her.

"Don't lose that."

He folds the paper and puts it in the bag with her vial, and then places the bag in a 'Biohazard' container.

"Please step out and to your left."

She follows directions, and outside, a soldier stands ready to direct her.

"Head straight on the road. Half-mile down, you'll reach a staging area for active military. Once you're cleared, you'll receive new orders."

"How long to be cleared?"

"Not sure, ma'am. If you would." He holds his arm out in the direction she's to go.

Taking her time, she walks slowly so some of the soldiers she'd been traveling with can catch up. Particularly, she was holding back for Ensign Naki. *He's young, but he's holding it together pretty well.*

Naki catches up, and he walks at her side for a few moments before speaking.

"What do you think's going to happen?"

"Hard to say. I'm still not sure what happened with China that their troops were allowed onto American soil willingly. I'm going to try and get in touch with Secretary Bates and find out more."

"What do you think is happening with that general? Truman?"

"His son was affected in the first wave. I'm sure he's working hard to find the cure."

They reach their holding area, and there are familiar faces there. Master Sergeant Thomas, some from the wall, and the remainder of her reformed EH-US-11 unit. Approaching, she salutes Thomas.

"Good to see you made it Corporal Fitzgerald," Thomas greets her and salutes back.

"I'm not sure I'm glad to be here, but we at least made it safely," she drops her salute and extends her hand for a handshake.

He grips firmly and gives a good half-shake.

"What can you tell me about what's going on?" she asks.

"Not much more than you probably already know. We arrived a few hours ahead of you. Looks like they're making sure we aren't some sort of infected sleeper cell."

She looks around. "I thought Chinese troops would be here."

"They came in through the bay, they're still gearing up to reinforce new and existing checkpoints."

She wonders what help they'll actually provide, except for extra bullets.

"Ever flown before?" the master sergeant asks.

"Yes, sir. Why?"

"Rumors are floating around of anti-nanite EMPs in development. Heard speculation of delivery via air."

Rumor or not, a sense of hope returns. It's the first she's felt safe since this all started, despite being in an apparent detention camp.

"Get some rest and some food. Need you and your unit at peak condition," he tells her.

Fitz takes it as an order.

"Sir, yes, sir!"

*

Alphaeus Lang hasn't slept well in weeks. He's been taking a few hours to himself here or there, but never enough to feel rested. His normally slicked back, white hair is unkempt. His eyes have bags under them, and he's thankful his glasses at least partially hide the dark circles.

Everyone, including the foreign programming experts brought in, were either working on the cure for the infected or designing an EMP device. He was running them ragged because of *his* failure to keep the public safe from their invention.

Morgan White perverted his idea, but he still holds hope the nanites will eventually be accepted as a cure for so much that's wrong with the world. *It's now going to be harder than ever. The public will be even more cynical.*

Small scale EMP tests on mice showed the nanites could successfully be shut down with no adverse effects, but the president was clear, she wants a non-destructive method of delivery to ensure safety of the people, and to preserve the nation's electronic infrastructure.

One team came up with a simple structure. A station people could walk through where a constant EMP field would neutralize all of the nanites at once. The hurdles were how much power it would require for a single apparatus, and curing people would be incredibly slow.

On the other hand, the other team's antidote nanite was close. Though Morgan had intertwined her devious kill command deeply and intricately, they had made several successes in rewriting without killing host mice.

His cell rings. The president and her staff had been calling for updates so often he doesn't want to pick up. Only in the interest of keeping her from sending in the military to keep tabs on him does he answer.

"Hello, this is Alphaeus Lang."

"Alphaeus," a whisper comes over the phone. "It's good to hear your voice!"

"Who is this?"

"It's Beth Greenwall."

"Beth? Where are you? Are you safe?" His attention is fully on her now, and the fatigue he was feeling is temporarily wiped away.

"No time for that. I can only talk for a few moments before I'm noticed."

"Noticed by whom?"

"General Truman. We did it. We created a cure. We programmed Gen-II nanites not to overwrite the programming, but to physically attack and dismantle the infected nanites. It averts triggering the kill command."

"What about a delivery system?"

There's silence, but he can hear her breathing.

"Beth?"

There's banging on the other side of the phone, and he can hear a man's voice, but it's muffled.

"I'm using the bathroom. I'll be out soon," she replies to the person on the other end.

"What's going on?" Alphaeus asks.

There's more banging and the male voice again.

"He can wait, my body can't!" Beth practically yells at whomever is bothering her.

It's silent again, and Alphaeus looks at his phone to see if the call is still connected. It is. Patiently, he waits for her.

"Reverse infection. The bitten distribute the cure. Our internet is being blocked, but I'll find a work around. I'm going to upload my work to the shared drive. Look for a file folder with my name—"

The line becomes silent again, and this time the phone beeps in his ear to tell him the call has ended. He tries calling her back, but there's no answer, and he's sent to the phone owner's voicemail. Moving over to the computer, he opens the folder she designated and waits for the upload.

*

Truman greets Beth as soon as she exits the bathroom. She scowls at him.

"Search her," he orders a serviceman.

The soldier moves to obey the order, and Beth takes a defensive stance.

"Fuck off. Don't touch me."

The soldier hesitates. Truman grabs her by the wrist and frisks her.

"Let go of me you son of a bitch!" she screams and takes a swing at him.

He dodges and finds a phone tucked into the backside of her pant line. It's locked, and he can't get in to see the call list.

"Who did you call?"

"Fuck you!"

He pulls her arm up harshly, practically lifting her off the ground, and shakes her violently. The phone rings, and an unknown number comes up. He silences it.

"WHO DID YOU CALL? WHO IS CALLING?"

"Alphaeus Lang! He knows how we're curing people. Your game is over because I gave him all he needs to do the same."

He turns the phone off. Motioning to the soldiers next to him, he directs them to take her to an interrogation room, away from the group. They walk her over, and she gives them a hard time by struggling against their grips.

"Let go of me!"

"We are at war, and you are conspiring with our enemy. You will be detained."

The commotion gains the attention of everyone in the basement, including Crawford. Gerald makes his way over.

"What is going on?" he asks with concern.

"One of my men discovered Beth making a phone call. She's confessed to providing intel to Alphaeus Lang. It's a reasonable assumption that Lang and President Ismail are in contact, and that he's assisting her with our extermination," Truman says loudly so others can hear.

"General Truman," his friend starts, keeping it formal in front of the others, "surely you can't make that kind of assumption—"

"Director Crawford, what kind of assumption do you think I've made? The president's orders are to exterminate the infected. The Chinese troops are amassing all along Washington, Oregon, and California's borders. A two-million-man army is being sent to kill us, and when they're done, the US will be in such a weakened state the complete takeover by foreign powers will be inevitable."

Gerald frowns, and Truman can tell he isn't buying it. He has to think of a way to get his friend on board, or he'll be forced to take drastic measures. *I can't let him jeopardize the future.* He motions for Gerald to follow to an area away from everyone while the soldiers secure Beth in the room.

"Norm, what the hell is going on?"

"Gerald, if we don't turn these infected persons into an army to fight off the Chinese, we're not going to make it."

"You can't turn millions of citizens into an army against their will."

"Morgan White opened Pandora's Box, and we lost control of the nanotechnology. Every country in the world is going to have it in their head that this should be a shared technology, and they're going to take it by force!"

"I understand your concerns, but I still think we can reason with President Ismail. Let me call her."

Truman sighs at his friend. He nods and extends his arm out. Crawford heads for the phones, likely to find his. *I'm sorry, old friend, but I'm going to have to use you as an example.*

Determined to keep his control, he pulls his pistol, aims, and fires. The deafening sound reverberating off the walls can't muffle the screams. Before Crawford's body settles, he enters the interrogation room where Beth is, and puts a bullet in her head. Emerging back out into the main area, Truman sees another person running for the phones, and he shoots them, too.

"Listen up! As of right now, anyone who attempts to contact the outside world will be regarded as a traitor. This is what happens to traitors!" He points at his dead friend lying in a dark pool.

Turning to the soldiers, he addresses them.

"You are under my authority. The president has allowed us to be invaded by China, and that means she is a traitor to this country. I am declaring her unfit for duty, and through my plan, we will reclaim the sovereignty of our nation. We are going to raise an army to take back the East Coast, and then we march west! Are there any objections?"

"No, sir!" came a unanimous reply from his soldiers.

No one interjected or refused, and Truman was pleased.

*

# Chapter 8:

He was in shock. His face and hands were cold, and he was laboring to breathe. General Truman had just murdered three people in cold blood, and Reese fears for *his* life now.

Sitting completely still, he hopes to avoid the general's gaze, but he locks eyes with him, and there's no stopping the tears. He manages to keep from sobbing, but the hot liquid pours down his cheeks.

"Can you finish programming the nanites?" Truman asks roughly.

He's unable to respond. He opens his mouth, but his throat closes. Nothing comes out. Truman glares. The fight or flight instinct pushes hard, and it takes every ounce of willpower not to do something stupid.

"Can you finish the job, *Reese*?" Truman gets closer.

He doesn't mean to answer at all, but his body acts on its own. Unwittingly, he nods and lets out an incoherent guttural sound. Truman holsters his sidearm, and ushers him to stand by tapping his shoulder. He does, slowly.

"The country is counting on you, son. I need you to be *very* clear. Can you finish programming the Gen-II nanites?"

"I…what…I don't know." There, finally something. "What do you want me to do?"

"I need full control of those who will receive the Gen-II upgrades, and I need to be able to issue remote orders to our soon-to-be army. Can you program the nanites for that?"

"Beth would know better how to do that… I mean, would have…"

"She was a traitor and conspiring to get us killed. It's on you now. I'm designating you as the team lead. The Gen-IIs are built to receive instructions, so work on that, and use some of Morgan's programming to make the Gen-II compliant to my orders," Truman was firm.

Truman turns to the rest of the TEAL team, the FBI agents, and Pentagon workers, most of whom have scattered from his position.

"Anything Reese needs, you provide. I know what just happened was shocking. It was an unfortunate, but necessary, action to save not only your lives but millions of infected above us. Your friends and families."

Truman turns his attention back to him.

"People are counting on you," he says loud enough for everyone to hear.

*

Alphaeus has tried calling Beth back several times now, but it goes straight to voicemail. The file hasn't appeared in the shared drive, and he can't wait any longer. He heads to the nanite research lab, where dozens of his people are working on their cure. He hates to interrupt them, but he picks up the phone and dials the intercom.

"I need everyone to stop what they're doing and join me."

The groups collectively come to a stopping point and join him, with Doctor Gray up front and center. Their weariness is as apparent as his own is to him. He hangs up the phone and addresses them.

"I just heard from Beth in DC. The small team we left behind made a breakthrough. Instead of attacking the programming, they chose to attack the infected nanites directly.

"She was supposed to send her file to us, but it hasn't come through. I'm unable to get back in touch with her, so we're scrapping the re-write project, and we'll start over with fresh nanites. I want a new nanite developed, one which has the ability to destroy the infected ones.

"Doctor Gray, please form three teams. Designing, programming, and distribution. Work together and communicate. I want a draft of the new nanite done in twelve hours, and a twenty four hour plan for development."

"Should we suspend the *EMP-Bridge* project?" he asks.

"Only long enough to work up our version of their Gen-II nanite. But before we begin, give me your dinner orders. I'm buying."

While everyone gives him their requests, he mentally readies himself to phone President Ismail and update her on the breakthrough.

*

"Corporal Fitzgerald!" a voice yells out, startling her from sleep.

Jumping up, she stands at attention while the officer calls additional names. She recognizes them. It's the EH-US-11 unit. The officer who woke her paces back and speaks loud enough so their unit can hear.

"You're being assigned to the checkpoint on Interstate 15 outside of Primm, Nevada. The Chinook you'll be riding in will be carrying supplies for the checkpoint. When you arrive, unload, and then report to the C.O.!"

She salutes, and her unit follows suit.

"Follow me!" he orders.

He leads EH-US-11 out of the tent and makes a beeline to where all of the helicopters are parked. Each of them receives a M4 rifle before climbing into the helicopter's cargo bay. Theirs isn't the only unit on the helicopter. Several other soldiers are already seated, and the pilot is going through pre-flight checks.

The engines whir to life, and the blades chop the air overhead. Though still mostly dark out, as they ascend, she sees the purples and pinks starting. Soon, the sun is peeking over the horizon, and when its rays hit her face it brings her a moment of peace.

It takes about an hour and a half to reach their destination. Once landed, they're greeted by the commanding officer of the checkpoint, a sergeant major. He directs them on where to put the supplies and issues out shift rotations and assignments. Fitz is put on duty, checking people through their checkpoint on the highway.

The area is narrow, with hills on either side. Fitz thought it was chosen likely as a way to funnel the zombies, and wondered if there was a bigger plan in place.  There was no sign of anything important going on, however. Vehicles were being checked through, much like she had been yesterday. *Maybe we're just a meat shield.*

*

Truman is antsy. The room is quiet in his presence, except for hushed voices and keys clacking on keyboards. He can't be sure Reese is being fully cooperative because of his lack of understanding programming code. He has to assume Reese is working on what he instructed.

Reese tenses every time Truman hovers over his shoulder, but it doesn't stop him from checking in once in a while.

"How long until I can input commands?" he asks.

"Not long, but the problem is going to be range. Their transceiver antennas are small. You'll only be able to give commands to anyone nearby," he replies.

"How do we increase the range?"

"Piggyback on cell towers? But that would take an insane amount of coding and time. Then if the signal was discovered, they could cut off access."

Truman scowls at the others who are supposed to be helping Reese figure things out.

"Well?" he raises his voice at them. "Give *him* solutions! How do we extend the transceiver range and maintain our access?"

The room is silent, and most of the people cower. Whether they don't want to answer, or don't have any ideas, he's not sure. What he is sure of is that they need more motivation. He pulls his sidearm from its holster and puts it on the table.

"I understand some of you still have reservations, but I need everyone here on board. We need to take the country back. If you have an idea and keep it to yourself, you are just as culpable as the president for allowing the foreign troops to invade!" he keeps his voice elevated.

There's a small sound out of a man across the desks. He recognizes him as someone who reported to Crawford. He rubs his chin and appears to be deep in thought. Truman clears his throat to get the man's attention. He looks up.

"What about a hive mind?" the man offers.

"Elaborate," he requests.

Reese looks across the desks and shakes his head ever so slightly to attempt to draw attention. But Truman sees it, and the man ignores it.

"If we network the nanites to wirelessly communicate to nanites in other hosts, you can reach everyone with the Gen-IIs in a much shorter time."

"What's your name?" Truman asks.

"Ivan Gregory," he answers.

"Smart idea, Ivan."

"I don't know how to do that," Reese interjects fervently. "Beth was the master programmer here, and *she's dead*!"

"Figure it out!" he lashes out, and scowls. "The nanites already talk to each other within the body, right? Build on that! In fact, I want everyone working on this hive mind idea. If we're going to survive World War III, this is our best chance!"

Ivan stands and walks to where Truman is.

"I'll work with him. I'm not a programmer, but I can be the ideas, and he can implement them," he says, clearly trying to be an overachiever.

"Sit down," Truman's sharp with him. Ivan does as he's commanded, sitting in Beth's spot right next to Reese.

He taps Reese's shoulder and motions for him to follow. Without looking to make sure he's coming, he walks away. A chair squeaks on the floor behind him, and footsteps approach. When he reaches the wall, Truman turns back to him and frowns.

"Make this happen." He lowers his voice, and watches everyone else. "The Chinese are coming to kill everyone. You, me, my son, your mother. They won't care. They're going to annihilate us unless you figure this out."

"I'm not sure you understand how bad of an idea this is. People have been writing cautionary tales about nanotechnology for as long as I can remember. Using it in this way *will* destroy civilization."

"Not if *you* do it right. Remember, we have the nanites programmed so we can issue a self-destruct command and have them break down with no harm done. Won't it also be easier if the army is linked together? Once we win, you issue the command, everyone goes back to normal, and we rebuild America greater than before."

Reese's brows are downturned, and it's clear he's hesitant. He nods and sighs. Truman places his hand on Reese's shoulder in a reassuring manner, despite the fact that once the army is started he plans to inject him with the new nanites. *His ethics and morals are too grounded in the past. He can't see what humanity can be. Even more so if they're united as one mind. No more wars, no more poverty, no more destruction. Just humankind cooperating as one.*

*

Alphaeus gauges the team. Their work on their own Gen-II nanites is only beginning, but he is enthusiastic. Working with Doctor Gray, they layer new security protocols. *Once implemented, even the strongest brute force attack would take incredible computing power to break through. I shouldn't have let General Truman push us into field testing so soon.*

Though the nanite cure would stop the infection, he intended for their future EMP-Bridges to return society to normal. Then he'd take the nanites back to the drawing board.

*The energy draw for the bridge is going to be enormous. We'll need to tap directly into a power grid.*

Doctor Gray turns to a colleague to discuss their Gen-II changes, and Alphaeus takes a few moments to envision the future. Most of his thoughts are devoted to this problem. But putting setbacks aside, he knows that if employed in the correct way, nanotechnology still had a place in improving the world.

*All I need is to show that this technology can work. Just because the hill we're climbing turned into a mountain doesn't mean we should stop.*

"Alphaeus, Mike wants to know if we're ready to implement the new security protocols into the active program," Doctor Gray interrupts his thoughts.

Alphaeus finishes the function he's working on and saves his file. "Yes, proceed and compile. Before we add anything else, I want to run some external attacks and make sure we don't have any gaping holes."

Doctor Gray nods and stands, taking the external drive with their work to join another team. While they prepare to implement, it gives Alphaeus a few moments to focus on readying to field test an EMP-Bridge. He reaches for his phone and dials President Ismail.

*

# Chapter 9:

Truman is antsy for the modifications to be complete. Their food is running low, and everyone is going stir crazy. He hides in the secured hall, trying to stay out of the way. Reese promised the completion of the Gen-III nanites today, and his anticipation is causing agitation.

Two days ago, they'd performed a small test, networking the remaining mice together, and then pushing an update to one. The hive mind programming had been successful. But he was unimpressed by the still very limited ability to issue orders. He tasked the team to figure out a way to incorporate giving them by voice.

Reese pushed back, likening it to mind control, but he didn't care. Truman threatened him with removal from the facility if he didn't cooperate, and this put him back on track.

He checks his watch and finds it's nearly noon. He exits the secure hallway and approaches Reese.

"Are we ready to test?"

"Yes."

"Good."

Truman waves his soldiers over, and they already know what's next because they roll their sleeves up as they join him.

Reese pulls a syringe from the table and puts it into some grey-looking goo. Pulling the plunger, he sucks some up, and wipes off the end of the needle against the petri dish. Master Sergeant Gorski's first, eagerly holding out his arm. Reese tries to be easy with the needle, appearing to copy what he'd likely seen at a doctor's office. The needle goes in, and Gorski grimaces at Reese's ineptitude with it. After he plunges a little, he pulls the needle and readies it for the next taker. One by one the soldiers are injected.

"How do you feel, soldier?" he asks after a few moments.

"Fine, sir," Gorski replies.

"Good. Reese, can I give commands by voice?" he asks.

"Yes," he answers. "You have to have your finger on the scanner while you speak or it won't allow any changes."

Reese hands a headset with a microphone to him, and he puts it on. Following instructions, he puts his index finger on the scanner and issues his first instruction. "Take out your knife and cut your palm."

Without hesitation, all of the soldiers take out their knives in unison and cut their palms. The direction was vague, so each soldier does it a bit differently, but the end result is the same. The nanites heal their hands, and Truman smiles. It was dramatic, but it was a way to ensure even an order with a negative consequence would be followed.

"What was that like, Master Sergeant?" he asks.

"It was strange, sir. I'm not sure how to describe it. My body just reacted to what you said."

"Did my giving you an instruction hurt in any way?" he asks.

"Only the cut, sir."

"Go stand over at the wall and wait for my next command," he speaks into the microphone.

They do as they're told, marching together, however, like before, each one of them takes their own interpretation of *at the wall* and end up at slightly different distances. Seeing they're off, they line up.

"Space yourselves out a foot apart, and then turn around to face directly at the wall," Truman gets even more specific.

He then whispers into the microphone so they can't hear him.

"Raise your left hand into the air."

The soldiers do as he commands, though they're not in hearing range. This excites him, but he holds his composure in front of everyone.

"Return and stop a foot from me, spread out."

They do.

"Look to your left and right. You are the cure. Your next mission will require you to head out into the world and begin the reverse infection. Are you ready to accept your mission?"

"Sir, yes, sir!"

"Good. Do not move until I say 'go'. You are to stick together as a team at all times. You allow yourselves to be bitten to start the reverse infection process. Master Sergeant Gorski, once the perimeter of the Pentagon is safe for us to come up, you are to radio me. Do you understand?"

"Sir, yes, sir!" they answer again, and he can't be sure if it was a voluntary response or nanite compliance.

"Go!"

The soldiers head for the elevator, and Truman escorts them. He inputs his security clearances, and when the doors open, they pile in. It whirs to life and they've gone to save the world. He returns to the group.

"Alright people. We've begun the movement to take back the country, but the work has just started. We are going to have to move back topside, as this was never meant to be a permanent facility for a department, and as you've seen our food is running low. You need to be inoculated against the infected."

"I'm not putting those things in me," a woman protests.

"I'm afraid you don't have a choice. We need every able bodied person to become part of the army," Truman is firm.

"You can't make us!" another speaks up.

*I don't have time for a rebellion.*

"Reese, inoculate them," he orders.

"General Truman, if we do, you'll dwindle my team, and any orders you give will be given to them, too. You need them just as much as me to maintain your army."

"That's not true. You can keep a group isolated from the rest of the army and task them to maintain the programming, with the nanites," Ivan interjects.

"This is all temporary, remember?" Truman offers the group. "We're doing this to take back the nation. Once it's free of traitors and other potential threats, we will rebuild and get back to our lives."

"I don't think everyone needs to be inoculated," Reese tries to bargain again. "If you have everyone injected with Gen-III, people will see you as a dictator, not the savior of humanity."

Truman stares at him.

*

He watches Truman intently, waiting to see if there's any flicker or waver in the way he's holding himself. He stands as the barrier between curing people and allowing them to be enslaved.

"We need everyone here to be able to regenerate if hurt. You all are invaluable to the team and restoring humanity and the country. What happens if you're shot in the head, *Reese*?" Truman is trying to scare him. "If *you* die, then who will become the lead programmer of the nanites?"

*No. He's just trying to get to me. I have control and can revoke his at any time. He knows it. I have to stand my ground.*

Ivan leaps at Reese while trying to grab at the syringe in his hand. He pulls back, and he has to fight to keep the syringe. Ivan pushes in hard, nearly knocking him over to get to it.

"Give me the syringe!" Ivan yells.

"Fuck off!"

Truman does nothing to stop him from attacking, appearing to be content to watch for a moment. Reese finds enough leverage to shove him away, and he moves to the computer.

"Back the fuck off, or I'll send the command to destroy the Gen-IIIs!" he yells. "And then I'll destroy the code!"

"You wouldn't. You'd be letting the terrorist win! The world will end!" Ivan yells back.

Truman steps into the opening between them. He holds his arm out to Ivan, keeping him at arm's length. Ivan is furious.

"Give me the syringe," Truman demands.

Reese shakes his head, his fingers are ready to push the command to dismantle the Gen-III nanites.

"You know full well if you destroy it, we're lost. Everyone we've ever known is or will be one of the infected. We need to be united right now, to come together and cure everyone. Then we move past all of this and onto rebuilding," Truman says.

"If I take the nanites, if we all do, there's no one who could disobey your orders. What if you wanted to set yourself up as the emperor of the world after this is over?"

"You make a good point. Then how about you inject me?" the general offers and rolls up his sleeve.

*Unexpected, but I'm sure it's calculated.*

"That's not what I was thinking. You need someone to balance things, who doesn't have the Gen-III and won't take blind orders," he projects his voice to sound strong.

"And that's you?" Truman asks.

"Bullshit he is!" Ivan chimes in and sparks a harsh glance from the general.

"What do all of you think?" he turns to the group. "Who would be a good candidate as *my* counterbalance?"

No one speaks up right away. It takes a few moments, but a woman stands.

"I don't think we need to take the nanites. The soldiers are up there right now, curing everyone. I don't think we're going to be in any danger."

"Is that so? What about the Chinese soldiers on American soil, and the Russian Navy off the West Coast? They're here, and ready to gun you down," Truman points out.

"I'll be your counterbalance," Ivan offers.

"Hell no. You've seen his actions," Reese protests to the group.

"Just because you don't have the balls—"

A man from the other side of the desks speaks up, and his deep voice echoes through the room.

"I vote for Reese."

"I second that," another says.

Truman looks to Reese again and speaks, "There you have it. You're it. I hope you are up to the task, because leading isn't easy."

The general could have acted by now and simply taken the syringe from Reese. It doesn't feel like a win, but as long as he can be the balance, it's enough for now.

"I want everyone here inoculated by Reese," Truman commands. "When we've secured the country from our enemies, *he* will enter the command for the Gen-III shutdown."

*Will he allow me to disarm the Gen-IIIs when it comes time? I need to start planning for the possibility that he won't.*

The survivors line up. One by one, Reese injects them. He wants to fake an injection on at least one person as a failsafe, but there was no opportunity. He had to inject them all, or risk Truman turning on him. It was done.

"We need to be able to isolate groups within our army in order to issue specific commands. Everyone needs to assist Reese with this new project."

He leaves it as a directive, not as a command through the headset.

Everyone returns to their spaces for the moment, and Truman leans over to whisper in Reese's ear. His hand sits right next to the syringe, and Reese is uncomfortable, positive he is going to pick the syringe up and betray him.

"I need you to come up with a way for me to issue orders without being tethered to this desk."

He sees Truman's hand shifts away from the syringe.

"I'll look into it."

"I'm confident you'll think of something."

Despite fearing the general would attack him, Truman straightens up and walks away. Relief washes over him, at least until he looks around and all eyes are on him.

*

Alphaeus takes in the fresh air, a fair distance from the sterile interior of the office and labs. Their quick successes in their Gen-II nanites gave them time to refocus on installing the first EMP-Bridge while they waited for clearance to deploy their cure. Consulting with the president's people, it was determined that the Ivanpah Solar Power Facility off Highway 15 would be the best place to start testing. The military had already established an outpost and checkpoint measures near there, making it the best choice.

It was blueprinted to reach twenty feet high, ten feet wide, and three hundred feet in length to cover the entire highway, plus some. Most of the bridge's construction was going to be a simple frame of pipes and cross beams, but it would be enough to support their mobile EMP devices.

TEAL employees unload the components, while power plant workers and the military work to lay enough cabling to reach from the plant. He helps bring down supplies from one of the semi-trucks they'd leased, but is distracted by the military's effort to screen for infected.

*There were always risks. People might have rejected the technology, but in time, the skeptics would have seen the benefits. Am I naïve to think we can still better the world with them?*

Setting down supplies near where the bridge was going up, he notices a soldier looking sideways at him. She's working to clear cars of any potential infected, and pass them through, but his presence is distracting her. He recognizes her face. She's from one of General Truman's units. *Ella Fitzgerald*. There's an urge to introduce himself, and to explain how sorry he was for all of this, but the timing wasn't right. Instead, he returned to his work and left her to hers.

*

"Excuse me Madam President," Vice President Abraham enters their makeshift video conference room, and interrupts a call between her and China. "I'm sorry to interrupt, but I urgently need your attention."

All eyes turn to him, and the translator on the other end of the call translates. President Ismail turns to him, and there's a panicked look on his face. Turning back to the screen, she stands up and acknowledges the foreign delegate.

"I apologize, but we'll have to continue discussing the terms of sharing the nanotechnology in-depth at a later time."

The translator relays her message, and the Chinese official, Premiere Lài speaks. She waits for the translator to communicate the message.

"Is there a problem with our soldiers?" the translator asks.

"No, sir, this is unrelated to any of the soldiers," he responds.

President Ismail turns to leave. When she's at the door, she looks over her shoulder and speaks again.

"I will give you an update later on our efforts. Thank you again for being patient with the negotiations."

The technician in the room ends the transmissions, and President Ismail questions her VP with a quirked eyebrow.

"What is going on?" she asks.

He doesn't respond verbally. He waves her along, and they traverse the house to the situation room. There are dozens of monitors to focus on, and through the satellite images, foreign and domestic news media, and more data than she could ever hope to read, nothing immediately stands out.

"Madam President," Secretary Bates addresses her while leaned over an analyst's station. "I would have come to get you, but sending Vice President Abraham to interrupt seemed more appropriate."

He leads her through the crowded room, and she's careful not to trip over the hundreds of cords strung out every which way. At a computer, she can clearly see what they're monitoring. It's the Pentagon in real-time, shown through thermal imaging view. There's a huge body of red amassing not just around the Pentagon, but inside, too.

"Are those infected people? What's drawing them there?"

"We're not sure, but look," an analyst responds.

They switch views to a zoomed in feed. The infected flood over to the Pentagon and attack, but curiously, they become docile. The group grows larger, with more of them becoming docile by the moment.

"What's causing this?" she asks.

"We have no idea," Secretary Bates responds. "We've been monitoring this area because it's General Truman's last known location. Now this. Do you think he succeeded in obtaining the terrorist's key?"

"It's possible. I've attempted to call Director Crawford, but had no luck. General Truman's phone has been turned off, and his voicemail box is full." She pauses to form an idea. "I want a UAV over the area as soon as possible."

"Yes, ma'am. We can have one in the air shortly," Secretary Bates tells her and turns to a couple analysts. "I'll make the necessary calls and coordinate with the Navy. If I recall, the USS Theodore Roosevelt is parked off the coast and has a small compliment of UAVs."

"Good. We need to know what's going on. If General Truman is still at the Pentagon, and has a cure, I want it secured."

"Yes, ma'am!"

She waits while Secretary Bates coordinates. Fifteen minutes pass, and the Pentagon group grows larger. On one of the large screens in the room they've accessed the UAV's camera and it's hurtling toward the Virginia coastline. It's a matter of moments before it's overhead of the Pentagon, and it swoops low enough to gather images of people looking up at it.

*

"General Truman, come in. Over," Gorski's voice crackles in over the radio.

"Yes, Master Sergeant? Is the perimeter secured? Over," he responds.

"Nearly, sir. But we have another issue to address. We just got buzzed by a Stingray. Over."

"Roger. Confirm the heavy munitions near the helipad are still there. Over."

"They are. Over."

"If you get a chance, shoot it down. Over."

"Understood. Over and out."

Truman looks to his tech group.

"President Ismail has launched a reconnaissance drone against us, likely to size up what's going on topside. Keep working on a way to isolate groups within the hive-mind, but know we're running out of time, fast. That drone would have been sent by a Navy ship off the coast, and it means we could be facing two sides of the same army."

He picks up the command microphone, puts his finger on the scanner, and issues another order.

"Addendum to all previous commands: There is to be a silence in all electronic communication. Do not make phone calls, do not text message, do not access the internet, do not use any form of radio communications until further notice."

*

"The question is, were they looking up because it was making noise, or did they recognize it?" President Ismail asks as the drone makes a hard left and circles back.

The room watches and waits. The UAV heads back toward the Pentagon and flies a little lower. As it nears, there are odd flashes coming from the ground. It only takes a moment to realize it's under fire. The UAV takes a sharp right, plummets to the ground, and the video goes black. Secretary Bates is still on the phone with the Navy.

"What the hell happened?" he asks. "Launch another, but stay out of range of whatever's happening at the Pentagon. I want as much intel as you can collect."

He leaves the phone line open and turns to her.

"Madam President, what we saw is confirmed. The UAV was shot down."

*What the hell is happening?*

"We need to know more. We need to organize a fact finding mission. Who is the senior officer of the EH-US units?" she asks.

"That would be Master Sergeant Thomas. I'll organize an EH-US unit and send them in."

"Alphaeus Lang has finished his anti-infection nanites and promises permanent protection from becoming infected," she informs the secretary. "Issue a directive; anyone sent on the recon mission are to be inoculated."

"Yes, ma'am."

*

"Excuse me, Corporal Fitzgerald?" a serviceman addresses her.

"Yes?"

"Master Sergeant Thomas has just arrived. He has requested you to meet him at the command center tent."

"Understood. Dismissed."

She immediately heads to the tent and finds Thomas conversing with Alphaeus Lang. She enters mid-conversation.

"…second generation is ready," Mr. Lang tells the master sergeant.

"Give me a rundown of the second gen." Thomas sees Fitz and waves her in. "Good timing."

"Gen-II has far more security protocols. We took a note from Morgan when it came to protecting the software. Everything is tied together now, so if the code is tampered with, the nanites shut down. The other new feature is that the nanites have been redesigned and recoded to recognize foreign nanites and dismantle them. Anyone bitten by an infected person will not become one of the infected."

"Good. I have orders to allow you to inoculate Corporal Fitzgerald's EH-US unit, and myself," Thomas says and looks to her. "You, me, and your unit are going back to the East Coast. Something is happening at the Pentagon, and the mission is to find out what."

"General Truman?" she asks.

"Possibly. Current intel is weak. What we know is that a UAV was shot down at the Pentagon, and that's his last known location. I won't speculate any further. If it was him, I want you present, since you were close to his son."

"Yes, sir."

"Gather your unit and meet back here in thirty to receive the Gen-II nanite injections."

"Sir, yes, sir!"

She does an about face, and before she's left the tent, Mr. Lang and Master Sergeant Thomas continue to discuss the nanites. Quickly, she's out of earshot and looking for the members of her unit.

*If the Gen-II nanites are as advertised, then we could be looking at the tail end of this epic disaster. The entire population of North America would need to have nanites injected in them, but at least it would stop the zombie apocalypse.*

Once she's collected her unit, she leads them into the tent. One by one, her unit of seven, plus Master Sergeant Thomas, are injected with the new nanites.

She moves around and waits for any difference in how she feels. When she was first injected, it was like a permanent adrenaline rush she just got used to. She felt no new physiological changes this time, though.

Thomas stands by the door and waits for them to assemble. When they're lined up and at attention, he addresses them.

"Nobody knows what the hell we're going to walk into, so I need you to be on your toes and ready for shit hitting the fan. What we do know is there's a growing mass of people at the Pentagon, and a Navy UAV was shot down there. We're to recon and report. Are you ready?"

"Yes, sir!" EH-US-11 responds.

"Follow me. We have a chopper waiting to take us to the airport!"

"Sir, yes, sir!"

Thomas steps out of the tent and begins to jog. Her unit follows, with her at the rear. Fitz feels exhausted, due to being shuffled off again, and intends to take a long vacation after this is over. At the helicopter, they climb in, ready to go.

*

Fresh air. The sun was setting, and there's a slight breeze blowing in from the east. Truman sighs in relief now they're recovering from Morgan's attack.

Reese's team successfully incorporated a way to task just an individual, as well as form groups and task them. While still time-intensive, he could now make the hive's *brain* work exclusively on the technological progression, while the army is tasked to spread out and cure. Strangely, the army had to be told when to eat, as they weren't doing so on their own. This meant sending them out to gather food, and ration it.

Back inside, he passes members of the hive-brain bringing the computer network back upstairs. Their orders were to not to plug into the Pentagon's main servers, until they found a way to keep the president and her ilk out.

He couldn't afford their work to fall into her hands. Ivan comes up in the elevator and approaches unabashedly.

"General Truman, we need to speak."

"What is it?" he says firmly.

"I have an idea to make giving commands significantly easier. What you need is a direct link to those who have taken the Gen-III nanites."

"What do you mean?"

"A nanite that taps into your brain, and you control it. You could think and it would send a command to the others around you who have the nanites."

"Take this up with Reese."

"I tried. He said it's too dangerous and won't listen to reason."

His plans for the near and distant future were achievable with the current methods, and to push Reese might stir him to send the self-destruct command to the Gen-IIIs. Still, the idea of a *master nanite* would bring success faster.

"I'll speak to him," Truman says and walks away before Ivan can say anything else.

The new command center is coming together nicely. Reese is working on setting up his station, larger than it was down in the basement. He's standing on top of a large desk, rigging up six monitors to the computers and machines for programming and creating nanites.

If he knew where Reese hid the syringe of nanites, he might take this opportunity to inject him right now, while he's unable to issue the self-destruct command. He could order someone to infect him, but because the computers weren't up yet, it would be a verbal order only. Too many things could work against him to stop him from infecting Reese, for now.

"Reese, step down and come over here," he orders.

*

Reese looks over his shoulder and continues to plug in the cables. General Truman has been especially vigilant of every move he's been making. *What's his next move? I have to anticipate so I can balance and counter...*

"I'm trying to get the system back up. Can this wait?" he projects in protest.

"This won't take long."

He sighs and takes his time climbing down off the desk. Unlike other times where he spoke to Reese independently, this time he doesn't seem to care.

"Ivan tells me you've refused to consider an idea for a master nanite which would increase the ability to issue commands to *our* army," he projects.

"You're damn right I did," he says, raising his voice some. "Like I told him, it would be irresponsible simply for the fact that it would remove all free will. We're borderline there as it is, except for the need to input commands into the headset."

"I understand your ethical reservations," Truman says condescendingly, "But what you need to understand is that, unless we have complete *unity*, this world will fall back into its old ways, and we'll be back here again in this type of predicament. The world is poised to tear itself apart if we can't save it here and now."

*God forbid he find out I already know how to do what he wants. But unless I can placate him further, the others might figure it out, too, and do it without me. If I have my hands in it, I can keep control of it.*

Feeling bold, he confronts Truman.

"I know what you're doing, General. I'm not an idiot. I'm playing along because in the end, I'll out maneuver you. I've already inserted an algorithm in the nanites to self-destruct if I don't input my password every hour."

The look of shock, and then anger on the general's face is satisfying. It gives Reese the courage to keep going.

"If you kill me, they'll self-destruct. If I sense any hostility from you, or anyone else here, I'll send the self-destruct command myself and let this world go to hell. I, and only I, will build your master nanite, but I'm putting in restrictions. I'll let you know what they are when it's complete."

Truman is silent, but Reese is sure he wants to kill him right now. He turns his back on the general and returns to his work. His face gets hot, and he dares not look back. The fact he hasn't been punched, tackled, or shot in the back yet only means Truman is evaluating if he's lying. Or perhaps contemplating injecting him with the Gen-III nanites.

*He'll get me in my sleep, I'm sure of it. I'm going to have to inject myself with Gen-IIIs with their transceivers deactivated.*

He climbs back up on the desk and continues hooking up the computers. Out of his peripheral vision, he sees Truman standing there, staring him down. He tires of gawking and leaves. Reese sighs in relief and repositions the computers in a half-circle at body height all around his station. *If he calls my bluff and decides to shoot me, he'll risk destroying everything. He'll have to get close, and I'll have the ability to initiate the self-destruct command.*

When he's finished rearranging, he powers the computers on and sits down.

*

Truman meets with Gorski, who is making rounds and checking on the newly cured. There's a general sense of confusion, but Gorski points out Truman and hails him as their savior.

"There, people! He is the one who cured you! Through his dedication, he never gave up on you while the president and her cabinet abandoned you!"

*This is better than I could have hoped for. It would look bad if I talked myself up, but he's doing the dirty work for me.*

The group turns to him, and he's bombarded by questions. He takes the time to explain *his* version of events to them, to jade them against the president. They're not very receptive to the idea their president up and left, and that she enlisted Chinese soldiers to come gunning, but he promised them footage. All he'd have to do would be to access the news in one of the many conference rooms of the Pentagon to show them it was true, and it would spread like wildfire.

"What we want is our home back, but since President Ismail has allowed foreign troops onto our soil, it won't be possible without a fight! Spread the word to others that war is coming to us whether we like it or not, and we need to be prepared!"

Truman smiles and retreats from the crowd. Gorski continues to spread the propaganda, and he's ready to begin the next phase of the reverse infection.

Back into the new command center, he sees Reese has rearranged the computers to surround him. *Smart son of a bitch.* He walks over and initiates a cold stare with the serpent in his garden. Reese is ready for him with the self-destruct interface on one of the six screens.

"Where's the headset?" Truman asks roughly.

"Over there," Reese replies and points without taking his eyes away from the monitors.

He looks and finds it at the far end of the desk, annoyed at being outmaneuvered. *I should have thrown his ass in with Morgan, and given him the same treatment. He has to sleep sometime. But what about his having to put in a password every hour?*

He picks up the headset and places his finger on the scanner. Forming his thoughts, he plans his wording carefully.

"Everyone who is currently inside the Pentagon, remain in the Pentagon and continue working on upgrading the command center. Everyone who is not inside the Pentagon is to follow Master Sergeant Gorski's commands.

"Master Sergeant Gorski, lead the army northwest to Joint Base Myer-Henderson Hall and bring back weapons and food by twenty-three fifty-nine tonight."

It's cumbersome to issue orders like this, but it can't be helped until the master nanite is complete. Putting the headset down, he stands and watches Reese.

*

The EMP-Bridge nears completion. The biggest issue was setting up enough transformers and capacitors to keep the high energy volume coming from the solar power plant from blowing out the whole array. The mathematical calculations were lining up for a successful test run, but still, Alphaeus could only muster cautious optimism. *If it's successful, we'll have to build more at choke points all across the west, and then herd people like cattle.*

While Doctor Gray oversees the final additions, there's time for Alphaeus to climb a hill and fully take in the situation.

The line of cars heading westbound extends through the hills, and the end is nowhere in sight. Despite the apocalyptic feel, he refuses to accept a dystopian future. He's learned from his mistakes, and promises himself he'll do better.

His phone rings, startling him. It's Doctor Gray. He answers.

"Yes?"

"We're ready to begin testing."

"Ok. I'll be there shortly."

He hangs up and heads back down, and Doctor Gray meets him.

"You need to stop scowling," he scolds. "We're at the tail end of this."

Alphaeus hadn't realized he was scowling. He nods and relaxes some, and they walk over to their team. *Now, more than ever, it's necessary to build up their hope.*

"Alright ladies and gentlemen, we're finally gaining traction on the problem set in motion by our failings, and the terrorist's actions. This is where we prove we can take accountability. You've put in long, hard hours, and I deeply appreciate it. So let's cross our fingers, say a prayer, or whatever it is you choose to do, and flip the switch."

It was as good a speech as any, he feels. Nothing fancy, something to show humanity and humility.

The team moves off the road, and the soldiers hold off from letting anyone else through. Doctor Gray moves to the terminal they'd set up twenty-some feet from the EMP-Bridge. Mike readies a lab mouse with nanites. The plan was for Mike to walk through with the mouse in a cage, but Alphaeus takes over. *If something goes wrong, I don't want anyone else at risk.*

Doctor Gray initiates the startup sequence. There's an audible crackle, and now a physical pressure in the air. Though the EMP wave is invisible, the gradually increasing hum peaks, and it's hard to hear anything. Alphaeus takes the cage from Mike, and Mike looks at him in question. He smiles and gives him the 'it's okay' look.

Stepping forward, he's unsure of if there will be any effects on his unaltered body, but he carries himself with dignity across the threshold. The hum intensifies under the bridge, and he walks straight through to the other side. There's been no harm to him or the mouse. Turning around, he nods in satisfaction. Back through to the other side, now was the moment of truth.

Handing the cage back to Mike, he draws blood from the mouse and puts it under the microscope. He's heartened when he sees the nanites there, but completely inactive. Not wanting to get anyone's hopes up prematurely, he moves the slide of blood around, and examines thousands of nanites.

It's a complete success. The bridge has nullified the nanites. Alphaeus turns and smiles. Doctor Gray shuts the bridge down.

"Congratulations! We've succeeded, but that means we have our work cut out for us now. I need to call President Ismail."

"What about the cars already on the highway?" Doctor Gray asks.

"Coordinate with the commanding officer here to start the funneling procedures. Give them the knowledge they'll need to operate the bridge, and then prepare our team to move to the next site."

"Got it."

Alphaeus steps away from the EMP-Bridge and dials the president. She answers on the first ring.

"Mr. Lang?"

"President Ismail, the EMP-Bridge is a success. Let's start implementing more wherever we can. I'll send you a list of what we need to start building more."

"I'm glad to hear that. We have additional sites already chosen. You'll have whatever you need to make this work."

*

President Ismail hadn't felt relief in a very long time, but now there was a hint of it. Hanging up with Alphaeus, it was time to put everything into overdrive. In the situation room, she briefs everyone on the success, and directs Secretary Bates to the next step.

"Now we know it works, we need to furnish Mr. Lang with anything he needs. I want you to coordinate a massive military effort to start gathering the resources."

"Yes, Madam President," he replies.

Looking to her vice president, she waves him over.

"What can I do?" he asks.

"Prepare for a press conference. I'm going to contact foreign delegates and inform them we're taking back the country."

"When this is over, you're taking a vacation. You haven't had a real one since taking office, and if this win isn't a reason to, I don't know what is," Vice President Abraham scolds but smiles.

She puts her hand on his shoulder and smiles back. "We'll see about that."

Back into the video conference room, she dials up the Canadian prime minister first. *The end of this nightmare is near.*

*

# Chapter 10:

"General Truman, this is Master Sergeant Gorski. Over."

He was resting his eyes when the hand radio crackled to life. He picks up the radio and responds.

"This is Truman. What do you need? Over."

"Did you see it? Over."

"See what? Over."

"An airplane landed at DCA. Over."

*Shit!* He thought he heard a noise, but with the vivid dreaming he'd been having about the Vietnam War, his mind had incorporated the sound into it. Now, as the grogginess was fading, he realized the plane noise was real.

"Status on your mission? Over."

"We're at the joint base gathering. The army is growing. Over."

"Continue and return at the scheduled time. If there are infected still at the airport, they'll take care of whomever landed, and then we'll cure them. Over."

"Yes, sir! Over and out."

*

Fitz has an uneasy feeling in the pit of her stomach. She can't pinpoint why. The tarmac is littered with infected, but despite the constant running from them, she knew they weren't the cause of the anxiety.

The wheels touch down, and the plane brakes. The unit unbuckles and begins gearing up. Master Sergeant Thomas is the first to the door and turns to them.

"Let's go troop, we have a nation to save," he commands.

The plane pulls into the terminal and up to the gate. Thomas pulls the handle to release the locking mechanism and pushes it enough to open it a sliver. There's an infected there to greet them. He fires a bullet into their skull, and uses the door to push them out of the way.

"When we're clear of the plane, close the door and get the hell out of here," he orders the pilots.

"Yes, sir!"

They form pairs, with her and the master sergeant at the front. Up the ramp, and out into the open, there are a dozen infected in the gate area. With precision, they gun down the group. A few stragglers come looking for the origin of the sound, and they're easily dealt with.

"Just because we have nanites to protect us doesn't mean I want to be swarmed and repeatedly bitten," Fitz whispers. "Remember, these things respawn! Naki, Moss, watch our six."

Other than the occasional zombie, and rifle fire, the airport is eerily silent. Devoid of normal activities, they're able to easily make their way through the airport toward the front doors. Their hopes of an easy out are dashed when they come to a large group hovering inside the exit.

Thomas balls his fist and holds it up to signal them to stop. He waves for them to back up. Fitz points up to the second level. He nods, and they backtrack. Up a stopped escalator, there are considerably less zombies, but enough to cause a problem if they aren't careful.

"Let's see if we can sneak past them," Thomas whispers.

One by one, they move between objects and obstacles to avoid detection. Moss becomes pinned down, separated from the unit as a lone zombie walks near the bench he's hiding behind. Fitz waves to catch his attention, and he sees her. Pointing to her boot, she directs him to pull his combat knife and take the zombie out.

He acknowledges with a nod and prepares. Another comes near. He watches her, waiting for a signal. She holds a closed fist up until the extra zombie passes. The attention of the first is drawn by the other leaving, and she motions for him to go. A swift leap, and he plunges the knife up through the soft spot on the back of the zombie's head. It slumps onto the bench, and Moss drops back down out of sight.

No other zombies are alerted, and he makes his way to the group. They continue on and find an area with minimal zombies. Despite not wanting to take them head on, the exit is blocked.

"Stay low and quiet. Use your knives if any of them come near," Thomas whispers.

He leads, and they work their way to the closed doors, taking out a half-dozen zombies quietly. When they reach the entrance, she and Thomas pry a sliding door open. They cover the group as they exit, and once outside, the fear of being overwhelmed lessens. Zombies are spread out on the roadway in between parked vehicles. Seeing an opening, Thomas directs them to a hotel's bus.

Fitz takes the lead up the stairs onto the bus. A couple zombies inside run to the front, trying to bite her. Fighting them back, she keeps them at bay. Naki slips in the back door and plants his knife in the back of their heads.

"Good work Ensign," she commends.

They carry the zombies off the bus while the other soldiers climb aboard. Thomas takes the driver's seat and familiarizes himself. Fitz sits at the front of the bus, kitty-corner to the driver's seat. He closes the doors.

"Ready your weapons and brace yourself," he orders and starts the vehicle.

Immediately, they have the attention of all zombies in the area. Thomas throws the vehicle into reverse, slams into a car, and then turns the wheel hard left. In drive, he presses the pedal to the floor and begins shoving through parked cars.

The EH-US-11 unit readies to defend themselves from all angles. The zombies are quick to run up to the vehicle, and Fitz is the first to fire a shot through the side windows. One zombie down. The bus is turned into a battle zone while Thomas pushes out of the impromptu parking lot.

A few shots miss their targets when they slam into a vehicle.

"Watch it!" she yells at the master sergeant in jest.

"Doin' the best I can, Fitz!" he yells back.

"Whoa, who the hell said you could call me by my squad name?"

He puts the bus in reverse and backs over some zombies, then goes forward again to slam a truck out of the way.

"Just trying to blend into your unit!"

"Keep up this shit driving, and I'll kick you out of *my* unit!"

"Can you two kiss and shut the hell up already? You're messing up my headshot accuracy ratio," Smith remarks, grinning.

"What's that, Lieutenant? You want to kiss my ass?" Fitz shoots back at her.

Between the banter, gunfire, and crunching noises, she feels at home, in the battlefield. A zombie smashes the front door open, but she puts a bullet in between his eyes and kicks him back out.

Thomas pushes the last obstacle out of the way, and they're free, leaving behind a still rather large wave of zombies trying to chase them down. He presses on the gas pedal, exceeding the horde's thirty mile an hour run speed.

They're clear of the airport, but the George Washington Memorial Parkway still has quite a few abandoned cars. Oddly, the number of zombies are minimal on the road, resulting in a much easier drive than she was anticipating.

"You really think something's going on at the Pentagon?" Welch asks.

"Could be a holdout of survivors who somehow found a way to protect it," Allen replies.

"I wouldn't count on that," Fitz chimes in. "The zombies would have found a way to overrun the building. I'm betting General Truman finally got answers out of the terrorist."

Because the road takes them up around the north side of the Pentagon before doubling back, their time to arrive is significantly longer. The guard shack is abandoned, and the way is open to the north parking lot.

Outside, the building is eerily quiet, with no one in sight. The claims of a massive group gathering here were either false, or the group has moved. Thomas picks up his phone and dials the first saved number. He puts it on speakerphone so everyone can hear.

"Secretary Bates, we've arrived at the Pentagon, but there's no one here. Where the hell did the group go?"

"The swarm went north. They're at the joint base."

"Should we follow?"

"Negative. Infrared shows there are still people gathered inside the Pentagon on the east side. Investigate there and see if you can get some answers."

"Roger. We'll check in when we have, or need something."

"Godspeed."

He hangs up, and they stand ready to disembark. He holds his hand up and gains their attention.

"Keep your guards up. My gut's telling me that whoever's in that swarm at the base is gathering weapons. Let's see what we can learn here, and bug out before they get back."

"Yes, sir!" they respond.

She and Thomas, and they assume their two-by-four formation. Inside the building, they head toward the east side, but before they get there, they run into a person, going about his business. He's oblivious to their presence for a moment, but when he looks up, he's confused.

"I thought General Truman sent you all to the base," he says with disdain and then mumbles. "Must be a glitch in the programming."

"What's going on here?" Master Sergeant Thomas asks.

It's clear the man is now more confused than ever, and after a moment his eyes widen in surprise.

"Where did you come from?" the man asks.

"Answer my question," Thomas orders him.

"My name is Ivan, and I'm not qualified to answer what's going on here. I think you should come with me."

*

The room is mostly quiet while the team works to build up their mainframe infrastructure. It's now wall to wall computers and monitors, tied into many of the different Pentagon operations.

Truman walks toward Reese, seeking an update. It wasn't enough to know the master nanite was in process, he wants specifics, no matter how technical. He hovers over Reese's shoulder, but before he can get a word out, the double doors burst open. Ivan struts through with soldiers behind him. He only needs half a second to know his own, and he smiles.

"Master Sergeant Thomas. Corporal Fitzgerald." He stands at attention and salutes them.

They look at each other, and then back to him with eyes wide in surprise. They lower their rifles, and straighten up with hesitant salutes.

"General Truman? What the hell is going on here?" Master Sergeant Thomas asks.

"We created a cure, and now we're working on retaking the country from the infected," he answers.

"What cure?" Corporal Fitzgerald asks.

"Our team here has dedicated a significant amount of time and efforts to use nanites to combat nanites. Our new nanites seek out and destroy infected ones. We've begun administering inoculations to everyone."

The master sergeant and corporal look at each other.

"It sounds like you and Alphaeus Lang had the same idea," Fitzgerald replies. "His team developed similar nanites to prevent us from being infected."

*Damnit, Beth.*

"Amazing how like minds operate," Truman deflects. "Alphaeus must be ecstatic we can now fight this on two fronts. Is the president okay?"

"As far as we know," Thomas replies. "I heard they lost contact with you. What happened to the drone? Who shot it down?"

"That was one of ours? Last I'd heard the Chinese were encroaching on us. I thought it might be one of theirs."

"It wasn't. The president was disturbed by the group amassing here, and then when the drone was shot down, we were sent," Thomas says.

"I'll give her a call in a moment, let her know that we're on the same path to curing people. In the meantime, make yourselves at home. I have a small group retrieving food, and they'll be back soon."

"How about Charlie? Is there a plan yet to save him?" Fitz asks.

He turns back around and smiles. Without batting an eye, he replies, "All in good time. The mission is not just a single person, but to cure everyone."

*

Reese watches this exchange between the general and the new soldiers. *There's an opportunity here somewhere to undermine him.* Ideas run through his head. He could try to delay the master nanite until the soldiers figure out what's going on. Or he could tell them. Truman would surely kill him over the second option, if he wasn't subdued first.

General Truman walks over to the desks and picks up a phone, but Reese is positive he has no intention of calling the president. This is reinforced by Truman coming close, fiddling with the phone, and whispering to him.

"Don't say a goddamn word."

Reese stares at him. The time for him to act isn't now, that much is apparent. Walking away, Truman heads to the headset and speaks so lowly into it he can't hear. Wondering if the speech recognition programming picks up anything at that low of a voice, he checks the inputs on the command screen. It took.

> You are loyal to General Truman only. Don't trust the new soldiers in this room. They were sent by the treasonous President Ismail. Make up convincing lies about what's going on, but don't tell them about the master nanite, the reverse infection process, or the plan to go to war to take our country back. If they come talk to you, question them to gain intel about the West Coast. Don't help them. Don't attack them.

Looking over his shoulder, he sees most of the soldiers conversing amongst themselves, but the two at the lead of their unit keep their eyes on Truman. He hopes they have a healthy suspicion about what's actually going on here, but there's no way to know without putting himself in jeopardy.

The general walks with the phone in his hand and waves to the soldiers while exiting. The soldiers disperse throughout the room and begin snooping. The questions begin, and Reese listens in.

"What's going on here?" the lead woman asks.

"We're trying to reestablish a network to connect to the internet," an analyst replies while continuing about her business. "Why are you here?"

Reese casually looks around for a piece of paper and pen while a half-dozen conversations are happening. There are disconnected printers, which haven't been removed from the room, and would have the paper he seeks. Approaching them means drawing attention to himself.

He risks it. Standing and moving away from the desk, he keeps his head down and heads for the printer. Pretending to look for a fictional lost object, he quietly opens the drawer for the paper, takes a piece, and closes it. When he turns around, Ivan is there.

"Don't fucking think about it," Ivan whispers right next to Reese's ear.

"Think about what?" he asks, not bothering to quiet himself.

He stays right by his ear. "If you think you're going to write a note and slip it to them, I'll let General Truman know. He'll kill you."

Reese hands him the piece of paper and retorts casually, "I needed some scratch paper to visualize an idea on how the master nanite should work. But if you're that paranoid, you can keep the paper."

Ears pick up on what was said. All eyes are now on him. Ignoring the palpable tension, he returns to his computer. *Letting that out, I'm sure General Truman will let me know his displeasure when he finds out.*

Pulling up coding, he continues working on the master nanite, but on a side screen turned slightly out of the view of the others, he works on his own concoction of code.

One of the soldiers comes over and hovers near him. Ivan follows.

"What's a master nanite?" she asks.

"A what?" Reese plays dumb.

"Excuse me, but he's very busy," Ivan tries to interrupt her.

"Master nanite. Don't tell me I misheard you," she ignores him. "I have enhanced hearing."

"It was the original version of our cure," he lies, but doesn't put any effort into making himself sound convincing. "It works, but I think it could work more efficiently."

"How is it different than what you're distributing as the cure?" she probes.

"What's your name?" Reese asks.

"Corporal Fitzgerald."

"Well, Corporal Fitzgerald," he adopts the most condescending tone he can, "it's a working prototype for making sure there are no compiling errors. The coding is complex, and we need to make sure nothing conflicts so there's no recurrence of infection."

She squints at him, appearing angry. He's confident he's pushed her to leave him alone. But she doesn't leave. He has to be ruder.

"Can you go stand somewhere else? I need my space to concentrate. Last thing you want is for me to make a mistake."

*God, I hope that sets off her internal alarms.*

That does it. She huffs and returns to her squad leader. Watching her out of the corner of his eye, he sees her speak with him. At the same time, Ivan whispers in his ear again. He wants to punch him, but he knows it wouldn't do any good.

"Get back to programming," he orders like he has authority.

Back onto the task, Reese continues to work until Ivan is satisfied. When he moves away, Reese switches back to *his* nanite's code. The race to save himself was on.

*

"There's something seriously wrong here," Fitz whispers to Thomas.

"Agreed," he whispers back. "The walls have ears."

With hand signals, Thomas directs the unit to leave. Naki opens the door, and every eye in the room turns to them, except for Reese. They exit, and Thomas leads them back the way they came.

They're not in the hall more than a moment when General Truman reappears and confronts them.

"Where are you going?" he probes.

"Taking a walk. Some of these kids haven't been to the Pentagon before, so I thought I'd give them a tour," Thomas smiles and plays off their leave.

"I'll accompany you," Truman smiles back. "I've spent years here, and I know of some nice little areas most people don't get to see."

"What did the president say?" Fitz asks.

"She was pleased we had a cure," he replies. "We're in agreement that I'm to continue working to cure the East Coast while the West Coast starts working their way in. We'll meet in the middle."

They stroll through the corridors of the Pentagon. Both Master Sergeant Thomas and General Truman play the game, showing off the different areas. She likens the exchange to chess. Each is looking for a way to one-up the other and take advantage of the board.

*He's buying time. Why?*

The sun was down, the night drags on, and Truman has led them all the way back around to the room with the computers. Still no sign of Truman's group. Her stomach growls, and it presents an opportunity to try and break away.

"General Truman, we need to eat. Since your group is still out collecting food, we should also head out and find some for us."

"Nonsense, we still have supplies here. With the growing population of cured, we just needed to start bringing in more. If you're hungry enough that you can't wait, we have rations in the third basement level."

Fitz turns her head and questions him with a look. She knows better.

"There is no third level," Thomas points out, picking up on the same note.

"It was a secret area developed for high level officials to convene without the presence of ears everywhere. We took refuge down there when the infected overran us."

Thomas stops the unit. Truman continues on, and when he realizes he's walking alone, faces them and smiles.

"Well, are you hungry or not?" he asks.

Leery and hesitant, Thomas calls him out.

"Sir, how about we drop the pretense and you tell us what the fuck is going on."

"You wanted food. Do you expect me to bring enough up for all of you by myself?"

"You know that's not what I mean, General," he replies.

"Where is this lack of trust coming from, soldier? Last I checked, I was still your general. Let two of your unit come with me down there and we'll bring up some food."

She pulls Thomas away, and the unit follows.

She speaks low, "I don't know what he's planning, but we're not in a good position. We don't know anything about the people he's cured. For all we know, they're like the people in that room, utterly loyal."

"Agreed. We need to walk out while we can," Thomas says. "Resume formation and return to the bus."

Thomas turns back to Truman.

"General Truman, we're not staying. We'll return at a later time."

Truman squints and his lip curls up a little. Thomas begins leading the unit through the Pentagon, while she and Smith cover the rear this time. She keeps her eye on the general, ready to draw on him if he makes any quick movements. He stands still, allowing them to leave.

Outside, at the north parking lot, they head toward the bus in darkness. Thomas speeds the unit up to a sprint, and Fitz and Smith turn around to keep up.

"Let's go! Get on the bus!" he hollers.

In the distance is a wave of shadows heading for the Pentagon. *Something's wrong.*

Before everyone is on the bus, Thomas fires it up. Fitz is the last on, and the moment her feet are off the ground, he's flooring the gas pedal to get them out of there. He tosses her his phone.

"Call Secretary Bates!" he orders.

She checks the recent calls, and dials. The wave of bodies approaches faster than normal humans, and there's nowhere to go but through them. The bus rolls over the first line in the wave, and he arcs away from the massive group. The phone continues to ring, and there's an answer.

"Master Sergeant Thomas?"

The bus is hit hard from the side with incredible force. It rolls, throwing everyone inside around like ragdolls. Her neck snaps as she slams into a metal pole, and she expects it to hurt. It doesn't. She can't feel anything. The vehicle comes to a rest on its side, and the unit is overwhelmed by masses pulling them free of the wreckage.

They're not free though. Pulled out and held on their knees, they didn't make it far from the Pentagon. They're stripped of weapons while General Truman strolls out and heads over to them.

"What the fuck?" Moss blurts out.

"General Truman, stop this," Fitz pleads. Feeling is slowly returning to her body, in the form of severe pain down her back. "I don't know what you're doing, but it doesn't have to be this way."

"I'm sorry, but curing everyone is only the start. There is a much bigger threat than the terrorist's nanites now. With the invasion of China into our sovereign nation, and Russia threatening us just off coast, our very country is at stake. We must repel the invaders."

"What?" Thomas questions. "China is here to help us!"

"Don't lie to me!" he yells. "Don't lie to these people! Can you honestly say they'll leave willingly after the threat has passed? Have you not taken notes from US history in the world? We sent our military to a multitude of places for *aid*, and we had more bases than any other nation in the world. Are you so naïve to think other countries haven't been itching to do the same to us?"

"That's bullshit. With the nanites, we're stronger than they are. We could easily repel them," Moss replies.

"Exactly my point!" Truman's face lights up. "With an army built out of the nation, *we* are stronger than they are. That's what this is about! We will rise up and push them out!"

"You're misunderstanding the situation," Fitz says.

"You tell *me* then. When they refuse to leave, what do *you* think will happen?" he probes.

She hadn't thought about what happens after all this is over. The idea they would willingly leave is unlikely, especially now because the cure of the infected means the American population will be enhanced.

"I can't see the future, but with all of the potential fallout of an international incident, I don't believe any country would be willing to risk it right now."

"You're wrong. Both Russia and China could wipe out two-thirds of the US, and reap the benefits. The world would fall into oblivion without the US to balance the powers."

General Truman walks along the lined up unit. It's reminiscent of a scene from an old zombie comic, and he makes her think he's going to kill someone. Except in this instance, the person he chose to kill would come back, and he could do it again, or target another.

"Master Sergeant Gorski, you and your team are to assist me. We're going to confine them in the basement."

"Yes, sir!"

Her unit is lifted forcibly, and they're led back inside the Pentagon, and to an elevator. She watches the security measures: a card swipe, a finger print, and a retina scan. The elevator is large enough to accommodate a half-dozen people, but because everyone here is matched one for one in strength, it takes three of General Truman's people per one of theirs. Master Sergeant Thomas is first.

The doors close, and the elevator hums. A minute later, it returns and the next captive is shoved in. One by one, they repeat the process until it's just her left. Truman steps out to get her himself.

"I'm sorry about this Ella," he uncharacteristically calls her by her first name. "But in time, you'll understand."

Inside, she finds he's said at least one truthful thing tonight. There's a third level below the Pentagon. The doors open and the sight is horrific. Her squad mates have all been executed.

"When you recover, think about joining me," he says.

She is shoved out, and a gunshot rings in her ears. The hot metal enters her skull, and she feels every moment of excruciating pain. Then nothing.

*

The group is on alert because of the unexpected soldiers, but they aren't paying much attention to *him*. He's had enough time to get his modified Gen-IIIs ready for his own injection. He puts a nanite into the coding dock and uploads the instructions.

His heart races with the feeling he's going to be caught. Looking over his shoulder, the hive-brain group is still working on bringing in more computers, creating a sort of server farm. Even Ivan is too busy to hover over him.

The upload is done, and the nanite is ready. He hears voices down the hall, and the sense of urgency becomes greater. Putting the needle into the solution, he draws it in, and then injects himself.

General Truman's voice is recognizable in the group coming, and Reese hurries to return to the master nanite programming. He hides the needle casually and stares up at the screen. Truman enters with Gorski, and they're discussing something he can't make out.

He isn't sure what he expected with a lone nanite in him. He knew he wouldn't have super hearing immediately, but that didn't mean he wasn't disappointed when it failed to happen.

Truman finishes his conversation and heads for Reese.

"How long until it's done?" he questions demandingly.

"There are some coding problems I'm coming across, and to top it off, I'm still not sure how your brain will receive information from hundreds to thousands of the cured. I need more time to research and test on mice."

"You're out of time. I need it now."

Reese turns to the general and stands up.

"The logistics of the master nanite are incredibly complex. I have to create an entire interface function just so the damn thing reads how your brain will send commands, and then have the master nanite transmit that to any Gen-IIIs around it! Then we have to test it!"

"If you'd take the nanites, you could increase your mental capacity and figure this out faster!"

*With every person he reverse infects, the greater likeliness he'll find new programmers to replace me. Just need to placate him a little longer.*

"I'm reassigning the hive-brain to help you directly," he says, angry.

"No. I told you, it has to be me so I can ensure there are restrictions. Also, too many voices in my ear will distract me."

"Then I'll have Ivan help you."

"That idiot wouldn't know a function from a hole in the ground. Find someone else who's more capable."

"Fine."

He regrets planting the idea, but it gives him a little more time since he'll now be looking for an aide, or replacement. Turning back to the computer, he continues working. Truman heads to the microphone at the end of the desk.

"Everyone take a nine hour break to eat and sleep. After nine hours, you are to await new instructions."

*

President Ismail and her cabinet sit around a table, all staring at one another in silence. They're brainstorming, but she is fuming. Though she hadn't heard it, she believed every word of Secretary Bates' recounting General Truman's plan to go to war with them.

She's not sure how to handle this new situation. General Truman has dived off the deep end, raising an army of cured to repel a fictitious invader. Not a single idea was a good one because every one of them involved engaging in the war Truman wanted. Every single one of the ideas resulted in the loss of lives.

"I want all of our military fitted with Lang's new nanites and coordinated for a strike. We need to take General Truman out now before he indoctrinates the whole East Coast," President Ismail orders. "We face annihilation if they gain control of weapons of mass destruction."

"What about the general population, ma'am?" Secretary of Homeland Security, Xavier Dominguez, asks. "We need to think about ways of saving everyone. Can we work with China for temporary relocation?"

She thinks about the prospect. While she doesn't want them having the nanites before the technology refined, it's been a good bargaining chip so far.

"I'll speak with them and see if we can come to an agreement. In the meantime, let's work on the plan to take out Truman. Minimum casualties."

She stands and readies to leave the room, but Vice President Abraham steps into her path. He turns his back to the room and speaks low.

"Ma'am, I know how you feel about it, but it may be time to think about allowing an EMP detonation over the East Coast."

"I know. We were so close to averting it completely, but it's better than letting Truman start a civil war."

President Ismail excuses herself and enters the video conference room. She dials up the foreign delegates to begin talks of evacuation.

*

Fitz gasps for air and sits straight up.

"That son of a fucking bitch!" she yells.

"Master Sergeant! She's revived!" Naki yells from her side.

Thomas heads over to her and extends his hand out to help her up.

"Welcome back to the land of the living."

"How long was I down?" she asks.

"Not sure," he replies. "We've been stripped of everything but the clothes on our backs."

She's furious. "I'm going to kill him."

"We have to get out of here first," Smith says.

"Well, let's get that damned elevator door open and climb to the next level," she responds, thinking of the B1 and B2 buttons on the panel.

"We were just waiting for you." Smith smirks and puts her fingers in between the doors.

The unit crowds around the elevator. Four on left and four on right, they pull hard to overcome the locking mechanism. Even with enhanced strength, forcing the doors open is a feat. The metal begins to buckle a little where the fingers are prying. There's a slight gap, and they each work their hands in farther. *Creaking* and *popping*, the metal gives way.

When there's enough room, Frederickson wedges himself in and uses his girth to open it more. He puts his legs on one door, and his spine into the other, and pushes hard. The mechanism gives way, and the doors snap open, depositing Frederickson onto his back with a *thud*.

They lift him back up and look inside the elevator shaft. It's dark except for what the lights from this level can illuminate. Fitz doesn't hesitate to jump in and grab the ladder at the back of the shaft. She bounds upward toward the surface. The others are right behind.

As she climbs, she looks for any sliver of light to indicate reaching the next floor. But it never comes. She finds the bottom of the elevator and deduces there are no other floors connected to this shaft.

Feeling for an entry way into the elevator, she can't find any sort of hatch. In anger she punches the bottom of the elevator and yells. It echoes all the way down.

"What's wrong?" Thomas asks.

"It's a dead end. The B1 and B2 buttons must have been dummies."

"What's going on?" Naki yells from several feet below.

"There's no way out," Fitz yells back.

Momentarily defeated, the unit climbs back down. Returning to the basement, they examine their surroundings. There are a few dead bodies stuffed in one corner, none with anything of interest on their persons. The vents are too small for anyone to fit through. The bathroom is plain. All the office areas and rooms have been stripped bare, minus chairs and desks.

Everyone circles around, and they converge on the double doors on the far end of the wall.

"A back door?" she questions out loud.

"Let's get these open," Thomas commands.

*

Reese is feeling tired, despite feeling a bit more able than he has since this started. He hoped with his new enhancements, he'd be able to stave off fatigue, but that wasn't reality.

Truman had been circling like a vulture, waiting for him to let his guard down. Eventually, he'd stepped out of the room, and Reese could breathe easier for a few moments.

Because the new soldiers haven't returned, Reese assumes the worst. Now more than ever, he feels it's his duty to counter Truman's nefarious scheme. *It's just a matter of when and how. I could try to kill him with my super strength, but it's likely I'd be stopped.*

He yawns, locks his computers to prevent tampering, and heads for the door. The *drones* in the room are asleep, and it's his opportunity to slip away. There was no actual escape, not yet. He needed sleep, and in sleeping there was an opportunity to set Truman up to think he can win. *He'll find me, no doubt, and he'll try to inject me. He'll think he can control me.*

It's quiet in the halls. Coming to a common area, there's a multitude of people sleeping on the floor. He tiptoes through. Off a branch from the hallway, there's an unlocked door, which leads to a waiting area. The soft cushions of a couch hug his body as he slumps down, and he drifts off.

*

Truman is both pissed and elated Reese snuck off. It gave his team an opportunity to install new hardware, which would allow him to use his cell phone's fingerprint scanner and microphone to replace the hardwired ones. He would now be able to give commands outside of the room, and more effectively lead his army.

But he also needed to find him immediately. The fear that Reese wasn't bluffing about the automatic self-destruct weighs heavily. Needle in hand, he intends to finally bring Reese into the army, and force him to remove the password.

A woman approaches. "We've found him."

She leads him to the east side of the Pentagon, to an offshoot office. Inside, Reese is restrained by three men. He struggles to free himself but fails.

"It's time," Truman says and holds up the syringe.

"Get that away from me!" Reese tries to kick him as he comes close. He's held down.

"I'm told that in time you'll come to appreciate the nanites enhancing your abilities. I'm looking forward to you finishing my master nanite so I can experience it, too."

Truman injects him and waits for the nanites to make their way to his brain. Pulling out his phone, he issues his first command through it.

"Everyone cease the search for Reese. He has been found. Gather outside the north end of the Pentagon for an assembly," he orders. "Master Sergeant Gorski, move a vehicle with a loudspeaker to the front of the group."

Reese grimaces in disgust. The men holding him release their grip, and everyone vacates the room except for Reese and himself.

"The nanites are working their way through your body. Take a moment to understand I'm about to unite the world. No more hunger, greed, sickness, war, or death. Before, I wasn't so sure utopia was the right term, but now it's clear. Humanity needs an intervention if we're to survive."

"Someone will stop you, even if it's not me."

"Reese," he holds his phone up to his mouth. "Disable the automatic self-destruct."

Reese stands there, unmoving.

He squints in skepticism, and issues another order. "Reese, raise your left hand."

Reese complies.

"Reese, I order you to answer me. Was there ever an automatic self-destruct?"

"No. It was just something to deter you from attacking me outright."

General Truman smiles and about faces.

"Come," he beckons.

Heading to the northern wing of the Pentagon, he glances over his shoulder to make sure Reese is following. He is. Outside, he points for Reese to take a place amongst the multitude gathered. Gorski has positioned a Humvee, and Truman speaks through its loudspeaker.

"We have a hard task ahead of us, and I'm going to ask much of you. I know some of you will be called to do things you are against, but I promise in the end it will all be worth it!"

He issues a new directive with his phone.

"We're breaking into groups. Everyone with experience in computer sciences, step forward."

Dozens separate themselves from the multitude of people, Reese included.

"This group that has stepped forward will be designated as the *Programmers*. Programmers, you are to do whatever's necessary to finish the master nanite."

The Programmers return to the building. Now they'll be working as a cohesive group, instead of Reese hoarding the task, he hopes it will be done soon.

He sets his sights on the rest of the group. There are many more waiting to be commanded, and with President Ismail now on the move with her own cure, he's on borrowed time.

"All active and former military personnel, step forward!" Truman commands.

He waits while all types of people step up, about fifty in total.

"Master Sergeant Gorski, separate the soldiers into four groups as evenly as possible."

As he does, Truman plans. *If Ismail figures out what's going on, she might launch an EMP. I need to send a contingent far, to both cure others, and return to re-inoculate people with the Gen-IIIs.*

Gorski finishes, and Truman directs the four groups. As he speaks, he points to the groupings of military personnel.

"You are now Alfa, Bravo, Charlie, and Delta groups. Alfa, Bravo, Charlie, and Delta Groups, split the army into approximate fourths, and from left to right facing from this direction, each of those groups will also be Alfa, Bravo, Charlie, and Delta..."

With all of this, he hasn't accomplished much, and he's tired of issuing verbal commands. They complete their task, slowly, and he can now issue orders to the groups in their entirety.

"Alfa group, you are to head north and spread out through the Northeastern United States, in all major cities, and allow yourselves to be bitten to spread the cure. Anyone you cure will become a part of your group.

Do not cross into Canada. Eat three meals a day, and rest for eight hours a day, in whatever timing you choose. Go, now."

Alfa turns and heads off, and he copies the method for Bravo and Charlie groups, sending them to the Midwest, and the south respectively. All that's left is Delta.

"Delta, your job is security at the Pentagon. President Ismail may send more troops to find out what happened to the unit she sent. Your job is to spread out in Washington DC and allow yourselves to be bitten by the infected to spread the cure. In four hours, return to the Pentagon to protect it."

With the groups now on their missions, his army will grow exponentially, and he will be one step closer to a united humanity.

*

The unit has beaten themselves up getting the secure doors open using anything sturdy enough to withstand a few blows, including a desktop as a battering ram. There'd been a little outrage at finding a second set, but it drove the team to push even harder.

When they're through, there's no time to rest. They make their way down the semi-dark hallway, smashing the handles on the first doors. She and Thomas look in, and she immediately knows what the remainder of the rooms are.

"I had no idea they even did this on the mainland," she blurts.

"What's up?" Naki asks from behind them.

Thomas turns to him. "Enhanced interrogation rooms."

Down the hallway, she smells death. They reach where it smells the worst, and she breaks the door open. The overwhelming smell of decay causes her to dry heave involuntarily. Thomas brings his arm up, as if breathing through a layer of clothing would act as a respirator.

She regains her composure and sees what's left of Morgan White. Along with her, there was a dead soldier, and a doctor. The master sergeant walks over to the serviceman and retrieves the fallen soldier's dog tags.

He shuts the door and waves the group on. They pass another dozen torture rooms. All of them have varying degrees in which to torture a person, but none of them have any other persons, dead or alive. The end of the hall is in sight, with another set of doors with similar security as the first ones.

"Check it," Thomas orders.

Fitz steps up and tries the handles. They're locked. The unit breaks it down, and inside is a medium-sized hospital ward. A dozen rooms with glass doors line the walls. In the center is a monitoring station, and it gives Fitz hope of establishing communication.

On the desk area, there are a few computers set up, and a desk phone. She picks up the handset, checking for dial tone. It's there.

"Do you remember any of the numbers in the phone you had?" Fitz asks.

"Give it here." Thomas reaches for the phone.

She hands it to him, and he punches some numbers. It's quiet enough to hear it ring, and the person answering on the other end.

"Hello?"

"Hey, babe, I need you to get in my go-bag and get the phone in there."

"Sure. Where the hell are you?" comes the voice from the other side.

"Nowhere you want to be," he says, and then turns to the unit and whispers. "Find a pen and paper."

Allen has already preempted the request and hands him what he needs.

"I have the phone. What do you need?"

"Find Michael Bates and read me the number."

"202-609-2321."

Thomas scribbles the number down and prepares to hang up.

"Thanks. I'll call back when I can. Love you."

"Love you too. Stay safe."

He hangs up, and Moss laughs.

"Awww. So sweet!" he mocks the master sergeant.

"Don't make me put you in one of those rooms back there, Sergeant," Thomas taunts back.

"You know, that kind of sweet talk usually signals the death of a character in a book or movie," Naki blurts out in an attempt to be humorous.

Nobody in the unit laughs, and Thomas stares blankly at him.

"Too much, bro," Welch comments.

"I'm…I'm sorry. I didn't mean…"

Naki's face pales, and Fitz is embarrassed for him. After a painful thirty seconds, Thomas lets a smile crack, and then laughs so hard it echoes through the room.

"Calm yourself, Ensign. I can take a joke. Shoulda seen your face, though," Thomas tells him.

The group laughs, except for Naki. His face relaxes and he sighs loudly. Thomas gets on with making the call to Secretary Bates. The phone doesn't even ring on their end, and the Secretary answers.

"Who is this?" he demands.

"Master Sergeant Byron Thomas, sir."

"Thank God you're alive." He sighs in relief. "We caught Truman's speech when you dialed me before. What the hell's he up to?"

"He's off the deep end, and there's something wrong with the people he's cured. The loyalty I saw from them makes it seem like he's their messiah. He trapped us in some third basement level of the Pentagon. Can't get out through the elevator."

"I know where you are. Hold on while I move to a more secure location."

They wait and hear shuffling on the other end.

"You're in the hospital ward?"

"Yeah."

"In room five, there's a false floor panel. It leads out."

Smith and Naki head there as soon as they've heard the words and begin tossing the room to find it.

"Your biggest obstacle is going to be a security door at the end of the tunnel, but I have confidence you'll figure out a way through them."

"Yes, sir, we will. Orders?"

"Work fast and look for an opportunity to take out Truman. The president is considering allowing high altitude nukes over the US, and your nanites may be rendered useless."

"Yes, sir."

"Godspeed, Byron."

They hang up, and Thomas looks to room five. Smith waves the unit over. Inside, Naki has pulled up a section of the floor to reveal a ladder down into the passage.

"Alright, let's go," Thomas commands.

Fitz is first in. It's dark, but there are electrical conduits at the entrance. Feeling around, she discovers a light switch and flips it on. A narrow corridor is lit up, and it appears endless. Everyone climbs down, with the master sergeant last. He pulls the false floor block back into place, and they get underway.

They reach the next doorway, about a half-mile from where they entered by her estimate. The door's smaller than the last ones, but still has a similar amount of security measures. They take turns kicking at it, and it eventually buckles, revealing a second door.

"Really?" Fitz grumbles.

They break it down to find a ladder to who-knows-where. Thomas climbs it cautiously, and at the top is another false floor. He pushes enough to break the seal, and then lifts an edge to peek through. He sighs in relief, and shoves the floor up.

Inside a small building, it's clear they're not in the Pentagon any longer. Outside is a marina outside, and no zombies in sight. Thomas points and everyone looks. They're across the water from the Pentagon.

"Makes sense. How else could they get suspected terrorists in and out without anyone noticing?" Fitz says.

"Now all we need are weapons. And a way back in. And access to General Truman," Moss says sardonically.

"The joint base is north west of here. I say we raid it for what we're lacking," Frederickson suggests.

"Let's get this over with so I can get some *real* shut-eye," replies Smith.

"Alright, troop, let's see what we can get done. Stay close, stay low, avoid everyone," Thomas directs.

*

# Chapter 11:

Fitz watches their six while Thomas leads them north on the George Washington Memorial Parkway. The plan is to cut through the Arlington National Cemetery and locate the joint base's secured building, which holds the firearms.

As they step into the hallowed grounds, she recalls the time she came here with her father, a decorated veteran, when they were younger. It wasn't important to her then, because she was a child. She understood the significance of the cemetery but hadn't yet adopted her father's patriotic fire. That came after his death.

She'd decided to serve, to honor his memory, and if there was an afterlife he could see her from, make him proud. Now they were in the midst of stopping the end of the world, the cemetery gives her a greater feeling of reverence for her fellow soldiers, both alive and dead.

There aren't many areas for them to hide, so they don't try. It's devoid of people, and far too quiet even for a cemetery. A looming sense of dread falls over her, and it feels like they're walking into an ambush. Deeper into the grounds, every one of them is alert, and finally there's somebody in the distance. Thomas signals them to find any cover.

There are a few sporadic trees, but not enough to give cover for them all. Fitz and Naki duck down between white headstones. Watching for a few minutes, the person just wanders. There's no sight of anyone else with them, and it's difficult to tell if they're one of Truman's cured, or still a zombie.

Thomas lets out a sharp whistle, and it catches the person's attention. Rather than running at them, like one of the zombies would, they look for where the whistle came from. The person returns to wandering aimlessly, and they're undiscovered.

She gains Thomas' attention, and uses hand gestures to indicate going around. He nods in agreement and signals the unit. One by one, they make a wide arc past the roaming person toward the north side of the base.

They reach the dividing road between the cemetery and some buildings. In a parking lot across the road are a couple more people. The unit takes cover near a grouping of trees. Thomas creeps over to her, and points to a building to their far left.

"That's the CIF building," he whispers. "If Truman hasn't raided everything, we should be able to get some protective gear there, maybe more."

"Infiltrate and confiscate," Fitz whispers back.

He nods and directs them with hand signals again; cross the road one at a time, stay low, take cover out of view, and wait. The people don't look like they're patrolling, but they do appear to be looking for something.

Because their *patrols* are random and sporadic, the unit's movements have to happen when they think they can make it. Fitz ducks down and begins crossing. In the middle of the road, a woman turns toward her and locks eyes with her. She's caught, but there's no rapid movement. *Definitely not a zombie.*

The woman stares, eyes glazed over. They're motionless, and she's unsure what to do. Because she was the only one seen, she doesn't want to expose her teammates. Standing upright, she moves away from her unit.

"What are you doing?" the woman asks her.

"What are *you* doing?" Fitz stands up straight, and answers with her own question.

*Need to distract her.*

"Trying to be bitten, to spread the cure…" she responds coldly. "Do you want to bite me?"

*What the fuck?*

"No." Fitz walks over to her while using hand motions behind her back. "I'm already cured."

"What are you doing?" the woman asks again, and Fitz steps past her to direct her attention away from the unit's location.

"I'm also trying to spread the cure," she replies.

"Okay," the woman responds and continues wandering.

The bizarre behavior leaves Fitz confused, but she's left alone. She slips away, wandering slowly so as not to draw attention. Around the corner of the building next to the one Thomas identified as CIF, her unit is already at the other end. Fitz catches up.

"Shit! I thought you were a goner!" Smith whispers, drawing the attention of the rest.

"These people, there's something seriously wrong with them. They've been cured, but it's like they're still zombies. Morgan's dead, and Truman's curing people," she says, using air quotes at the word *curing*. "I have a sickening feeling he got what he want out of Morgan, killed her, and now he's building his own version of subservient zombies."

"Oh God," Welch blurts.

"Good news is, we can feign being one of them, at least for now," Fitz tells them.

"All the more reason to take out Truman as soon as possible," Thomas says.

"We should check those," Naki points at a few remaining military vehicles behind secured fencing. "Might find what we need without having to go into the building."

"They're usually not supplied when parked, but if someone stocked them in preparation for deployment, we might be in luck," Thomas says.

"Stay here. I'll go look," Fitz offers.

Though the cured don't travel in groups, she half-expects that the moment she steps away from the building she'll be swarmed. Her fear is quelled when it doesn't happen. Free to move, she heads to an opening in the fence surrounding the area. Inside the closest vehicle, a Humvee, she doesn't find much of use, just a few rations and a tire iron.

She brings her find to the opening in the fence and sets it all down. Another vehicle has nothing useful, but the one following gives her some hope. Someone had stashed two M9 Berettas, a box of ammo, a combat knife, and several rations. *It's not enough, but it's a start.*

Meticulously, she combs the few vehicles on this side of the lot, but they were either never stocked or already pillaged. She returns to the unit to report.

"Nothing else here. I'm heading over there," she says and points to the farthest area of the parking lot. "Eat while you can."

She heads for the last vehicles in the area, convoy trucks. Empty crates. Empty boxes. Out of stubbornness, she digs into the third truck and is rewarded for her efforts. Stashed in a black case underneath a seat is a M110A1 sniper rifle, ready to be assembled. Along with the rifle is a blue, plastic ammo box filled with 7.62 NATO.

*Can we lure him out somehow? There are no real vantage points around the Pentagon.*

Pleased with the find, she closes the case and heads back to the group. As she gets close to the unit, she smiles when they see what she's carrying.

"Found something good?" Thomas asks.

"Hell yeah I did," she says and sets the box down to open it.

The unit's excitement is audible, and they begin to chatter amongst themselves. Thomas hands Fitz a ration, practically shoving it at her.

"Good work, Fitz. Now eat."

"Let's get out of the open, and make a plan," she suggests while digging into the ration.

"Affirmative. Let's move!" he orders.

*

Reese keeps his head down in the mainframe room, and sticks close to Truman any time he's there, so he can hear the commands being given. He fears, at any moment, the subterfuge of pretending to be infected with Gen-III will be uncovered and his life will be in danger.

He's stood by and watched Ivan and others gut the fluff programming he stuffed into the master nanite. Ivan had pointed it out, however, rather than implicating it as a purposeful act, he used the opportunity to try and build himself up by calling Reese incompetent.

Though he isn't at the helm of development anymore doesn't mean he's helpless. He actively seeks ways to hinder the progress, including accidentally tripping on a major power cord and forcing them to lose time and work. It wasn't much of a setback, but it was something.

While no one is paying attention to him, he uses a terminal at the opposite end of the room to build and imbed a quick denial-of-service bot to interrupt the command transmissions. Once activated, he won't have much time to do whatever it is he's going to do because the Programmers will track it quickly and shut it down within minutes.

*Could I kill Truman when I activate the DoS attack?*

With a plan formulating, he follows the lead of his mind-controlled colleagues. They all take one MRE from the pile in the corner of the room, and he determines they were given a directive to eat. He follows.

Keeping his head down, he makes sure to have eye contact with no one. Only when he'd finished the MRE did he look up to see what other people were doing. They, too, had finished, but continued sitting there, staring off.

He keeps still until the group starts moving as one. They stand, and he's quick to copy. They dump their garbage and exit the room. Down the hall, the men and women separate into their respective groups and head into the bathrooms. He waits his turn, and Ivan waits next to him.

"How does it feel being beaten?" Ivan goads.

He remains silent. *Better to let him think what he wants.*

They move up as the line of people rotate through.

"Did you think you could last forever?" Ivan continues.

Ivan's trying hard to be the prodigal protégé, even when his master isn't nearby. He steps out of the line and into Reese's view. Facing him, it looks as though he wants to push more.

"One day you'll thank *him* for keeping you involved, whatever his reasoning."

Reese makes eye contact and steps away from the wall to intimidate him. Ivan flinches. Passing him by, Reese moves to an open urinal.

When he's finished, he washes up, and rejoins the Programmers inside the mainframe room. Truman has made an appearance and is discussing updates with them. He sees Reese enter but makes no acknowledgement. Taking a place amongst the rest, he turns and listens. The few remaining Programmers enter and take their place amongst the group.

"Ivan, give me a status update on the master nanite," Truman commands.

"Most of the specifications you requested have been programmed, but unlike the nanites stimulating the brain to create action, we have yet to test if a human brain can communicate back to the master nanite. We need human test subjects, people who can tell us what they're experiencing."

*Test subject my ass. He's going to volunteer himself.*

"I will get you some—" Truman starts but is interrupted by Ivan.

"Sir, I'm willing to try it on myself. I understand the code which should govern the communication between the brain and the nanites."

"Won't the Gen-III attack the master nanite?" he asks.

"It's coded the same as the Gen-III, so it won't be dismantled upon insertion," Ivan responds.

"We can't have *test subjects* able to control the army," Reese speaks up. "We need to change the frequency in which the transceiver communicates on for the test version of the master nanite, and then cure a single person with the new frequency."

With his interjection, he's certain Ivan's trying to burn a hole in the back of his head with a stare. Quite pleased with himself, he keeps his eyes forward, and Truman nods.

"Good thinking. I want you to set up a separate station to monitor this test. Once we have confirmation it works, then we'll move to the final phase."

Truman pulls up his portable microphone and speaks into it.

"Master Sergeant Gorski, take one other person and find an infected and capture it. Do not let it bite anyone. Do not cure it. Bring it to the Pentagon and restrain it."

He returns his attention to the Programmers and commands them through the mic.

"Programmers, prepare for a master nanite test." He points to a woman in the group and speaks, "You, your job is to recode the master nanite to operate on a different frequency, and then recode a slave Gen-III to that frequency. When ready, you are to inject it into Ivan. Ivan, you are to sit on the opposite side of the room from the main computer and wait."

The group accepts his commands, and they begin preparations. Reese makes himself look busy about the support systems while not actually doing anything of importance.

Truman paces and watches. Reese avoids him as much as possible, but he approaches anyway.

"I hope one day you'll understand why I had to take this course of action. Humanity can't be trusted not to destroy itself," he tries to rationalize. "Before Alphaeus came up with this technology, we were on a collision course with extinction. His goal for it was not only to bring us together, but also send us out to the stars. I'm going to see this through."

Reese stays silent and keeps an unfocused gaze. He does his best not to tip his hand to any of the sabotage he's planning.

"Do you not have anything to say?"

"No."

Truman nods at him, and he provides a courteous nod back.

*

Truman exits the mainframe room and heads to his office. He anticipates he has some time before Delta Group is back, enough to continue planning humanity's course.

Inside his office, he reviews papers he's taped all across the walls. His manifesto isn't yet complete, and he wants to have as much of it written down as possible before he's injected with the master nanite.

At his desk, he returns to where he left off. With a virtually immortal army behind him, he would take the west, then Canada, and Mexico. *The biggest issue will be injecting those not infected with Morgan's abominations with the Gen-IIIs.*

*I need to diversify Delta group. I need missile defense against an EMP strike and ground defense. I'll have to split them into three. Delta to continue curing, Echo to take complete control of the Pentagon's infrastructure and US missile system, and Foxtrot to cover ground protection.*

Scribbling, he continues to lay out the utopian ideology and creates what he believes is a solid opening paragraph to the world.

> I believe in a world where there is no more chaos, where everything and everyone has a place, and death is conquered. The world has been separated for far too long over petty ideals, and humanity has faltered in its destiny to be the greatest organism on Earth and beyond. We've let ourselves be conquered *by* ourselves, and now is the era to end that. By establishing a new order where everyone is fundamentally the same, we will be able to grow like never before. We will reach a new level of civilization, by becoming more than human. But in order to achieve this goal, we must establish rules for our new society; Truman's Laws of Transhumanism.

He re-reads it and is pleased with himself. It shows intent and reasoning for *Unity*. He feels a twinge of regret for his friend whose life he took, and the others who opposed him before this could be realized. He knows the opposition they would have posed, and this idea wouldn't be anywhere near to realization if he hadn't done what was necessary. He foresaw and quelled a rebellion before it started. *A few lives lost saves the many.*

Looking at his watch, he's spent more time thinking than working on the Unity Manifesto. Out of the office again, he wanders outside. Gorski returns with an infected man. He and two other people keep him from biting anyone.

"Master Sergeant Gorski, and the two soldiers holding the infected man, bring him into the Programmers' room and keep him restrained," he commands through his phone. "Delta group, except for Master Sergeant Gorski and the two soldiers holding the infected, form up as evenly as possible, in rows of nine."

It takes fifteen minutes for Delta to group, and when he does he enacts his plan to form Delta, Echo, and Foxtrot from them. With their new tasks, they disperse.

Truman heads inside to the Programmers' room to oversee the master nanite test.

"Has the recoded master nanite been injected?" he asks.

"Yes," Reese replies. "We are ready to test it."

"Good. Inject the infected man with the frequency modified Gen-III," Truman orders through the microphone.

Reese brings a syringe over and plunges it into the infected man's arm. The soldiers hold him steady and wait for a response. Truman pulls his sidearm and waits. It takes a few minutes, but he snaps out of the infection's haze and regains awareness.

"Who...are...you?" he asks.

"We're the ones with the cure," Truman says. "It's an ongoing process, but you can count yourself lucky we got to you first."

"Thank you! It was such a nightmare! It was awful." He starts crying.

"Ivan, can you sense him?" Truman asks.

"Yes. I…I can connect to…oh, my God. I can feel everything. I'm receiving input directly into my mind," he answers, giddy. "There's this weird sensation. It's a second consciousness?"

"Do you have control?"

"I don't know."

"Ivan, try to move around," Truman orders into his phone.

Ivan raises his left arm, and the man raises his, too. Ivan stands, and the man stands. The cured man's face switches from relief to terror.

"What are you doing to me?" he cries out.

Ivan stops moving and returns to a neutral stance, but the man continues. He raises his other arm, and then puts both down. His mouth opens and shuts but no words come out. He steps forward, and then back.

"Is this you, Ivan?" Truman asks.

"Yes! Oh, wow. It's…it's…it's…" Ivan stops mid-sentence, and his eyes glaze over.

Both Ivan and the test subject begin seizing, and they both fall to the floor. Their eyes and noses hemorrhage. Truman steps back and looks to Reese. His initial reaction is to blame this on him, but his eyes are wide in fear.

"What the hell's happening?" he yells.

"I-I have…no idea!" he stammers. "Synaptic overload? Feedback? The nanites have never been interfaced or interlinked like this before."

"How do we fix this?"

Reese is silent, watching the two men spasm on the ground.

"Reese, issue the self-destruct for the test subjects," Truman yells into the phone.

Reese moves to a terminal and types frantically. The men stop seizing, but now they're likely dying due to not having active nanites.

"Inject them with standard Gen-III nanites," he orders.

A woman brings two syringes over and injects both of them. Everyone stands around, waiting to see if the nanites will be able to reverse the damage done. The men lie there breathing shallowly. After ten minutes, there are signs of life, albeit abnormal signs.

Ivan is the first to sit up. He shakes his head violently and becomes agitated.

"That shouldn't have happened! That wasn't what was supposed to happen! This wasn't a failure! Try again! Try again!"

He falls into a repeating loop before his eyes roll back, and becomes unresponsive. Truman anticipates there's permanent brain damage, and the nanites can't repair it. The other man is still on the ground, in the fetal position. He's showing no signs of recovering either.

"How can we stop this from happening?" he asks roughly.

The room is silent.

"Programmers, I order you all to tell me how we can prevent brain damage like we just saw, while still implementing the master nanite plan!" he yells into his phone.

Unanimously the group responds, "Create a buffer."

Except for Reese. Reese didn't answer.

"Why didn't you respond?" he asks him.

"Hmm?" he looks up from the damaged men.

"Why didn't you answer when I gave an order?"

"I didn't have an answer, but the consensus of the group is a buffer, and I agree. A buffer would disallow the feedback loop these men suffered."

He looks at Reese suspiciously, and his glare is ignored. *Is he not under my control?*

"Programmers, analyze what happened between the test master nanite and the test subject, and then create a buffer to prevent this from happening again," Truman orders.

The Programmers disperse and begin working, including Reese. While Reese isn't looking, he lifts his phone up to his mouth and whispers.

"Reese Gordon, place your left hand on the top of your head."

He doesn't comply with the order given. Truman watches him intensely, wondering how he'd circumvented the transceiver code. *How in the hell did he get one step ahead of me, again? This can't continue.*

Moving to Reese, he raises his sidearm, and places it at Reese's temple.

"How'd you do it?" Truman asks.

"What?" He glances at him, a hint of fear in his eyes.

"You're not under my control. How'd you do it?"

"I'm doing as you—"

"Reese, disarm me, put my gun's barrel in your mouth, and pull the trigger," Truman commands into his phone.

He stands still.

"I injected myself with a modified version of nanites," Reese confesses. "There's no way you can control me. And yet I'm still here, doing as you asked. Have the Programmers check my work."

He's skeptical.

"Let's go," Truman directs and moves out of Reese's way while keeping the gun pointed at his head. "I can't trust you anymore, and so I'm going to put you in the basement until I can figure out what to do about your modified nanites."

Reese walks toward the door.

"Master Sergeant Gorski, come with me," Truman orders through the microphone.

The three of them make their way through the halls to the elevator. He goes through the motions to open the doors, enter, and select the third basement floor.

"Master Sergeant, be ready to shoot any of the soldiers down here if they try to rush the elevator."

He raises his rifle, and flicks the safety off.

They descend, and when the doors open, he's baffled. The soldiers are nowhere in sight, and there's a mess of destroyed furniture. His eyes find the security door on the other side of the room, and it's open.

"Son of a bitch! Gorski, investigate! Search for the soldiers!"

"Yes, sir!" he replies.

"If you twitch, I'll put a bullet in your head," Truman warns Reese harshly.

He shoves Reese into the main area, keeping him in front as they head to the detention block. Gorski returns, and shakes his head to indicate no signs of Master Sergeant Thomas or his unit.

All of the doors to the enhanced interrogation rooms were open. Gorski clears each one before they continue. Passing the room, where Morgan, Doctor Tseng, and the serviceman lie, Reese's face pales. He dry heaves and turns away from the room.

"What...what the fuck did you do?" Reese yells at Truman.

Truman puts the muzzle on Reese's forehead.

"What I had to. Keep moving."

Every door in this wing is open, including the ones into the hospital ward. There's no sign of the unit. Truman's face reddens, and he knows how they got out, just not how they knew the hidden hatch was there.

"Master Sergeant Gorski, keep an eye on him," he orders. "If he attempts to escape, shoot him."

He nods and trains his rifle on Reese. It frees Truman to head to the fifth room. It's disturbed, and there's signs the false floor has been opened. Back into the main area, he looks in each of the rooms. No others have been touched.

*They knew it was there. How? None of them would have had the knowledge of it.*

At the desk, he heads to the phone, picks up the handset, and presses the redial button. It rings and only takes a moment for the other end to pick up.

"Master Sergeant Thomas?" comes a voice over the phone, and he recognizes it; Secretary Bates.

"I'm afraid not, and now I know they've escaped, I'll have my army looking for them," Truman taunts.

"Truman? What have you done?"

"I'm curing people over here."

There's a change in the sound, and he realizes he's now on speakerphone.

"We're doing the same thing. Let's work together," Secretary Bates says.

"I assume you've put me on speakerphone because you're in a war room. President Ismail, are you there?"

"I'm here, Truman," President Ismail replies.

"Have you stopped calling me *general* now? I assume you've stripped me of rank. It's of no consequence, though, not like the Chinese invasion is."

"There *is* no invasion, Truman. They're here to help us," she says.

"It won't matter, we've already begun curing the United States and will move onto Canada shortly. We won't let you *kill* any of the infected."

"We're not trying to kill anyone!"

He ignores her and continues, "There is hope for recovery and movement toward humanity's next advancement. We can achieve unity."

"What are you planning?" she asks.

"You'll find out soon enough, but I can't let you interfere," he replies, and then brings his cell phone up. "Echo Group, locate all connections to US defense and computer infrastructures which aren't ours, and terminate the connections."

"What—" President Ismail starts and is interrupted.

"Ma'am! We've lost connection to the satellites," Vice President Abraham's voice comes over the phone.

"Damnit, Truman! Stop what you're doing and let us handle the infection!"

"President Ismail, I'll arrange a face to face soon, but until then, I have a mission to continue spreading the cure until Morgan's infection is stamped out."

"Truman—"

He hangs up on her, and then takes the phone off the hook.

"Gorski, bring Reese. We're going back upstairs to prepare for the master nanite integration."

Back in the Programmers' room, he puts Reese in the corner where Ivan lies, barely alive.

"Watch him," he orders Gorski. "Don't let him get up."

He nods and aims his rifle.

"Programmers, I need your attention now!" he commands.

The Programmers stop and turn to him.

"Pull up footage from the other night when Master Sergeant Thomas and his unit were captured. I want all of the faces of that unit run through the facial recognition database and each of those soldiers' information distributed to the hive-mind."

Where once this request would have taken significant time to accomplish, the Programmers work to capture the data, and have immediate results. They've isolated the eight individuals, images, profiles, and background information.

"Has it been distributed?" he asks.

"Yes."

"Good," he replies and brings the microphone to his mouth. "Attention: the profiles of eight individuals have just been uploaded to your nanites' databases. If you see any of these individuals, you are to apprehend and bring them to Master Sergeant Gorski for execution!"

He continues, "Master Sergeant Gorski, if any of these eight soldiers are brought to you, shoot them in the head, and then burn their bodies."

He reassigns another soldier to watch over Reese and commands them both to follow him everywhere. Satisfied he's now protected from the rogue element, he takes a cleansing breath. *It's time to unity to the world.*

*

The unit devises their plan.

"There is only one way we're going to get to Truman, catch him outside," Fitz tells them.

"I'll find a position with a good vantage point to take him out," Thomas follows up. "Lieutenant Smith, you're my spotter."

"Yes, sir!" she replies.

"The rest of us will head toward the helipad at the Pentagon, incognito. Civilian clothes, hats, anything to avoid recognition," Fitz explains. "When we're close enough, Naki will break cover and call attention to himself and insist on joining Truman's army."

"What happens if he doesn't come out?" Naki asks.

"Then we do whatever's needed to infiltrate. We only have the two M9 Beretta. Captain Frederickson will get the first, and I'll have the second," she answers.

The six not on the sniper team make their way to the civilian area beyond the joint-base and elude Truman's drones. Nearby shops provide opportunity to find clothes. Fitz puts on slacks, a button-down shirt, a tie, and a suit jacket. To top it off, she puts her hair into a bun and puts on a stylish hat. She looks in a dressing room mirror and examines herself.

*Like a superhero with an alter ego.*

Though the style doesn't quite fit the standard look of a Washington politician, she likes the look. She'd never thought of being a politician before now, but the world was facing new threats, and they were going to need someone who had firsthand experience.

The unit almost looks ready. The new clothes make them stand out worse than before, and would be a dead giveaway they hadn't been part of the infected.

"We're too clean. One by one, we'll leave the store and tear these clothes. Make yourselves look like shit. I want blood and dirt on everyone.

"If anyone says anything to you, just parrot them. Once we're there, only Naki is to break cover. If this shit goes south, I want to be able to retreat and regroup." She's firm in her tone.

"Ensign Naki, the sacrificial lamb," Welch jokes.

"Only for a bit while we take out Truman, and give this nation a rebirth," Fitz reassures him.

"It's alright. I understand the mission," Naki says, showing some resolve.

Being a Marine for a number of years now, the idea of failure causes her to recoil a little internally. Pushing the feeling down, she gives them the signal to move out.

Their exits are staggered, and she's the last out. She tears her clothes in random ways as to make it look like she'd been attacked. With her knife, she cuts her palm, and before the nanites can heal her she smears it on her neck and face.

On the long walk back to the Pentagon, she keeps her head down to remain undiscovered. From afar, she sees the whole northern section outside the Pentagon is packed with people, vehicles, and munitions caches. Her gut tells her to pull back a little. She takes a hard left away from the rest of her unit.

Thomas and Smith had purposely not explained where they were going to be shooting from, but there weren't many locations which had a vantage point on where Truman would come out, *if* he came out. Looking around, she tries to find where she'd shoot from.

From the highway, she makes her way to the parking area underneath the helipad and up the stairway. Before she gets to the top, she takes a few deep breaths. On the helipad, she mingles with the crowd, making her way slowly forward. No one is paying her any attention.

A hundred people deep into the sea of bodies, she hears someone yell out. She can't search for whoever it is without calling attention to herself. A group of the brain-washed start to swarm, and then another person calls out. It feels to her like their plan was falling apart before they could even get into place.

"Let go of me, you son of a bitch!"

Following, the swarm splits into two groups, and they push toward the front of the building. *At least we're going in the right direction.* Keeping her head down, she follows the yelling on her left. Getting close enough, she sees Welch being hauled along. He's facing away from her, left unknowing she's there.

Near the stairs up to the entrance, the group stops, and Welch is forced to his knees. Another of her unit, Moss, is brought right up alongside him.

Rather than Truman coming out to confront them, Master Sergeant Gorski exits the building. He speaks no words, and aims his rifle. She waits for some announcement, some ultimatum. Anything at all. It never comes.

"What the fu—"

*BANG!* He shoots Moss in the head.

"Hey! Hey! Let's talk this out! Let me talk to General Truman! I want to join the army!" Welch pleads, trying to play Naki's role.

*BANG!*

Both of them are let go, and they slump over. The master sergeant waves for people to move away from the bodies, and they do. He retrieves a flamethrower from a nearby Humvee, and lights it.

*Oh God, what is he doing?*

Everything in her is screaming to stop him, but she knows the moment she makes a move she, too, will be murdered. Even looking away risks calling attention to herself. There's nothing she can do except swear to get revenge.

The flash of a muzzle and sound of a gunshot ring out overhead, from the top of the Pentagon. The bullet rips through Gorski's skull. He topples, and then another bullet is fired. It punctures the gas tank on his back and causes an explosion. His body burns, instead of her teammates. The group closest to him scatters, screams filling the air over the sound of fire crackling. Now's her chance.

Fitz makes a break for the doors. *He's definitely not coming out now.* Hoping not to be recognized, she throws caution to the wind and enters the building.

Soldiers exit the building as she's heading in, but they don't bother to look at her, let alone stop her. She's infiltrated the Pentagon, but unlike the other day, the halls are now bustling with life. Keeping her head down, she moves with purpose, blending into a quick moving group.

Thinking Truman would likely be found in the room with the computers, she keeps mental track of where she is and where that room is.

*

Reese sits in the corner and watches Truman start spinning. He's talking furiously to one of the other departments on the only phone in the room. Unable to hear the other side of the conversation, he only knows what he's hearing. There's been an attack, an explosion outside of the building.

"Foxtrot group, I want exact details of what just happened, and whomever just attacked us caught and killed!" Truman practically screams into his phone.

Truman's attention on him has lapsed. *Is this my chance to do something? I can't let him take the master nanite into himself.*

The soldier assigned to guard him was still there.

*With only one person looking over me, I might be able to break away and activate the DoS attack*, he reasons. *Then what, though? The soldier's probably going to shoot me, and the DoS attack will only last a few moments.*

"Is the buffer ready yet?" Truman yells.

"We're bringing it online now," one of the Programmers replies.

"Hurry up, goddammit!"

*

The groupings of people in the Pentagon's halls shift their direction back toward the door in which she came, and now Fitz is directly in the sight of fifty-some people. Seeing her, they stop dead in their tracks and gravitate toward her. Every one of them able to put their hands on her finds a way to do so. In the most eerie way possible, they all speak at the same time.

"Did you attack us?"

She's baffled. Her first instinct is to lie.

"No," she answers.

Instead of continuing on, they stand with their hands on her. Testing to see what they'll do, she tries to step away and break free. Some try to hang on. New people grab onto her. They don't stop her, but they're hindering her significantly. The number of people who've seen her is now growing. Pushing through, every single one of them attempts to grab onto her. Having dozens of hands on her all at one time unnerves her. It reaches a point she can't help but verbally lash at them.

"What the fuck are you doing? Get your hands off of me!"

In the same eerie manner as before, the entirety of the group answers in sync with one another.

"Capture Corporal Ella Fitzgerald. Error. Directive Failure. Master Sergeant Gorski not found."

Their cryptic response, and lack of action other than to grab onto her, leaves her speechless, but not without thought. *This isn't brainwashing, it's mind control…*

It's harder to move now, but with some effort, she barges through and starts gaining momentum. She manages to keep most hands from getting a solid grip and starts running as fast as she can. Left, right, and center, she knocks people over.

*

"What is going on out there? Someone tell me what happened!" Truman screams into his phone.

The door to the mainframe room bursts open, and Corporal Fitzgerald, dressed in civilian clothing, bursts in. He's given only a fraction of a second to respond as she levels a pistol at him.

"Stop her!" he yells in the microphone.

The soldier guarding Reese tries to get to her, but it's too late. She fires the gun, and the deafening sound resounds off the walls.

*

In the sudden chaos of everyone in the room running to tackle Corporal Fitzgerald, Reese jumps up and runs over to the computer he planted the DoS attack program on. Truman's hit, and bleeding, but he's not dead. He grips onto his side, trying to stifle the blood.

"You dumb fucking bitch!" he yells at Fitzgerald.

Reese activates his attack, and the script begins running.

"Give me the master nanite, now!" Truman hollers into his phone.

Not a single one of his drones stop what they're doing to accommodate him. Trying to prop himself up, he sees Reese and yells.

"What the hell did you do?"

Truman turns to where the master nanite is stored and moves to it as fast as he can. It's up to Reese to do something before it's too late. He leaps over the desks in between them. Truman picks up the syringe and draws the plunger. Reese tackles him to the floor. His newfound enhanced strength makes it easy to rip the syringe out of Truman's hand.

He accidentally exerts so much force he shatters the syringe in his hand. The glass cuts him, and the liquid inside mixes with his blood. He drops it and stands up, frantically trying to wipe the liquid away on his pants. *Oh shit! Oh shit!* He's unsure if his brand of nanites will destroy the master nanite or not.

Looking up, he sees the shock on Truman's face, and he knows his expression is the same.

"What have you done?" he stands up and slumps against the consoles behind him. "Do you know?"

"I...I don't know...I didn't mean..." Reese is now completely unsure of his actions.

"I gave you too much leniency...my mistake."

Truman slides back down to the floor, sapped of any energy to continue fighting. His clothes are soaked with his blood.

Everyone is now looking to Reese, waiting for what's next. If he assimilated the master nanite, the moment he stops the DoS attack, he'll be in control of the Gen-IIIs, if the buffer even works. His eyes find Ivan on the floor.

"You're in control now, Reese. You can still see my plan through. Find my manifesto."

"Let me go!" Corporal Fitzgerald screams.

There's a choice to be made: self-destruct the Gen-IIIs now or to continue to cure. The question of which one to choose seems apparent, to finish curing everyone first. But he might face significant opposition to that course of action once he freed everyone's minds.

"They won't let you go. They have orders. I can't countermand those orders while the DoS attack is blocking the transceiver. If I turn it off, I don't know what's going to happen," Reese tells her.

"What do you mean?" she struggles against them. "Get off!"

"Truman was using mind-control through nanites on these people, and I might have a nanite in me now, which would allow me to mentally control everyone we've cured. It's was his goal."

None of the mind-controlled chime in, and he wonders what they're thinking, what their counsel would be. *Whether I'm going to issue the self-destruct command now, or later, I'll have to stop the DoS attack to return everyone to normal.*

"Don't...waste the...opportunity," Truman interjects, his breathing labored. "The Unity Manifesto...in my office...read it."

Knowing he would now shape history going forward, he takes Truman's phone from him. He moves to the computer attacking the command server, and with a few keystrokes, he shuts the attack down.

*

It's been too long having not heard from the unit in DC, and she feels it's likely the worst case scenario has played out. President Ismail is sure that EH-US-11 failed to take out Truman, and that his plan to use the North American population to wage war is progressing.

In the video conference room, she bites her nails hoping to hear from them, but she can't wait any longer. She connects to the heads of other countries, and questions everything she stands for. She doesn't have long to think, as those that matter are online within a few moments.

*

Truman lies dying on the floor of his second home, the Pentagon. His dreams of leading the world into a utopian society are gone. Broken, he feels regret not for his actions, but for not taking the nanites out of fear that he, too, could be controlled.

He reflects on what's left, and how he'll be perceived to the world. His name won't go down as the unifier of humanity but scribed as deranged like Morgan White.

*

Reese screams out in pain. His vision goes white, and then red. Voices flood into his head, overwhelming every sense. The buffer kicks on, and the pain subsides. His face is wet with blood from his eyes, ears, and nose. But unlike Ivan, he's still standing.

He senses the people beyond the buffer, allowing him to issue commands to anyone connected. His first action is to 'order' everyone to stand down and return to their homes and lives, regardless of where they're from.

The group lets up Corporal Fitzgerald, and disburses. The room clears out, leaving him and her standing.

"What the hell?" she exclaims.

Reese thumbs through Truman's phone, and all of the numbers are unlabeled.

"Corporal Fitzgerald, I need to talk to someone high up. Maybe the president. Do any of these numbers look familiar?"

Looking through them, she shakes her head.

"I don't, but my C.O. might recognize one."

She waves for him to follow, and they head out together. She's silent, but looks back at him every few feet, maybe to see if they're being followed. While she leads, he gets a feel for the legions of people he is connected to.

*All these minds Truman wanted to control. It's not hard to romanticize a perfect world based on one's own morals and ethics applied.*

*A new era of technology is barely born, and it's already been abused. No doubt when I deactivate the hive-mind, this technology will continue to exist. Other countries are going to race to create or modify their own. What happens to the world then?*

He realizes he's stopped in the middle of the hallway, and Corporal Fitzgerald is trying to get his attention.

"What the hell are you doing?" she asks.

"I don't know. What was I doing?"

"You stopped and just stood there. Your eyes glossed over, and it was like there was no one home."

"Sorry, I was thinking."

"Let's go, now," she demands with a scowl.

He follows her out of the Pentagon, and in the distance, a great many people are leaving the area. A few feet past the charred remains of someone, two soldiers are sitting on the ground. Corporal Fitzgerald jogs over to them.

"You alright?" she asks them.

"You mean other than being shot in the head a second time?" one responds.

"Shit, that's the least of your worries. That was about to be you." She points back to a charred body. "Master Sergeant Thomas took him out."

As they're joined by a few others, he hears a noise overhead. When he looks, he doesn't see anything, but something's there. Its high-pitched whine through the air is interrupted by an explosion in the atmosphere farther inland, and it heralds the worst of scenarios. A shockwave disperses the clouds high up and, immediately, he can no longer sense the hive-mind. Powerline transformers explode in a spectacular display of fireworks.

"Is that what I think it is?" a younger man asks.

"Yes," Reese blurts, and a sense of dread falls over him. "It's all gone."

"Orders?" Corporal Fitzgerald addresses a man he recognizes from before; Master Sergeant Thomas.

Reese interjects before the man with the rifle can respond, "I need help either protecting or completely destroying any computer that held any information about the nanites."

"Why? Didn't it all just die?" a woman in uniform asks.

"Not necessarily. Though the electronics are dead, the actual disks could still hold the data. Last thing we want is for someone to salvage the components and recover the sensitive material," he explains.

"What do we do about the west?" the younger man questions.

"For now, nothing. We're the only leadership on the East Coast. We're going to be looked to for answers. Your orders are to secure the Pentagon. Once we've established a temporary government here, we will send someone west to connect."

*

Three HEMP devices had just been detonated over North America, but no one sat and wondered what they were going to do. Everyone in the Western White House had a job or task, preparing to begin local recovery operations.

Years prior, the Department of Energy had designed the Electromagnetic Pulse Resilience Strategy, a way to explore the ramifications of such a situation. Through careful refinement, past administrations had designated ways to mitigate and recover. Prior to the UK launching their devices, they'd shut down electrical grids in the west for preservation, but an evaluation of how much damage had occurred would come much later.

Exactly ten minutes after the detonation, the local power plant was scheduled to turn the electricity back on. It was a small consolation in relation to the loss of everything with circuitry, but it was better than nothing.

President Ismail wasn't stagnant, but she keeps an eye on an old grandfather clock as she moves from one task to another. Ten minutes pass. Then fifteen. No lights yet. Vice President Abraham rests his hand on her shoulder.

"It'll come back," he consoles her.

She nods and sits to write a memorandum. Pen in hand, she barely has it to the paper when an electric hum fills the air, and the lights come back on. There's cheering throughout the house, and Vice President Abraham smiles at her.

"It's only the beginning," she states.

"Of course. But it's a new beginning."

*

Arturo sniffs around a trash can looking for a bite to eat. The dog has scrounged for his meals since last with his owner. He misses her. He jumps up to look inside a large green metal trash bin and digs to find morsels. There isn't much, but it's enough to satisfy until he can find more.

When he jumps out, there are people there. He hadn't been avoiding them, they just weren't where he was. A young man was there and saw the dog.

"Here, boy," he calls.

He's shy, but when the child gets down on his knees and holds his hand out. It entices him to go to him, in hopes that he might be offering something to eat. There's nothing, but he sniffs anyway, and licks his salty palms.

"Good boy," he says and plays with the box on his neck. "What's this? Arturo? Are you a good boy, Arturo? Yes, you are. Come."

The young man stands back up and pats his leg, beckoning him to follow. He does. The boy takes to him, and he takes to the boy.

"Mom? Dad?" he calls out and begins wandering. "Mom? Dad?"

Arturo follows the friendly boy willingly.

*

# Epilogue:

It's neither the end, nor the beginning. The course of humanity has been altered due to Morgan and Truman's actions. Though things haven't gone according to anyone's plan, humanity will recover. But to what extent? Some, like Fitz and President Ismail, seek to bring the country back online and give people back their lives. Others, like Alphaeus and Reese, contemplate what comes after Pandora's Box has opened, and how humanity will learn and grow from the mistakes made.

In North America, governments draft former and current soldiers to keep the peace. There's an incredible amount of work to do to for the three countries to rebuild. Relief efforts pour in through the west, east, and the south to many of the coastal regions in an attempt to stabilize the continent before it falls into anarchy and chaos. Pockets of self-governing communities begin developing, some with the idea of annexing themselves and their land from government control.

Internationally, Russia leaks the names and profiles of the international Enhanced Human units, and puts a bounty out on the recovery of any team members. The Enhanced Human units retreat into hiding, ready to protect the nanites coursing through their veins to the death. A Chinese spy makes his way across the Pacific with a stolen vial of blood, ready to turn over the technology to the Ministry of State Security, but not before he injects some into himself.

Nothing will be the same. The destiny of the world depends on not just those in power, but every single individual. How will they reshape it?

A new future awaits...

# About The Author

Thomas W. Everson thinks you're awesome for reading his book(s). For his stories, he takes inspirations from many places, people, and events, all in the hopes of entertaining and encouraging thought.

His free time at home is spent with his amazing wife, Brandi, and their wonderful son, Bubby. From books, to movies, to video games, they currently favor science fiction *everything*.

Want to get in touch with Thomas? He'd love to hear from you!

http://www.tweverson.com

https://www.facebook.com/AuthorThomasEverson

https://twitter.com/WriterThomasE

www.ingramcontent.com/pod-product-compliance
Lightning Source LLC
Chambersburg PA
CBHW071509110726
47908CB00003B/780